Killing the Fatted Calf

Killing the Fatted Calf

SUSAN KELLY

This edition published in Great Britain in 2002 by
Allison & Busby Limited
Bon Marche Centre
241-251 Ferndale Road
Brixton, London SW9 8BJ
http://www.allisonandbusby.com

A catalogue record for this book is available from the British
Library

ISBN 0 7490 0511 4

Printed and bound in Spain by
Liberdúplex, s. l. Barcelona

SUSAN KELLY is the author of nine previous crime novels. She lives in west London with her solicitor husband and cat. *Killing the Fatted Calf* is the second book in a series featuring Gregory Summers.

Bring quickly the best robe and put it on him;
and put a ring on his hand, and shoes on his feet;
and bring hither the fatted calf and kill it,
and let us eat and make merry.

Luke 15, 22.

Prologue

A telephone ringing at midnight seldom brought good news, or not to a policeman. When the midnight in question was two days before Christmas it was likely to be very bad news indeed for any plans Superintendent Gregory Summers had made for the holidays.

He'd been hoping for a restful few days as well, what with the recent arrests in Operation Cuckoo and nothing on the horizon but the exhumation scheduled for the day after Boxing Day.

It would be raining. It always rained for exhumations. He would slither ankle-deep in mud and somebody — preferably somebody *else* — would fall into the hole.

He was cleaning his teeth in the en-suite bathroom, taking more time over this tiresome ablution than had been his custom, since a recent visit to the dentist at which he'd been asked 'Do you want to lose all your teeth?'

And what kind of a stupid question was that?

So he was preparing himself mentally for ordeal by dental floss when the phone began to ring. He assumed that Angelica would answer it but, after four or five rings went uninterrupted, he darted into the bedroom, literally foaming at the mouth. Angie was propped up against the pillows, wearing his striped pyjama top and reading a psychology text book. In answer to his unspoken question, she said, 'It's bound to be for you.'

He wiped his mouth with the hand towel draped over his shoulder, picked up the receiver from the cabinet on his side of the bed and snapped, 'Summers!'

'Sorry, sir. Did I wake you?'

The ever reliable Sergeant Barbara Carey who would never disturb him this late for anything trivial.

He said, 'No, no,' and sat down on the edge of the bed.

'Only we've got a suspicious death. It looks like a householder came home, disturbed a burglar and got stabbed. That's all we know at the moment. The person who dialled 999 wasn't too coherent.'

'Where?' he asked, already shrugging off his dressing gown.

'Alderbright. The house is called Alders End. Belongs to a Lady Weissman. It's at the west end of the village —'

'I know where it is,' he said quietly. 'I'll meet you there in twenty minutes.' He hung up and sat for a moment in silent thought until Angelica said, 'Trouble?'

'Looks like a murder.' He leaned across the bed and kissed her gently on the cheek. 'See you when I see you.'

She smiled mischievously and said, 'If you're not home in time for Christmas dinner with my mam, then you'll really know the meaning of the word Trouble.'

As he hurriedly dressed, Greg wondered if he was imagining, with hindsight, the sense of foreboding that had grown on him over the past three months, since that morning when he'd first noticed Elise Weissman and Antony Lucas in the street in Hungerford.

Seeing double

The woman was in her early forties, if Greg was any judge. The man was younger, a lot younger, maybe thirty. He noticed them as he walked up the hill that Saturday morning in early October because it was she who was driving the yellow Lotus Elise, manoeuvring it with confidence into a narrow space between two prosperous-looking cars, a Jaguar and an Aston Martin, parked at an angle to Hungerford High Street a few yards above the Corn Exchange.

The young man got out of the passenger seat and she waited as he walked round the front of the car and opened her door for her, sliding sidewards in her seat, kicking her long legs in the air with a youthful exuberance and descending gracefully to the pavement like an advertisement for a finishing school. Her companion plucked a cream silk jacket from the back ledge and closed the door softly behind her.

He draped the jacket over her shoulders and she turned her head to him and laughed.

Greg watched her with detached admiration as the young man felt in the pockets of his elegant lounge suit for change and bought a ticket at the pay-and-display machine. She was tall, about five-seven, and not as thin as society women tended to be, filling her knee-length skirt with attractive curves above shapely nylon-clad legs, which ended in narrow feet encased in the best leather. Her hair was dark, matte, almost sooty, cut short, curling around her heart-shaped face and, as she glanced his way, he saw that her eyes were unexpectedly blue.

Her gaze lingered on him for a second, or so he thought, but then she turned back to her escort and he told himself that he had imagined it. She locked the car and took the arm that the young man offered her. They disappeared into the Hungerford Arcade and were soon lost from view among the antique shops within.

Greg continued up the hill and thought no more about them.

He was surprised to find Piers Hamilton's photographic studio locked, the closed sign up on the door. Surprised and disappointed. Perhaps his friend had been called out to capture for posterity a wedding or christening. He rang the bell for the flat above the shop and was rewarded a minute later with a scamper of feet on the internal stairs and a smiling face as Piers unlatched the door for him.

'Gregory! I'm glad you stopped by. There's someone here I want you to meet.'

He was off again without waiting for a reply and Greg followed him slowly up the wooden stairs. He'd come to terms with the fact that one of his closest friends was as queer as a three-pound note but that didn't mean that he wanted to meet Piers' latest 'partner'.

But the man perched on a hard chair by the window of Piers' bedsitting room could hardly come into that category. He looked about a hundred years old, for a start: shrunken in height and dramatically bald, with the wrinkles of his brow marching back over his head to merge into the craters of his tanned neck. His baldness made his ears look huge, but they said that ears were the one thing that kept growing in old age; apart from an abused liver, and he looked as if he might have one of those as well.

His florid corpulence filled out a tweed suit, well-tailored but old, thick for a bright day in early autumn. He twirled a black, silver-topped cane in his hands like an Edwardian dandy and his shoes looked hand made in supple brown leather, as well worn by time as their owner.

'This is my friend Gregory Summers,' Piers announced in the slightly raised voice that the care-free young use to the incalculably old, 'of the Newbury *Sureté*. Gregory, this is my great-uncle, Piers Hamilton.'

'Confusing, ain't it?' the old man said, seeing Greg's surprise. He tottered to his feet before Greg could tell him not to and offered him an unexpectedly firm handshake. 'They named him after me, thinking I'd leave him everything when I popped my clogs, but that was more than thirty years ago and I've no more intention of popping them now than I did then.' He grinned at his great-nephew. 'So tough luck.'

'I can wait, Unc,' Piers said demurely.

'Huh! Who said I was leaving it to you anyway?'

He scrutinised Greg with small, pale eyes that glittered with some strong feeling: whether a joy of living or simple malice, Greg couldn't tell. He must have been fair, he thought, like Piers, in the days when he'd had hair. Probably handsome and willowy once, arrogant in his youthful beauty.

'You a shirt-lifter too?' the old man enquired bluntly.

'Me? No! No. Not at all. No.'

'He isn't,' Piers added, in case Greg hadn't made himself clear. 'He has a young girlfriend, to whom he is devoted.'

The old man sank back down in his chair with a sigh. 'Makes me bloody sick!' he bellowed, to Greg's alarm. 'When I was a lad you couldn't get a girl to lie down for you. Even after the first war, when there was supposed to be a shortage of chaps, they wouldn't lie down for you, not for love nor money.' He pointed his stick at Piers. 'Then by the time this whippersnapper was born the girls were giving it away for free all over the place and I was too old to enjoy it. And he turns out a shirt-lifter and shirt-lifters never had any trouble getting a bit of the other, which is why the rest of us hate them. Heh?'

He looked to Greg for agreement. 'I've never really thought about it in those terms,' he said, seeing that the old man genuinely awaited his reply.

'Well take my word for it. Uncomplicated sex. Just think: no women whining to be told you love them, no pregnancies, no demands for marriage. Queers have got it made. Do admit.'

'You may have a point,' Greg said readily, since he'd been brought up to be polite to his elders, an increasingly minority group. It still didn't sound like a good reason for jumping over the fence onto the other bus, if that wasn't a mixed metaphor, which it probably was.

The old man was still elaborating his thesis. 'All those bathhouses, half a dozen good screws in an afternoon —'

Greg flinched at the old man's surprisingly strong vocabulary, although he wasn't sure why he should expect the elderly to be more mealy-mouthed than anyone else.

'That was all a bit pre-Aids,' Piers murmured, 'We have to be more careful now.'

'Mind you,' Mr Hamilton went on, 'I did go to an orgy once. Must have been thirty years ago. In Salisbury, of all places. Pious sort of town, I always thought: bunch of God-botherers with nothing but that damned cathedral as far as the eye could see.'

Greg glanced at Piers who raised his eyes heavenwards like the most devout of Salisburians. He had heard this story too many times.

'Quite a night,' the old man was saying. 'There was one girl, I remember, fresh young thing — different from the other sordid old boilers — pretended to struggle, make a game of it.'

Greg stared at him, shocked at the implications,

but no doubt the old man was exaggerating for effect, as old men did.

'Could have done with more nights like that.' Mr Hamilton grinned wolfishly at Piers, eyeing his namesake with affection. 'The money *will* be yours one day.' He wagged his finger. 'But not yet. So!' He slapped his thigh. 'Let the merrymaking begin. Kill the fatted calf for the two black sheep of the Hamilton family.'

'Are you staying here?' Greg asked. 'On a visit.'

'Well, not here.' Mr Hamilton glanced round at Piers' cramped and untidy quarters without enthusiasm. 'Too many bloody stairs for a start. The lease has expired on my little mews house in Chelsea. I don't know! You buy these places with a sixty-year lease and the next minute they're telling you your time's up and you've got to move. I'm holed up at Boxford Hall till I sort something out. It's not too bad.'

Greg raised his eyebrows. Not too bad, indeed. Boxford Hall was the most expensive hotel for miles: a Georgian manor house overlooking a lake and velvet lawns, a chef with two Michelin stars and a Scottish temper that allowed him to refuse service to guests he didn't like the look of, even when they *had* booked the statutory month in advance.

'I believe Giacomo McFee does a very good fatted calf *à la façon de Touraine*,' young Piers remarked.

'All right,' old Piers said. 'Dinner at the Hall it is.'

* * *

Boxford Hall was a provincial parvenu's fantasy: a French chateau built in the Berkshire countryside by the first Lord Boxford in 1780. He had been an arms manufacturer and the American War of Independence had made him a very rich man, ennobled by his grateful country.

Deeply eccentric, Boxford had spent the last thirty years of his life here as a virtual recluse, tended only by male servants. He never left the Hall, even when a burst of anti-French feeling during the Napoleonic wars had led the local peasantry to attempt to raze this Gallic invader to the ground.

They failed — Lord Boxford being well supplied with his own weaponry — and their ringleaders were summarily hanged in the Market Place in Newbury.

He hated and feared women and legend had it that when, stepping into his gardens one fine summer's morning before breakfast, he had caught sight of a sprightly young milkmaid making her delivery from the local farm, he'd seized a scythe which the gardener had left lying on the lawn and flailed at her with it, wounding her in the neck. Fortunately the attack had not proved fatal and the girl's vengeful family had been pacified with gold coin.

Unsurprisingly, he had been the last as well as the first Lord Boxford: a short and undistinguished line.

Greg remembered the place as a prep school during his youth. On dull evenings he and his pals would sometimes cycle over with their catapults and hold a competition to see how many 'Boxford

Bolloxes' they could hit. In their purple and silver uniforms the boarders were hard to miss.

It had stood empty and mouldering during the eighties until, in 1991, it had been lavishly refurbished in its present incarnation. It was years since Greg had been here and he looked about him with nostalgia. He had demurred when included in the invitation — it was hospitality that he couldn't hope to repay — but the old man had been adamant.

'I can't take it with me,' he'd said. 'And the boy here will only spend it on drink and loose men.'

'Aha!' Piers said. 'Loose men come free, Unc.'

His uncle snorted. 'And bring your girlfriend too,' he suggested, his small eyes twinkling with a look that could only be described as lubricious. 'Young, you say? How young?'

Greg was glad to be able to reply, truthfully, that Angelica, having just started her course in psychology at Reading University, was staying over at college that night and would be unable to join them.

'Still at university?' Mr Hamilton eyed Greg with a new respect. 'Damn me!'

'A mature student,' he protested hastily, although Angie had only just turned twenty-four.

He'd gone home and put on his best suit before meeting the two Pierses in the bar at Boxford Hall at 7.30. Now he felt overdressed. Did no one want to look smart any more, he wondered, even in this holy of holies? True, no one was wearing jeans, but he seemed to be the only one in a tie. Smart casual. What the hell did that mean, anyway? It was so much easier just to put on a grey suit, blue shirt and plain tie.

No matching, no mixing, no possibility of error.

Mr Hamilton was wearing the same tweeds he'd had on that morning. Greg suspected that he'd been wearing the suit for weeks without sending it to the cleaners as it had that old-man smell about it: a whiff of sweat combined with the musty refusal to open a window on even the finest day. Young Piers was effortlessly elegant in that way he had which Greg envied; he consoled himself with the thought that it was a gift peculiar to gay men, though he was aware of the political incorrectness of this idea.

He looked round the place and breathed in the clean smell of money. He didn't know what it cost to stay here for a night but it seemed that Mr Hamilton was staying for weeks if not months. He could hardly bear to think what that would add up to.

They drank gin, with tonic for him, orange for the young photographer and pink for the old man. Greg found himself trying to work out exactly how old his host was as he regaled them with colourful stories of girls he had known — invariably in the biblical sense. Well over ninety, surely, to have been chasing women in the 1920s.

'Oh!' he exclaimed, after one particularly lurid reminiscence, banging his crystal tumbler on the polished table like a fractious infant and jolting out some of the pink liquid. 'What a cruel joke nature plays on us, Summers! The days of wine and roses, they are not long.'

'You never married?' Greg asked, thinking that Mr Hamilton had stretched his own wine-and-rose days out pretty well by the sound of it.

'*Pas si bête*!' His French accent was good and confident and he launched into tales of time spent liaising with de Gaulle and the Free French in 1943, which quickly segued into the pros and cons of French women versus their English cousins.

'Hairy armpits,' he reminisced. 'Always did something for me. The French know that a girl shouldn't be too clean, like when Napoleon sent Josephine that message telling her he was coming home so not to wash. American girls!' He shuddered melodramatically. 'Never out of the shower. It's like they've been sterilised. Heh?'

Greg was saved from having to answer this when a waiter sidled up to Mr Hamilton and murmured that his table was ready. He threw the youth a grateful look as his host rose with surprising alacrity and pronounced himself starving.

As they made their way into the dining room they had to pass a tall, lean man of about forty, his face familiar from newspaper and magazine articles, even television. He was immaculate in chef's whites, standing guard over the entrance to his kingdom, arms folded belligerently across his chest. His hair was bleached a platinum blond, making an odd contrast with his dark eyes, and cropped very short, which gave him a thuggish look.

He wore a single earring in his right lobe, a golden dagger.

Greg was the first through the door and made eye contact with the infamous chef. He smiled weakly and got a cold look in return. He felt like flashing his warrant card; that should get the man to show some respect. Then the chef saw Mr Hamilton and his face relented at the sight of his milch cow. He nodded them through. Greg was embarrassed to feel relieved, very English in his dislike of scenes.

Piers, bringing up the rear, blew the surprised chef a kiss.

Waiters fussed them into chairs at their table by the window; it was a round table, a good five feet in diameter, weighed down with a starched white cloth, matching napkins the size of tea towels, enough silverware to feed a small platoon, delicate china, three different glasses at each place and a big bowl of hothouse roses in the centre.

The menu, by contrast, was one page, hand-written, although the wine list made up for it: a leather bound volume like a small telephone directory which Mr Hamilton scrutinised as if memorising the contents, while conducting a muttered conversation of great length and complexity with the head wine waiter. Greg could make out the words 'biscuity' and 'a hint of vanilla'.

'Does that chap actually do any cooking?' he whispered while they waited for the conclusion of this conclave.

'Far too grand!' Piers murmured, his menu concealing his laughing lips. 'The kitchen is full of his slaves, toiling in heat and grease like damned souls.

A small boy turns the spit, blackened with soot, half roasted by the flames —'

'Yes, all right,' Greg said. 'I get the picture.'

The wine waiter finally departed with a big grin on his face and a girl came to take their order. She was in her late teens, slender and flat-chested as a boy, with a pointed face like a fox's, an effect enhanced by a shock of sleek ginger hair which contrasted well with her dour black and white uniform.

'What can I get you?' she asked in the rolling tones of rural Berkshire.

She wasn't pretty but something in her sheer youth made her appealing and Greg saw the tip of Mr Hamilton's blotchy tongue protrude to lick slowly round his full lips.

'I'll have the smoked duck,' he said hastily 'then, er . . .'

He glanced up from his menu as a flurry of gravel outside announced the arrival of another diner. It was the yellow Lotus and he watched the now familiar pantomime as the driver waited for her beau to come and open her door for her.

She wore a short but dressy outfit — what his mother would have called a cocktail dress — very plain, perfectly cut, black and cerise. The young man had on a cream suit that Greg thought must be silk, with a scarlet t-shirt under it. He had brown curly hair and pale skin and the splash of colour flattered him. Clearly some heterosexual men knew how to dress.

They handed the car over to a valet and disappeared from sight, only to reappear almost at once in the dining room. The chef jerked out of his laid-back demeanour in an instant, took both the woman's hands in his and kissed her first on one cheek, then the other, then the first again for good measure. She seemed to be introducing her companion and the two men shook hands.

Odd, Greg thought, to see the couple twice in one day. It was like when you heard a new word and, suddenly, you were hearing it everywhere. He thought that she glanced his way again, her eyes lingering on the threesome in the window, but then she turned away.

He finished giving his order and the waitress silently left.

Giacomo McFee led his new guests to their table and tended to them himself. Once they were seated, Greg could no longer see them and turned back to the job of earning his exorbitant dinner by being the ideal guest.

'Someone you know?' asked Mr Hamilton, who didn't miss much.

'I don't think so.'

'Not bad,' the old man commented, 'for her age. Heh?'

Greg didn't bother to answer this but sampled his wine, which was excellent, although he could detect neither biscuits nor vanilla.

He was certain that he had never seen the man before that morning, although there was something indefinably familiar about him: in the shape of his face, maybe, or the way he walked. But the thought that he knew the woman from somewhere, from another lifetime, nagged at him all evening.

Elsie Riley

He had no idea how long he'd been in the cupboard under the sink. Time did not operate here as it did outside where the sun shone and the air was scented with flowers. It must be some hours: long enough to soil himself, that was for sure, and that would earn him another punishment.

He moved carefully. The space was cramped and even an underfed boy of ten could bang himself on the crude wooden edges, forcing a splinter into flesh that was already sore. The cold white bulge of the kitchen sink above him made movement awkward.

Avoiding as best he could the damp patch that smelled of ordure, he flexed his legs against the far wall and heard the scuffling of mice behind the wood.

He wasn't afraid of mice; they'd never done him any harm.

He was chilly in his nakedness, although it was summer. When the nearby stove was lit in winter he was too hot, feeling the sweat running down his clammy back and a choking sensation in his asthmatic chest, as if iron bars were slowly tightening round his lungs and heart.

Cold was better: he could breathe in cold.

He was bad. That was obvious. Only a very bad boy would merit so much cruelty and so often. He was bad through and through. He was rotten to the core and had been born that way, the bastard spawn of a whore and her pimp.

And yet it seemed to him that the severity of the punishment bore no relation to the wickedness of his crime. When he did the twenty sums his father set him daily and got only nineteen right; when he tarried on the way home from school and was five minutes late; when he broke a cup or plate through clumsiness, trying as he was to skip out of the way of his father's fist: clearly those sins merited punishment.

But today all he had done was to answer his father with something other than a 'Yes, sir', saying 'But I didn't —' to the unfair charge that it was he who had damaged a rose bush in the garden when he had not been near it.

He had seen Isobel stifle a giggle. So she had trashed the bush. There was no point in his saying so.

He pushed at the door in the futile hope that it had somehow unlatched itself. He wanted to shout, to yell that he could no longer bear it, that he must have light, air, clothing for the pre-pubescent body that so embarrassed him, but there was no one to hear, for which he was thankful.

In the darkness he put his thumb in his mouth and found comfort in the contact the way an infant does, in the salty taste of his skin. It was something he often did when alone, in his hard bed at night, but a sin which would bring retribution as surely as the rest.

'The boy's a retard!' his father had shouted once, on catching him in the act. 'Do you see him, Annie, sucking his thumb like a baby? A retard and an ingrate.'

Ungrateful: he must be, for they had given him so much — he, who had no real claim on their kindness. The house was a large one, comfortable enough if slightly

*old-fashioned. It was full of beautiful things that had been
in the family for generations, things that he scarcely dared
to touch. His mother kept it clean and shining. There were
rooms where no one ever went, since they had no visitors,
rooms that were kept locked and unheated.*

*The lovely gardens were the envy of the neighbourhood,
tended not by a jobbing gardener but by his father's own
hands, so gently pliant as they caressed flower or shrub.*

*He went to a private day school in the nearest town
and it wasn't cheap, as his father told him repeatedly, and
probably wasted on him since he was a dullard, a retard, a
disgrace to the honoured name he bore. He didn't mix
with the local children because they went to the village
school. They didn't like him, anyway, made fun of the way
he spoke.*

*His one attempt to make human contact had ended
when an older boy had set his dog on him and they'd all
laughed as he sprinted for home, arriving so breathless
that he'd curled up on the flagstones of the hall floor and
waited for death to rescue him, sobbing in disappointment
when it had not come.*

*The house had been silent for hours but now he heard
the car pulling up outside, a metallic slamming, the
scratching of a key in the front door, murmured voices.*

Footsteps approached his prison.

*They were light footsteps, the carefree scamper of a girl
of nine, his sister Isobel. The door was unlatched and a
shrill voice shouted, 'Pooh! Daddy, Antony's wet himself
again. Daddy!'*

He was about to be set free.

He began to wheeze.

Greg knew that Sir Joachim Weissman, RA, had been in his eighties at the time of his death two years earlier so he assumed the widow to be of similar vintage. The sight of the yellow Lotus parked on the gravel in front of the sprawling house called Alders End made him reassess.

Lady Weissman had reported a prowler and, since her husband had been something of a local celebrity — a Jewish refugee from the ghetto of Salzburg turned grand old man of British art — and she sat on the same committees as his chief super's wife, he'd been volunteered to call in on her on his way home one afternoon, to see if there was genuine cause for concern or just an old woman's fancies.

'She's got some valuable stuff,' Chief Superintendent Barkiss said, 'out of the usual league,' and added rather dismissively, 'Arty stuff.'

She lived on the edge of the village of Alderbright not five miles from his own modest house in Kintbury and three miles by road from Boxford Hall. Probably used it as her local café.

No one would describe Alders End as modest: it rambled charmingly over two floors in an acre of immaculate garden. The front of the house looked Georgian, but Greg could see that much of it was earlier, maybe sixteenth century, and deduced that a new building had been added in the eighteenth century and the house turned so that it faced another way, leaving the original and humbler dwelling as a side wing.

Honeysuckle covered the stone porch, fading

now, shedding the last of its flowers in the October winds. He pulled an old-fashioned bell. A late wasp fell from the climbing plant as he waited, falling dead at his feet. He ground it under his heel to make sure.

The smile she gave him as she opened the door was warm and genuine. It was her, all right: sooty hair, blue eyes, that rare and enticing combination found only in certain parts of the Celtic fringes. He realised that she was a little older than he had thought in Hungerford that Saturday morning two weeks ago, betrayed by a slight wattling of the neck.

She was his own age.

She wore the sort of casual but well-cut trousers that he associated with old Katherine Hepburn films, pale beige, with a navy silk blouse and a cashmere cardigan of the same hue. A thick rope of coral strands hung round her neck, echoed by two neat studs in her long-lobed ears.

'Lady Weissman?'

'I'm Elise Weissman.'

He introduced himself and showed her his warrant card. She took it from him and scrutinised the photo, then the reality. Her eyes were laughing as she handed it back and he thought he must be missing something.

'You reported a prowler,' he reminded her.

'Indeed yes. How good of you to respond so promptly, Superintendent. Please come in.'

She turned away and he followed her into the house, shutting the front door behind him. The scuttling of claws on the hall floor at that moment announced the arrival of a terrier. It stopped at Greg's feet, sat back on its haunches and lifted one small paw to his knee. He felt neutral about dogs but this one's brown eyes looked up at him with such trust, such confidence that its attentions were welcome, that he hadn't the heart to disappoint it and bent to scratch behind its ears.

It emitted a mew of pleasure, almost like a cat.

'Bellini,' Lady Weissman said, by way of introduction. 'She's a Westie: a West Highland Terrier.'

The dog's coat was immaculately white, like a world without sin. 'Must be hard work to keep her so clean,' he commented.

'Not at all,' the dog's owner said wryly. 'When we reach a puddle or a patch of mud she waits patiently for me to carry her across.'

'She's got you well trained!'

They both laughed then, with good will established, she told him her story.

'I was getting ready for bed last night and I heard something in the garden, a noise like somebody . . . *scrambling* is the best description I can come up with. I looked out of the window and thought I could see movement near the back wall. I put my dressing gown on and hurried down. When I switched on the outside lights, I saw a figure run for cover. He vaulted back over the wall.'

'Could you see anything of him in the darkness?'

'I can't give you a useful description, I'm afraid. Tallish, thinnish, in something like jeans and a bomber jacket. That's all. He was moving fast, though, like a young man, even a teenage boy.' She smiled down at her hairy companion. 'Bellini's not much of a guard dog, I'm afraid, though she has a surprisingly loud bark when she chooses.'

'There's been a spate of burglaries round these parts lately.'

'So I hear.'

'Almost certainly the same man and we'd like to catch him. He takes mostly portable things — cash, jewellery — and there's been some vandalism: sheer spite, by the look of it.'

'That's what worries me most,' she said, with a faint shudder. 'I don't keep much cash in the house and I don't care about jewellery, but wanton destruction . . .'

'May I see the view from your window?'

She led the way upstairs. He had been right about the history of the house since the old and new parts were separated by an oak door so stout as to be all but soundproof. Lady Weissman took him through this, down a single step and into the older part. A brief corridor opened almost at once into a low-ceilinged room overlooking the back garden.

The room was wide and long but its lack of height gave it an intimate air. Greg could have reached up and touched the ceiling on his tiptoes. It was an irregular shape too, with pleasing corners in unexpected places. Two mullioned windows jutted out at the side and back, one slightly ajar.

It was blissfully uncluttered: a single bed, draped

all in white muslin, stood at an angle between the windows; a bedside cabinet bore a glass of water and a paperback book; in the side window stood a polished table on which a bowl of chrysanthemums neared the end of their life.

'Joachim and I chose this room for ourselves, away from the hubbub of the rest of the house,' she explained. 'Now it is mine, my sanctuary.'

Two plain wooden doors stood open to his left. He could make out a bathroom and a dressing room — more of a walk-in cupboard — with racks of clothes, mostly neutral colours but with the odd splash of turquoise or fuchsia. He crossed the room to stand in the rear window.

'This one?' he asked.

She nodded, joining him. 'As you can see, it gives a view of the whole garden.'

The grounds were neatly laid out without being regimented, an English hotch-potch of lawns and shrubs, fruit trees and rose bushes. A series of black alders, rather overgrown, stood guard over the path that snaked down to a wooden structure which Greg initially took for a summerhouse. It was the oddest summerhouse he'd ever seen, though; built of pale wood, it had no windows in the sides but the whole of the sloping roof was one giant skylight, tilting south.

He looked a question at her.

'Joachim's studio,' she said. 'He had it specially built. No one has set foot in there for the past two years. Rather a waste.'

More pedestrianly, a car port nestled against the side fence, housing an open-tailed van which bristled with gardening impedimenta. A wiry old man who had clearly spent his whole life out of doors was methodically raking up leaves into a wheelbarrow.

'Mr Weatherby,' Lady Weissman explained. 'He comes twice a week. We call him Mr Weatherbeaten, though not to his face.'

'Does he live in the village?' Greg asked.

'Cottage near the church, with his teenage son and daughter.'

'Teenage?' Greg squinted harder at the old man. He wore a shady hat and it was hard to make out his features or colouring. His arms were lithe and well muscled, bare beneath a tee shirt that had once been white and a sleeveless quilted jacket the colour of sludge.

'He married late,' Lady Weissman said, 'then lost his wife young. Worst of all possible worlds.'

The old man wheeled his loaded barrow to the far corner of the garden where a bonfire was steadily growing, emptied the leaves onto it and weighed them down with a couple of wood trimmings. He made his way back, leaving the barrow by the bonfire, and, without seeming to look up, raised his rake in greeting to the lady of the house who waved back.

He threw the rake into the back of the open-tailed van, skipped into the driver's seat with the speed and grace of a sprinter, fired the engine, reversed

adroitly out and was gone with a small puff of
smoke from the dodgy exhaust pipe.

'Joachim did a sketch of him once,' she said. 'It
was superb, one of his best, but when he offered it to
Silas he reacted as if Joachim was trying to steal his
soul. He was offended.' She shook her head in
amazement. 'He could have sold it for thousands!'

'Show me where you first saw your intruder.'

Elise Weissman pointed to a place in the rear wall,
to the left of the studio. 'That was where he came
over the wall, I think, certainly the way he left. Even
on a bright night the shadow of the studio falls on
that spot. As you see, we have a wall on one side,
wooden fencing by the road and hedges leading
onto the fields. We are nothing if not inconsistent.'

Walled gardens were a suburban dweller's
dream and a policeman's nightmare.

'I can't bear to put barbed wire on that wall,' she
added, as if reading his mind, 'or broken glass. It's
so ugly.'

'Do you live alone?' he asked, for she had said
'we' more than once. He remembered how his
mother had gone on using the plural pronoun for
years after the death of his father: for the rest of her
life, in fact. 'He is still with me,' she would say when
he queried it, 'and I never make any changes without thinking "What would Donald have done?"'

Lady Weissman was answering his question and
he dragged his thoughts back from his moment of
nostalgia. 'I'm a widow but my daughter looks in
often and, just lately, I've had my son staying at

weekends.' She fiddled with the coral strands, twining them in her fingers with an unexpected awkwardness. 'Antony, my son.'

Was that the handsome young man he had taken for a boyfriend, even a gigolo? He felt embarrassed at his own assumptions.

He cleared his throat.

'Yes,' she said. 'That was who you saw me with in Hungerford a couple of weeks ago, and at Boxford Hall that same night. My son.'

Alert, he thought. Observant. Not self-absorbed. Her smile was teasing; she could read the conclusions he'd jumped to as easily as she read her *Times* each morning. But why the sudden awkwardness?

'He looks a fine young man,' he said lamely.

'That remains to be seen,' she said, a little oddly. 'Come.'

She led the way downstairs into a sitting room at the back of the Georgian part of the house. The dog dodged ahead of them and installed itself on a chaise longue by the cone-filled fireplace. It was a large, square room with tall windows looking onto the terrace. It was cool and dark with polished oak floorboards and a single rug which he assumed was Persian.

There were no ornaments, no photographs; furniture and curtains were of the plainest cuts and colours though of the best fabric. He realised that it was designed as a background to show off her husband's pictures, nothing allowed to detract from them.

On the wall opposite the windows one massive painting hung in solitary grandeur. Each side wall displayed two smaller canvases: a portrait, two landscapes and a still life. He stood in front of the large painting for a moment, hoping for inspiration, for something to say.

Lady Weissman clicked on a light above the canvas and he caught his breath in admiration.

It was a seascape: somewhere far out in the ocean, he thought, judging by the cold grey of the water and the height of the waves. A sailing ship, its main mast shattered, plunged desperately in the storm as her sailors fought for their lives. He could almost hear their shrieks of fear as the ocean prepared to claim them for its own, their prayers as they begged the Lord for mercy.

He felt his breath quicken, his heart beat faster, and he stretched out a hand towards the painting, wanting to reach into it and help them, to restore to them their lives. He snatched it back at the last minute, feeling foolish, but the gentle smile on his hostess's face told him that she understood, that she did not think him a fool.

He no longer sought for something to say: words were superfluous. No wonder the thought of vandalism had made her shudder.

'Journey to the New World,' she said, her voice faint to his ears. 'It depicts the French Huguenots fleeing from persecution after the Edict of Nantes, which had given them freedom of worship, was revoked.'

He wished he had paid more attention in history classes; he wasn't even sure what century they were talking about and he didn't want to parade his ignorance by asking.

In the bottom left-hand corner he saw the flourish 'Joachim' in scarlet, no more than that, no need of surname.

'How could he ever bear to sell one?' he asked.

'He said it was like selling his soul each time and he was most particular whom he sold to, but there is a sort of companion piece to this — The Massacre of St Bartholomew's Eve — which is in the Met in New York. We went to visit it on our honeymoon. That was how he phrased it, to visit it, as if it were a relative. There were people, collectors, he wouldn't sell to at any price and he used to make anyone who bought his work promise by all they held dear not to sell it on during his lifetime.'

She laughed. 'There's been a lot of selling in the last two years, since his death, and at the most inflated prices, but these five paintings will leave the house only over my dead body. Literally.'

'Could these be what the prowler was after?' he asked. If so, it was not the same man who stuffed his pockets with cash and jewellery. You would need a van to shift this lot.

She switched the light above the seascape off and motioned him to an armchair, sitting down opposite him. 'I wondered that myself. They're not even insured.'

'What!'

She shrugged. 'What would be the point? To me they are beyond price and if I lose them then no insurance money will make up for it.'

'But they do have some definable monetary value, I take it?'

'Perhaps three million pounds. Altogether.'

He gaped at her, speechless. She explained further.

'When we enquired about insuring them the insurance company wanted us to turn Alders End into a fortress — a virtual prison, with locks and bolts and bars everywhere — instead of the happy family house we intended it to be. We did not choose to live like that.'

He said, 'But you have a burglar alarm, at least. I saw the box on the front wall.' Half hidden by the honeysuckle.

'Mmm.' She grinned like a naughty schoolgirl caught out in a prank. 'But I don't set it all that often — not at night, anyway. Bellini sleeps on my bed but she sometimes likes a nocturnal wander round her territory. After she'd set the alarm off for the third night running, I rather gave it up as a bad job.'

'Perhaps you might keep her shut up till we sort out this prowler,' he suggested.

'Perhaps, but I thought burglaries mostly took place during the day.'

'Opportunist burglaries, yes,' he said, 'kids looking to heist a video and some bits of jewellery, but a proper art thief, that's another matter. He'd be watching you, perhaps for weeks, learning your habits and movements, until he thinks the time is right.'

She turned to look at her garden for a moment, her vivid eyes fixed far away, and he admired the nobility of her profile. Then she turned back to him and said, 'Would you like some tea, Greg?'

He didn't answer, momentarily surprised by her use of his Christian name. She said, 'You don't remember me, do you?'

He frowned. Somewhere, deep inside, there was memory.

'I'm not surprised,' she went on. 'It's been — what? — thirty-five years, although I recognised you at once. Perhaps women change more than men do.' She rose again and went to the side wall, illuminating the portrait. 'Does this help?'

He joined her. It was Elise Weissman, clearly, but much younger, about twenty. Her hair was longer and dishevelled as a gipsy's. Her tanned body was naked except for some modestly placed flowers. She seemed to be dancing, or about to dance, or just to have stopped dancing, perhaps, because there was a sense of movement in the background which he couldn't quite place, of music.

She was beautiful, as beautiful as any woman he had seen. He felt himself blushing, since he was rarely invited to admire a middle-aged woman of his acquaintance naked, but he forced himself to look at the real thing again, the forty-something woman, still handsome despite the wrinkles round her eyes and mouth.

'That was the first portrait he painted of me,' Lady Weissman said. 'He called it "Tinker Girl" and he would never sell it.' She sighed and extinguished the light. She stood looking at him in mild exasperation at his stupidity, her hands on her hips.

'Badger's Copse?' she prompted him. 'Those endless summer evenings in the early sixties, climbing trees, skimming stones across the pond, catching cockroaches and making them race. Waterman's Farm and my mother's griddle cakes dripping with her gooseberry jam. Gregory Summers and —'

'Elsie Riley!' he finished for her. 'It can't be.'

'But it is.'

'I thought you gave your name as Elise.'

'Obviously I wasn't going to go through life saddled with a name like Elsie. When I got up to London at the age of eighteen everybody laughed at me, so a boyfriend suggested a tiny amendment, two letters swopped, and I've been Elise for thirty years.'

He sat down with a bump and muttered 'Elsie Riley'.

'I assume you want that tea, unless you need something stronger.' He didn't answer and she left the room with her quick, light step as he sat lost in reminiscence.

She had been his best friend when they were ten, eleven. Those were the days when a rigid apartheid ruled between girls — who were soppy — and boys — who were rough — and he'd taken a lot of stick for having Elsie Riley as a best mate. But she'd been a regular tomboy and his match in everything, not squeamish about spiders and mice, snakes and bats.

Her parents were Irish by birth and worked on Waterman's Farm, her father looking after the cattle while her mother helped in the house and with the poultry and the dairy. Those were the good old days when mixed farming was the norm and the fields weren't full of yellow rape as far as the sun shone.

It was as if he could hear her strange hybrid accent — half Irish, half Berkshire burr, quite different to the ladylike way she spoke now — calling to him across the years as she urged him into some new mischief. 'Come on, Greg!' That had been her battle cry as he, her cowardly lieutenant, protested that their parents would never approve.

At eleven, their paths had divided. He'd passed the eleven plus and gone to grammar school; she had failed — their class teacher, nasty Mrs Sheedy, making a point of telling the whole school that Elsie Riley had come bottom in the test for the county — and been consigned to the secondary modern.

They'd sworn blood brotherhood, solemnly pricking their thumbs with his blunt penknife and mingling the red drops.

He examined his thumb as if expecting to see the scar.

The inevitable had happened: they no longer saw each other every day at school, had to make an effort to meet up. Then there'd been a row at the farm and Mr Riley had moved his family to another place near the Savernake Forest which raised whole new logistical problems.

Meanwhile he, Greg, had homework to fill his evenings, along with the chess club and the third-eleven football team and, as he realised only years later, his parents had subtly discouraged the friend-ship, wanting better things for him than a simple Irish girl who flitted through the woods like a dryad.

Elsie Riley, who had once been a sister to him, but whom he hadn't thought of in more than thirty years.

If they could see her now, he thought, with a strange pride: ragamuffin Elsie Riley with her skinned knees and grazed knuckles, barefoot on her horny feet, with grit in her hair and the torn clothes that Mrs Riley mended with the patience of Grizelda.

She came back into the room carrying a tray of tea things and he rose and took them from her. He placed them reverently on an old oak chest that did duty as a coffee table and turned to her with tears in his eyes.

'Elsie Riley!' He hugged her to him so hard that she let out a little squeak of protest and Bellini sat up on her sofa and growled a warning. 'Elsie. I am so glad. So glad!'

'I wasn't thick after all,' she explained as they drank tea from Meissen china. 'I was dyslexic, which no one had heard of then. I never did get on academically because my condition wasn't diagnosed but I could draw and paint, a bit.'

'You went to art school?'

She shook her head. 'You needed A levels for that too. No, I went into the business on the other side of the canvas, as it were. I was an artist's model. As it turned out, I scrubbed up okay under all that tomboy dirt.'

'You certainly did!' he said, looking once more at the portrait of the young Elsie. Elise, as she had become by then.

'Joachim was already middle-aged, of course, but he had more life in him than many a man half his age. He asked me to marry him and I didn't hesitate. All oddly respectable for Bohemian artists. I soon realised that he wanted his home life settled — meals ready when he was hungry, clean clothes to pull on when the old ones got too dirty. That way he needn't think about anything but his work. Chasing girls took up too much time and energy that would be better devoted to his art, so he didn't bother.'

She glanced over her shoulder at the portrait. 'The day he finished that was the day he asked me to marry him. It has always held a special place in our hearts. Tinker Girl is not allowed out on loan to exhibitions. I doubt if more than fifty people in the world have ever set eyes on it.'

'I'm honoured. And you have a daughter and a son.'

'We had Cressida. She's twenty-six. Married, twin

boys. They live in Marlborough. Her husband, Stephen, teaches at the College.'

'Not far, then.'

'As I say, she pops over often, especially if she wants me to watch the boys for her. So, what about you? Married?'

'Briefly. Long time ago. I live with Angelica now. She's a mature student at Reading. Psychology.'

'I do admire women who can let their lives take a different course in middle age.' She made assumptions about Angie which he didn't choose to correct, although he knew that Elsie Riley wouldn't judge him. 'Children?'

He was always cagey about this question but Elsie was his oldest friend and he wouldn't dissemble with her. 'One son, Frederick. He died of leukaemia eighteen months ago. He was twenty-two.'

She spared him the customary exclamations of dismay, but her eyes bored into him, seeking to know how deep this pain went. He couldn't tell her all of it, or not yet: how Angelica was his dead son's widow and the love of his life; how he was still full of guilt and shame, knowing that he could have her only because Fred had died.

'But you too have a son,' he said quickly. 'Antony.'

'Antony Lucas.'

He was puzzled. 'You were married before?'

She shook her head and put her tea cup slowly down on the chest. 'Antony was born when I was eighteen, a mistake. I gave him up for adoption. We have found each other only recently. Rather, he found me. He contacted me a few weeks ago. We've been getting acquainted. It was a hell of a shock.'

'I'll bet.'

'I'm glad it didn't come earlier. I never told Joachim, you see. He was, in some unexpected ways, an old-fashioned man.'

They sat in silence for a moment and when she next spoke her words seemed strange to him, although he would come to understand them better before the year was out.

She said, 'Greg Summers and Elsie Riley, playing in the woods in those endless sunny days of childhood. If we any of us knew what the future held, would we have the strength to go on?'

He walked round the garden before he left, examining the wall and the ground around it. It was an old wall, perhaps the original from when the house was built, and the pointing was worn away, making useful hand- and footholds. He decided that he could climb it himself easily enough although his wall-climbing years were long behind him.

There was a flowerbed immediately in front of the wall, giving way soon to lawn which would have kept no footprints from the previous night, springing back up with the morning's dew. He crouched down and brushed aside the trailing leaves of a pale clematis that snaked creamily up the brickwork.

'Ah!' he said.

'I forbade Silas to go anywhere near this flowerbed today in case he disturbed evidence. That's right, isn't it?'

'Quite right.'

'I never miss an episode of Inspector Morse.'

The footprints were blurred, overlaid, the lower ones coming, the upper going. He wouldn't be able to lift a decent print from it but as least he had a good idea of the size. An eight, he thought, in a trainer. Medium to small.

Greg went straight to the collator's office when he got to the station the following morning. His first thought with any type of burglary was an inside job.

'Know anything about a man called Weatherby?' he asked without preamble. 'Alderbright.'

The sergeant snorted. 'Do I! Bloody little toe rag.'

Greg was puzzled. 'Are we talking about the same person? Silas Weatherby, works as a jobbing gardener.'

'Not the old man!' Sergeant Clifton said impatiently, as if he expected Greg to be a mind reader. 'The boy, Dickon, his son. Been in trouble since he was ten. Before that —'

'Below the age of criminal responsibility.'

'The lads were practically camped on his doorstep on his tenth birthday.'

'What's he into?'

'You name it: shoplifting, car theft, burglary, vandalism, pick- pocketing, a little light mugging, nothing too violent. His social worker says it's because his mum died when he was seven, but — I ask you — what sort of excuse is that?'

'Has he done time?' Greg asked.

'Couple of spells in Borstal — maybe fifteen months all told — but mostly he gets off with a slapped wrist.'

'Is he out now?'

'Last three months. Says he's going straight. Right! Once a toe rag, always a toe rag.'

What *was* a toe rag, Greg wondered. 'Dickon, you say? Unusual.'

'His sister's called Jennet. Nice girl.'

'Dickon and Jennet, how charmingly medieval.'

'The only medieval thing about Dickon Weatherby is that he's a great plague,' Clifton said.

Greg looked at him with respect. 'That's quite good!'

'Thank you.'

'What's the address?'

Clifton didn't need to look it up. 'Victoria Cottages, Numero Uno.'

'*Muchas Gracias.*'

Cuckoo in the nest

Twenty to ten on Monday morning found Greg sitting in the conference room on the top floor of the police station, drumming his fingers on the oblong table before him.

It was a soulless place which gave a sensitive man no incentive to linger and he glanced impatiently at his watch for the third time in ten minutes, wondering if it was on a go-slow. Five chairs were arranged haphazardly round the table, three of them unoccupied. Along one wall stood a row of desks, each with a computer, currently switched off.

Dusty Venetian blinds had been closed to block out a sudden burst of cold autumn sun.

In the other occupied chair sat his immediate subordinate and, after Greg had doodled the words 'Operation Cuckoo' on the pristine pad in front of him and filled in all the Os in red biro, he thought he might as well use the time while they waited for their colleagues by getting to know him better.

Newbury CID had been without a detective chief inspector since the abrupt departure of Harry Stratton during the Jordan Abbot investigation last summer. Greg had recently been sent an acting DCI from another part of the Thames Valley force, a colourless young inspector named Timothy Monroe, known in the canteen, with a predictable lack of originality, as Marilyn.

Monroe was in his early thirties. He was a fast-track officer with a degree in Politics and Economics, reputed to be clever. So far, Greg had merely found him diligent and thorough. The man seemed to him to lack imagination, but perhaps he was being unfair. As yet, he had hardly had time to get to know him: with his home being in Slough and his wife having recently given birth to their first child, he lacked the time to socialise and join the rest of CID in the pub at the end of a long day.

'So, how's it going?' he asked. 'Settling in all right?'

Monroe, relieved that the superintendent had stopped ignoring him, replied heartily. 'Fine, thank you, sir. I'm glad to be given this opportunity so soon . . .'

He broke off, running his fingers awkwardly through his sandy hair. He wasn't sure exactly what had happened to DCI Stratton, knew only that he'd resigned from the force one step ahead of the boot. While he didn't want to rejoice in his fellow officer's misfortune, it had been the opening he had been praying for.

With a new baby, the extra money was particularly welcome. Why did nobody ever tell you how bloody expensive babies were?

He wasn't sure, either, what to make of Gregory Summers, who was so different from his old guv'nor. In the three weeks he'd been commuting to Newbury he had yet to hear him bawl anyone out, for one thing, or reduce them to a quivering wreck with the sharp edge of his tongue. He was also a lot more hands-on than his former boss who'd seldom set foot outside his office except to go to a Rotary dinner.

Not wanting to appear tongue-tied and seeking a neutral subject, Monroe began talking about the force's problem-solving initiative, of which he was a firm supporter.

Under the initiative the perpetrators of trivial offences — minor thefts or vandalism — were called into the station where a policeman would talk informally with them, trying to find out what lay at the root of the crime, be it boredom or lack of guidance at home, showing to a cocky lad or girl the human face of the law guardians.

Nipping the bud of a hardened criminal while it was still soft.

That was probably where his talent lay, Greg thought, slightly bored by his subordinate's unemphatic voice: formulating policy, peddling ideas to politicians from an ACC's uniform. He was not against the problem-solving initiative himself, thought it was worth a try even if it did smack of social work, but nor did it exactly thrill him.

After a while he let the man drone on without even trying to listen, observing him instead, trying to read the DCI's character in his appearance and body language. He was of medium height and build, not made to stand out in a crowd, which was an asset when it came to covert police work but not always when promotion was in the wind.

Greg thought that he wasn't good-looking —
with his angular face and too short nose, his eyes
that were neither blue nor grey, his freckles — but
he'd learned over the years that women had
strange tastes and would fall for a nondescript man
on the grounds that he had 'a twinkle in his eye' or
'a lovely voice'.

Monroe was wearing a suit, as he had every day
since his arrival. He appeared to have three which
he rotated strictly. This one was a navy blue two
piece with a subtle red stripe that matched his tie.
Greg had seen it in the window of Marks and
Spencer.

The DCI seemed to have stopped talking. He
cleared his throat and Greg realised that he had
asked him a question.

They stared at each other in horror.

He was saved when his sergeant, Barbara Carey,
finally arrived, holding the door for a tall man wearing what was clearly a more expensive suit than
either Monroe's or his own, Italian cut. They were
followed by a shorter man in casual clothes: an
open-necked shirt and sports jacket over a pair of
khaki chinos.

Barbara introduced them as Chief Inspector Stan
Krepski and Inspector Trevor Faber of the NCS.
Greg threw her a grateful look and she raised her
eyebrows in query.

The men exchanged firm handshakes, a competi-
tive sport. Krepski took one of the spare seats next to
Greg, who scrutinised the newcomer while he settled

himself, taking his time about it. He was just the right side of forty and substantial without being fat, relaxed, pushing his chair back and spreading his limbs so that he took up more space. His dark blond hair was carefully cut to disguise thinning and his eyes, while on the small side, were dark and intense.

A man's man, Greg thought, probably a rugby player like Fred. Many women would find him attractive.

Barbara, who did not, sat down at the end of the table. Faber sank into the last empty seat and produced the smallest laptop Greg had seen from his jacket pocket. He flipped it open, pressed a few keys and looked expectantly at his colleagues. He had a thin face, framed with hair that was an indeterminate colour and a shade too long. A shrewd intelligence looked out of his eyes as he met Greg's gaze and held it for just the right length of time.

Pushing thirty, Greg thought. Young for an inspector. Ambitious.

'Hope we're not late,' Krepski was saying, his voice harsh, even ugly. 'Traffic was terrible on the M4.'

'Always is on a Monday,' Monroe offered.

'I thought we'd be going *against* the rush hour traffic, but when we tried to join the motorway at Chiswick —'

Barbara interrupted this peculiarly masculine discussion before it could deteriorate further. She plonked her heavy leather briefcase on the table and took out a set of five files which she passed round.

'Got the papers you biked over last night photocopied, as you asked, sir,' she said to Krepski.

'Sorry I was so late sending them,' he said, not sounding sorry at all. 'Well, shall we start? I'm very pleased to meet you all as you have a vital role to play in Operation Cuckoo.'

Operation Cuckoo was a project under the oversight of the NCS, which stood for National Crime Squad and not, as some people cynically suggested, No Crimes Solved. The United Kingdom did not have an integrated police force but was divided into fifty regional forces which did not always co-operate as well as they might.

The NCS had been set up to co-ordinate problems which were nationwide in their scope and serious-ness, then been divided into three regions just to break things up again. Krepski and Faber were from the southern region, based, inevitably, in London.

The task of Cuckoo was to deal with illegal immi-grants: stopping them from entering the country, where possible, tracking them down when they did, arresting and punishing those who imported them and those who used them as a source of cheap labour.

The series of brutal wars in the Balkans in the 1990s had exacerbated the problem both of asylum seekers and those who attempted to circumvent the ponderous and sometimes arbitrary asylum system with more direct action. Recently the British public had come to perceive both groups as a major threat to their quality of life.

Politicians, who knew better, pandered to these fears, anxious to avoid accusations that they were 'out of touch' or 'not listening to the man — sorry, *person* — in the street'.

Cuckoo was not an operation that was likely to see a definite end. Like the war against drugs or money laundering, it would be keeping the police busy long after the five officers round the table were drawing their pensions or pushing up daisies. In that sense it was doomed to frustrate them.

'Reason I emphasise your importance,' Krepski said, after his brief introduction, 'is that we consider the Thames Valley a prime target for these criminals — perhaps *the* prime target after London.'

Greg had no argument with that. Prosperous Newbury was bound to catch the eye of these smugglers of human flesh, many of whom were little better than slave traders, selling illegal immigrants as cheap labour, knowing that they wouldn't dare to complain about pay or conditions.

The bizarre difference from the slave merchants of the eighteenth century was that the slaves themselves paid for the trip.

So a family in China or Iraq would scrape together everything they possessed to send one son to England, and mortgage their future too. Often, in addition, the immigrant had to keep paying his 'benefactors' out of his earnings to avoid reprisals to the family back home.

'What with Heathrow airport a short ride away by car,' Krepski went on. 'I expect you know it's the busiest international airport in the world.' They all murmured agreement. 'Then there are good roads south to the harbours at Southampton and Portsmouth.'

'You could hide a herd of elephants in some of those container ships,' Monroe said. 'Plus there's a good ethnic mix here. No one sticks out, whatever their accent or complexion.'

'Like in the Smoke,' Krepski said with a snort. 'Bits of it look like down-town Calcutta.'

'You know there's no unemployment in Newbury?' Greg said.

'None?' Krepski said, startled, while Faber glanced up from his keyboard, interested.

'Effectively. Just the literally unemployable,' Greg explained, 'drug addicts, alcoholics, people with serious mental health problems.'

Companies paid substantial bonuses to staff members who recruited friends to work for them. Other businesses were threatening to leave the area altogether and settle in some part of the country where people were grateful for the work.

'You can't get anyone to do unskilled jobs,' Barbara put in. 'Every pub and café in the area has a sign up begging for staff.'

Roads went unswept and public parks unweeded.

But then they said that if police recruitment didn't pick up soon they'd be bringing in officers from overseas. And imported officers would be demanding handguns, incredulous that the British police kept the peace in the 21st century with batons.

'So maybe we could do with some fresh labour,' Barbara concluded. 'Is economic migration such a terrible thing?'

Faber indulged in a faint smile. Krepski looked at her as if she had just spat on the portrait of the Queen that graced the otherwise bare walls of the conference room but Barbara was not so easily deterred.

'Immigrants have *died* trying to enter this country,' she said. 'There were those people baked in that airless van in Dover earlier this year. And one man fell to his death from 30,000 feet after clinging to the frozen undercarriage of a jumbo jet for hours. You're talking desperation here.'

'We have problems of our own,' Krepski snapped. 'We can't be sentimental about migrants. The interests of our own people have to come first and they're sick of beggars on the streets, refugee camps full of dole scroungers, their council tax rising every year to meet the cost.'

His voice was getting louder, more emphatic and the three officers from Newbury watched him uneasily, while Faber studied his own fingernails.

'People who can't even speak the language half the time —'

'I'd like to get one thing straight.' Greg's intervention was deliberately repressive; he didn't like the turn the meeting was taking.

'Sir!' Krepski snapped to attention in his seat.

'Is the main point of Operation Cuckoo to catch illegal immigrants or to stop the people who traffic in them?'

Krepski shrugged. 'It all boils down to the same thing.'

'I can't agree.'

'Well, I'll put your question to the Commander in charge of the operation.' Krepski was pulling rank vicariously, his plump cheeks smiling without mirth. 'I'm sure he'll get back to you.'

'Pompous twerp,' Barbara said when she got back from seeing Krepski and Faber to their car. 'That's a good old English name, isn't it? Stanislav Krepski. Was it his parents or grandparents who came here as economic migrants. Any bets?'

'All right, Babs,' Greg said with a smile. 'I didn't take to the man either but let's not get personal. With luck, we won't see too much of him.'

'His friend was a bit taciturn,' Barbara remarked. 'If he hadn't said "How do you do?" downstairs, I might have taken him for a mute.'

'My guess would be that he uses his eyes and ears a lot more than his mouth. Not a bad character trait, at that.'

'If rare in a policeman,' she said. 'In a *man*, come to that.'

'I'm glad you picked him up on the main purpose of the operation, sir,' Monroe said. 'I agree that they are two different matters and that we should be concentrating on stopping the trade, not on persecuting the immigrants. In a sense, they're victims of the crime too.'

'Fine!' Greg clapped him on the back. 'I hereby

appoint you as our liaison with the NCS, Tim. You can keep in touch with DCI Krepski.'

Barbara tried not to smile at Tim Monroe's look of dismay.

Victoria Cottages dated from the 1890s, Greg surmised, from the old Queen's diamond jubilee. There were five of them, a two-up-two-down terrace, presumably built to house the deserving poor of the village.

The centre of Alderbright was compact around a green whose pond was still covered in algae from the hot summer. Its pub and shop had long gone, its link to the outside world of commerce consisting of one bus a day into Newbury and one out again. The church remained locked except on the first and third Sundays of the month when Evensong might be heard.

On the far side of the church was the Old Rectory, a handsome stone dwelling with a builder's sign outside. Opposite it was the brick bungalow where the team vicar — an alarming woman called Daphne — now lived, central to the three churches that were under her command: cheaper to run and more suitable to the era of the plebeian clergyman.

This was the first chance Greg had had to pay the colourfully-named Weatherbys a visit.

Number one was nearest to the church. He could probably have identified it from the garden which, while small, was overflowing with autumn flora, clearly the work of a professional although it was usually the cobbler's children who went unshod. The house looked trim and clean and the front door had recently been repainted a rich burgundy.

He knocked.

Silas Weatherby answered the door, hatless now. He was largely bald but the rim of hair remaining was sandy in hue and had probably once been ginger.

Greg displayed his warrant card and asked if Dickon was at home.

The old man stepped back and motioned him in without a word. Then he picked up his hat from the newel post and walked out of the front door before Greg could stop him, leaving him to his own devices.

He glanced round the hall and called, 'Dickon?' There was an answering shout from the upper floor and the boy appeared at the top of the uncarpeted stairs. Greg held up his warrant card again and said, 'Could I have a word?'

Outside he could hear a spade being wielded with considerable force against the innocent clods of the front garden.

Dickon Weatherby came slowly down the stairs. He had the same reddish hair as his father but cut so short as to render it almost colourless. He was tall and thin and matched the description Elise had given of her prowler, so far as it went, which wasn't far. He peered more closely at Greg's warrant card and gave an incredulous laugh. 'Superintendent? I'm honoured. Can I expect the chief constable for tea?'

'Is there somewhere we can talk?'

Dickon shrugged and led the way into a cramped room at the back of the house. A galley kitchen led off it to the rear. The boy pulled up a wooden chair and turned it round, straddling it, his bare arms folded along the back. His sleeveless singlet displayed a well-developed musculature — probably the result of a prison gym — and Greg wondered that he wasn't cold. He made no offer of hospitality but rested his chin on his forearms and waited for Greg to speak.

Greg helped himself to a similar chair but sat more conventionally. He glanced down. My, he thought, what big feet you have, grandma. For Dickon Weatherby's bare feet were no size eight, more like an eleven or even a twelve. Probably had to wear the boxes they came in.

'I'm clean,' the boy said, but more in sorrow than in anger.

'Oh, yes?'

'So whatever it is that's been done, I didn't do it.'

'You were released from a young offenders' institution three months ago,' Greg said. 'Is that right?'

'August the 25th, two days after my eighteenth birthday. I'm putting my juvenile record behind me.' He raised his head and looked defiantly at Greg.

'Got a job?' Greg asked.

'You ever tried getting a job when you've no qualifications and have been in the trouble I have?'

'Plenty of unskilled work about.'

'I'm looking. I'm looking real hard. Do you know

in the States when you turn eighteen your juvenile record is sealed so no one can refer to it? We should have that here.'

'So you know nothing about the series of burglaries being committed locally over the last few weeks — just the time, coincidentally, that you've been out.'

'Nothing.'

'Do you ever help your dad with his gardening?'

'Here?'

'No, his paid work.'

'I wouldn't mind, actually, but he'd never let me. Says I can't tell a flower from a weed.'

Greg had the same problem himself. 'Do you know Lady Weissman, at Alders End?'

'Course. Now she's a real lady, she is.'

'Ever been to her house?'

To Greg's surprise he replied, 'Yeah, loads of times.' He explained. 'When Sir Joachim was alive, they used to have a Christmas party for the village children.' His face lit with enthusiasm. 'It were great. They gave us all presents and everything and Lady W played games with us like she was a kid herself.'

Noblesse oblige, Greg thought. Elise playing her chosen part to perfection. He said, 'So what are you planning to do with your life as a respectable, law-abiding citizen?'

The boy examined Greg's face for sarcasm but found none. 'I got interested in stuff in my last stretch.'

'Stuff?'

'Books and stuff.'

'Any particular type of book?'

The boy smiled, looking very young. 'History, maybe. I thought it was crap at school but now it's quite interesting.'

'Somebody once said that those who learn nothing from history are doomed to repeat their mistakes: that might apply to you.'

'Yeah,' the boy said thoughtfully. 'Yeah, that's right. You know what'd really suit me? Working in a bookshop. That'd be brill.'

'Then I wish you luck.' Greg got up.

Dickon was startled. 'Is that it?'

'For now.' Greg looked round the room. The furniture was old but had been polished regularly. A shelf of well-thumbed paperbacks stood beside the bricked-up fireplace. Many an old lag had told him what a godsend books were inside. 'Your sister lives here too. Yes?'

'Jennet moved away six months back. Got herself a job where she lives in. Why?'

'No reason. I'll see myself out. I'll let you know if I hear of anything that might suit you.'

'Ta very much!'

As Greg walked back down the garden path, Silas Weatherby was still attacking his flowerbeds as if he hated them and the look he turned on Greg told the policeman where he would really like to bury his shovel.

He said something inaudible as Greg reached the gate.

Greg turned back. 'I beg your pardon.'

'I said, "Give a dog a bad name".'

'No one has been hanged, as far as I know.'

Greg left. It occurred to him that Silas himself was lithe enough to pass for a youngster in the dark. He looked to have large feet like his son, a family trait, but it was hard to tell in Wellington boots.

* * *

'Don't go yet, dear boy,' Mr Hamilton said. 'Stay and have another brandy. Heh?' He waved the bottle in offering.

'I'm driving, Unc. Besides.' Piers looked at his watch. 'It's gone midnight and I have to open the shop in the morning. If I don't get my eight hours beauty sleep then I'm good for nothing.'

With some complacency the old man said, 'You *are* beautiful, you know. You remind me of me when I was your age. Make the most of it. And whatever you do, don't live as long as I have.'

'I'll do my best.' Piers added, without much conviction, 'There must be some compensations, surely.'

'The only pleasure I have left is that of laughing at the folly of others, which is poor comfort compared to my own spectacular follies. As for beauty sleep.' Mr Hamilton sighed. 'I'm lucky if I get five hours, and that not all in one shift. You lie awake, in the small hours, listening to the noises of the outside world, of people who still have lives. Heh?'

'It seems pretty quiet here,' Piers pointed out. 'Is everyone in this hotel in bed by eleven?'

Mr Hamilton gave a sudden grin, his face gnome-like in the lamplight. 'You'd be surprised the things I hear in this old house in the middle of the night. I could tell some tales —'

'I must go.' Piers rose hurriedly and planted a kiss on his great-uncle's withered cheek. 'I have a little girl coming for her first communion photos at half past nine.'

'Dear God!'

'That would be the man in question, yes.'

'Chap in Paris, I remember — 1947, it must have been — asked me if I wanted to sell my soul to the devil.'

Piers made for the door. 'See you soon.'

'Thank you for coming, dear boy.' Mr Hamilton refilled his own tumbler with brandy, to the brim. 'You know the way out.'

In the doorway, the younger man paused. 'And did you?'

'Heh?'

'Sell your soul to the devil.'

'Of course I didn't! I'm not bloody stupid.'

A walk down memory lane

Mrs Lucas had fallen pregnant with Isobel just weeks after the adoption was finalised. It was not uncommon, apparently, when a woman had been trying for a baby for years without success and had finally taken the adoption route, for the miracle of nature to happen.

Call it sod's law.

He supposed that the Lucases must have wanted him when they adopted him — on some level, at least — and he had no memory of what his life had been like for the first year or so, until Isobel came along.

But with Isobel in the cradle, her demanding mouth and her tiny tantrums, the Lucases felt themselves complete. They no longer had a need for the cuckoo they had freely taken into their nest.

But cuckoo wasn't the right analogy, he realised later: baby cuckoos push the legitimate offspring out of their nest; here it was the biological child — the 'real' Lucas — who had destroyed the interloper.

For Isobel was even better at the game than her parents. She was the one who hid his asthma inhalers, until he learned to hide them better.

Greg felt no great surprise when Elise rang him one Saturday and asked him to go for a country walk with her.

'Antony has to get off straight after lunch

tomorrow,' she explained and I thought we might go out to Badger's Copse, if you're free, a trip down memory lane.'

'Yes,' he said at once. 'I've nothing special on.'

He didn't think to check with Angie till later but she raised no objection. She'd never shown any tendency to jealousy — not that he had given her cause — and there were moments when he wished she would.

'It'll be nice for you to talk over old times,' she said, not looking up from her pile of textbooks, rather as if she expected the two middle-aged people to reminisce about the good old days when Queen Victoria ruled an endlessly sunlit empire.

'You could come if you liked,' he suggested politely.

'Thanks, but I've got this essay to finish. Besides, you know me and exercise . . .'

She played no part in the youthful quest for muscle at the gym that featured so strongly in modern times. At her tender age her figure was still naturally trim and her flesh firm.

Just you wait, he thought with affection, as he bent to kiss her top of her head, once more buried in a book.

Not that Elise wasn't trim and firm too; with her khaki trousers and red lambswool sweater, her short tousled hair, she looked like a teenage girl from the back. She was wearing proper walking boots, a fact for which she vaguely apologised.

'I own no trainers,' she explained, 'but Joachim was a keen walker and we used to take a trip to the Lakes at least twice a year. We climbed the hills and he sketched the landscapes and we drank beer in local pubs to wash down the cheese and onion crisps.'

'Sounds idyllic.'

'It was. Simple.'

'In the old days I remember you as always being barefoot, although that can't really be right.'

'Almost!' She laughed. 'The minute school was over, it was off with the nasty Clarks sandals. My feet were tough then but years of soft living and expensive pedicures have seen to that.'

He wore trainers — sensible, white leather things with no designer name, a little scuffed — jeans, a short-sleeved shirt and his old brown corduroy jacket. He was fond of that jacket; he'd bought it as a thirtieth birthday present to himself and was proud of that fact that it still fitted him. It was shabby and he no longer wore it except for occasions such as these.

They'd arranged for her to pick him up, since he was on her way, and he enjoyed the powerful feel of the engine as the Lotus negotiated the narrow country roads under her expert guidance. If ever he had a mid-life crisis he would buy one of these, assuming he won the lottery at the same time.

The terrier, Bellini, sat on the ledge at the back, leaning forward occasionally to lick Greg's right ear lobe.

'She likes you,' Elise said, 'but then she's not very discriminating.'

She drew to a halt under some beech trees at the end of a deserted lane less than three miles south of his house. It was perfect walking weather: overcast but dry, a small breeze blowing from the west. Released from the car, Bellini ran round them both in circles, anxious to be off.

Greg picked up a fallen beech stick and stripped the leaves and twigs from it, perfect for swishing nettles.

He paused by the stile that linked the lane to a farmer's field and took in the scene. In his youth this had been a field of corn, now it was clearly EU set-aside: overgrown with grasses, cornflowers, poppies and flax, a habitat for insects and small vermin. From an aesthetic point of view it was an improvement, even if, to a layman, it seemed like economic nonsense.

'Pity it's a bit late for butterflies,' he commented as he swung his leg over the stile, turning on the other side to hand her over as the dog wriggled through the gap at the bottom. Bellini had found a stick of her own and was proudly clutching it in her jaws, although it impeded her passage through the stile.

'Have you been here lately?' Elise asked, her small hand resting in his, the fingers cool and smooth.

'Not for years.'

'I suppose it's all changed.'

'Inevitably.'

They stood in silent mourning for the lost world of their childhood. Then he struck out along the footpath that ran round the edge of the field, Elise easily keeping pace at his side. In the distance he could make out the hill on which Badger's Copse stood. He hoped they wouldn't find it screaming with mountain bikes

'Superintendent,' Elise mused. 'You've done well for yourself. Funny: I never had you marked down as ambitious.'

'I wasn't really. It just happened.'

'Some have greatness thrust upon them?'

'That's it!'

'They must pay policemen better than I thought,' she remarked, 'if you can afford to eat at Boxford Hall.'

'I wasn't paying,' he protested. 'I was a guest of the old man you saw me with. He's staying there.'

'A relative?' she asked.

'No, I'm remarkably short of relatives, as it happens.'

'I remember that you had no aunts and uncles. Whereas me, I had more than I knew what to do with, mostly in Ireland, luckily.'

'As the only child of two only children, how I envied you all those cousins.' She made a derisory noise. 'No,' he went on. 'Mr Hamilton is the uncle — great-uncle, in fact — of a friend of mine and I just got caught up in the invitation.'

'Clearly a generous man, this Mr Hamilton.'

'Not short of a bob or two, I gather. He's staying at the hotel indefinitely.' She whistled surprise. 'I can't say I took to the proprietor,' he added. 'McFee.'

'Jack? It's a bit of an act, that boorish Scotsman thing. He's always very civil to me.'

'I expect you're a good customer.'

'I do go there quite often,' she agreed. 'My husband was a real gourmet and he and Jack became good friends because Joachim appreciated cooking of that quality and Jack laps up adulation the way a miner sups beer. I've sort of inherited him as a friend.'

'Good luck!' He paused to massacre some nettles, although they were some distance from the path, since there was no point in wasting his home-made walking stick. 'But speaking of families, what became of your parents?'

Elise came to a halt and looked at the ground for a long moment. 'I had no idea what to do. I ran away, you see, when I found out I was pregnant. I thought of writing to them from London after Antony was born and disposed of, letting them know I was well and happy, but in the end I thought it'd only make things worse.'

He considered this as they walked on, across another stile, the ground now rising steadily, slowing their pace. Another middle-aged couple were coming the other way, a golden labrador, arthritic with age, preceding them like an outrider. The two couples exchanged greetings and the dogs dutifully sniffed each other's rears.

Greg was reminded of a coarse song he'd heard about how all the dogs in the world met for a conference and left their arses in the cloakroom on the way in. The meeting was disrupted and they all fled, grabbing the first arse they could find. Ever since that day, when one dog meets another he sniffs, hoping to be reunited with his lost arse.

He wasn't about to sing this song for Elise. But what was he thinking? This genteel lady was Elsie Riley to whom the pre-pubescent Gregory Summers had told anything and everything.

Even so, he kept his ditty to himself, and said, 'How would it have made things worse?'

'They'd have come to terms with my running off by then. Getting in touch would only have reopened old wounds. And after my marriage . . . I mean, it's not as if they were fanatics or anything but . . .'

'Oh, yes. Your husband was Jewish, wasn't he?'

'As I was Catholic. That's to say that we both lost our faith a long time ago. He because he couldn't accept that Jehovah would allow the Nazis to overrun his homeland and kill his friends and family.'

'And you?'

'For the same reason, I suppose.'

'The problem of pain?'

'Just so.'

'But then you moved back here, or near enough.'

'Yes.' She laughed. 'Dear Joachim. He was always rather high-handed; masterful, you might call it. One day about ten years ago he came home and told me he was fed up with Kensington and wanted to spend his declining years in the country, so he'd put down a deposit on an old place on the Berkshire downs.'

'Just like that?'

'Just like that. I was horrified at first, but I fell in love with the house, as he knew I would. Cressida was sixteen and absolutely furious. Just as she was getting to the age to fully appreciate the bright lights of London, we were dragging her out to a place she described as "the middle of nowhere and the arsehole of the universe". Joachim had to promise her driving lessons and a car for her seventeenth birthday to stop her sulking for the rest of her life.'

Spoiled brat, Greg thought.

As if reading his mind, she said, 'We never really refused her anything. That's supposed to be bad for people, isn't it? But Joachim and I both had impoverished childhoods and it seemed petty to say no when she asked for something, just out of principle. I don't think you spoil children by giving them material things, anyway; only by giving them things in place of your time, love and attention.'

He said, 'Lucky girl.'

'She's led a charmed life, in many ways. She met Stephen when she was twenty-two, straight out of university, and I think he was the first man she really loved. He was steady and sensible and she was married to him within six months. So easy.'

'And you are a grandmother.'

'And proud of it.'

The ground began to rise more steeply and Greg

felt himself beginning to sweat. The sun appeared as the clouds dispersed in the breeze.

'And you've been settled here for ten years?' he said.

'It wasn't as if there was any danger of anyone recognising me.' She glanced sideways at him, her mouth curving in amusement. 'You didn't.'

'But I'm not your loving mother,' he pointed out. "Cause there's nothing like a mother's love . . . Sorry!'

She waved the apology away. 'After we'd settled in I made discreet enquiries. It wasn't hard: you know how country people like to gossip.'

'Mmm,' Greg said. 'Almost as much as city people.'

'I learned that the Rileys had moved back to Ireland years ago. An old uncle died and left them a smallholding and since, as my informant told me with great authority, they'd suffered a terrible bereavement — lost their only daughter, a girl of twelve, in a car crash — they had nothing left to keep them in England.'

'Maybe that was the story they told people,' he suggested.

'But why should they change my age?' He shrugged and she said, 'No, it was Chinese whispers. That's all.'

'So was that the end of the line?'

She nodded. 'Joachim once suggested the west of Ireland as a change from the Lakes but I raised so many wild and implausible objections that I quite alarmed him and he never mentioned it again.'

'You family comes from the west?'

'Connemara, but I don't know it. They couldn't afford to take me there on holidays, although I referred to it always as home, since they did.' She looked about her. 'This was *home*.'

They had reached the summit of the hill and walked into the cool shade of the copse, picking their way with care over the rough ground where fallen leaves could hide a treacherous root waiting to send you sprawling flat on your face. The autumn sun shone through the branches, dappling their faces.

'It's smaller than I remember,' Elise said.

'We are larger.'

She said, 'Funnily enough, Antony was telling me how you can track people down easily nowadays, using the Internet. That's how he found me. I'm not really up to speed on it. Are you?'

'We've got it at the office and Angie's bought a laptop to use for her college course. She has access for research and so forth.'

'Perhaps I should give it a try,' Elise said, 'but you get used to the idea of someone being gone, even dead. I would be like a ghost to my parents and ghosts are seldom welcome visitors in the land of the living.'

He peered at her as she stood in the shadow of an old oak. Her face with its porcelain-pale complexion, free of make-up, *was* almost ghostlike in the gloom of the copse, and it was then that he first felt afraid for her.

He told himself that the gooseflesh came of standing too long out of the light. 'Come on,' he said quickly, 'let's enjoy the sun while it lasts.'

They emerged at the far side of the copse, looking down the hill, across the fields to the farm where she had grown up. It was a most peaceful scene: a ragged patchwork of crops and woods and streams. No battle had been fought on this land for more than 350 years and the people of Berkshire had been left to tend their cattle and plant their wheat and grow strong and rich.

He glanced at her to see if it affected her but she seemed unmoved.

'Looks like our cottage has been turned into a holiday home,' was her only comment.

Greg squinted, wishing he'd brought his binoculars since her distance sight was obviously better than his. He saw what she meant: a hanging basket, past its best at this time of year, dangled from the lintel of the ugly brick building known only as Riley's Cottage back then. There was a wooden bench outside and a picnic table. A child's swing stood nearby, motionless. Generations of farm workers had given way to the everburgeoning leisure industry.

'Season's over,' he said.

'Do you remember the chicken?' Elise asked.

'God, yes!'

'I've never forgotten the look on your face.'

Mary Riley had sent Elsie out to get a chicken for Sunday dinner and he had trotted after her, as he usually did, all unaware. She had led him down to the bottom of the garden where the Rileys kept half a dozen hens in a makeshift wire compound and, after a few minutes' scrutiny of the birds, had selected one and promptly wrung its neck.

When Greg squawked in protest, a noise not unlike that of an affronted hen, she explained, 'You have to do it just right, see. Too hard and the head comes off. Too soft and it's only stunned and then it starts struggling while you're plucking it.'

She'd returned to the cottage, the chicken slung from her hand by its bizarre feet, Greg trailing reluctantly behind her. Chickens came from the butcher's, ready plucked and drawn, all clean and white and wrapped in paper. There was no way he would have eaten that one, not if Fanny Craddock had cooked it.

'I tried to give Cressida the sort of carefree, secure upbringing I had myself,' Elise said, 'but it seems to be much harder to allow children the sort of freedom we had.'

'I know what you mean.' The arrest of the Moors Murderers in 1965 had hardly impinged on the adolescent Greg's consciousness — boring, grown-up news story — but he had rapidly become aware of a tightening of boundaries, of a demand that he state where he was going, with whom and what time he could be expected home.

'You would do anything to protect your children,' Elise added.

Except that sometimes, Greg thought, even *anything* wasn't enough. Fred's grave in Kintbury churchyard was testament to that.

Beyond the copse a meadow of short, soft grass sloped downhill to a dried-up stream, little more than a ditch. Almost forty years ago they had sat in this field for hours after school, listening to the water splashing over the pebbles as it ran cold and fast to join the Kennet just shy of Hamstead Lock.

They looked at each other and, with unspoken accord, tore off their socks and shoes and ran shrieking down the hill, Bellini barking joyfully with them at this new game. The grass was damp and tickly and Greg stubbed his toe against a clod of hard earth, finishing up panting on the edge of the ditch, rubbing the sore place and grimacing. Had he forgotten for a moment that he wasn't twelve any more?

Mr Hamilton had been right: the days of wine and roses were *not* long.

Although the weeping and the laughter went on.

Greg felt tired by the time they got back the Lotus, gleaming so yellow among the trees and hedges. Once he had run and jumped all day in this landscape; now a four-mile hike after Sunday lunch was enough. He left his makeshift stick propped against the stile for another walker.

Elise opened the boot and took out a flask of coffee and two china mugs. She poured for him and handed the welcome beverage over. He tasted a hint of whisky in it and felt it warm his insides.

'Good,' he said. He felt contented. Even the tiredness would translate, after a hot bath, into a good night's sleep.

She sat perched on the bonnet of the car, sipping her own drink. 'Soon,' she said, 'I must introduce Antony to Cressida, and explain.'

He was startled. 'They haven't met yet?'

'She doesn't know of his existence. I've been putting it off. Cressida doesn't come at weekends, except once a month when she and Stephen and the twins come for Sunday lunch, and I put them off last time. I said I had a stomach upset.'

'It'll be worse if she gets wind of it from someone else,' Greg said. 'People have seen you with him and will gossip. She might get the wrong idea entirely.'

'As you did?' She laughed at his protests. 'Yes, I must tell her next weekend.' She sighed. 'I just don't know how she'll react. And there's still a small part of me that feels ashamed of admitting to an illegitimate child.'

'No one cares about that sort of thing these days.'

Elise looked at him thoughtfully but didn't reply. They drank up their fortified coffee, restacked the boot and drove off.

'Are you coming in?' he asked as she drew up outside his house. 'Say hello to Angie.'

'Some other time. I wanted today to be just the two of us, like the old days.'

'Sure.' He leaned across to kiss her on the cheek before getting out. 'Talk to you soon. And good luck with Cressida.'

He stood watching as she drove away. Usually, when you tried to go back to the past, it was a dismal failure, nothing like the way you remembered. Today he and Elise had proved that it was sometimes possible after all.

Room service

He had occasionally thought of talking to a teacher, of confiding his misery and fear. Deep inside, he knew that it was wrong, the way things were at home, but how could he be sure?

Perhaps all boys went through what he went through, with only a conspiracy of silence to shield the truth from him.

There was one master, Mr Walton, the English teacher, who seemed kind, who told him that he had brains, that he would do well. Once Mr Walton let his hand linger on the boy's shoulder and called him 'Old son', an endearment that came close to bringing tears to his eyes.

But adults stuck together. The most likely thing was that Mr Walton would go straight to his parents with the allegations. They were plausible, he knew, even charming when they wanted to be. They would shake their heads in sorrow; his mother would ruffle his curls and say, 'Antony, what tales have you been telling, darling?' She would kiss him, a fine dumbshow for the teacher, petting his fragile body, make him apologise for troubling Mr Walton with his fairy stories, and that would be that.

Until they got him home.

There had been talk of sending him to his father's old school to board at thirteen and he had longed for it as a lifer longs for parole, but they had changed their minds, said it was too expensive, a waste of money in his case since he was stupid and not a real Lucas.

Cressida and Stephen didn't stand on ceremony, letting themselves into the house through the kitchen door with only a chorused 'Yoo-hoo' to warn of their arrival.

They came through into the sitting room, laughing at some shared joke. Each held a carrycot with a sleeping twin in it.

They stopped in surprise on seeing that Elise was not alone. 'Oh, sorry,' they said, in chorus and deposited their burdens on the floor.

'Darlings.' Elise got up and kissed them both.

Stephen handed her the bottle of red wine he'd been holding in his free hand. He was an ordinary-looking man in his early thirties, neither handsome nor plain, with a thick mop of brown hair receding slightly at the front. His wire-rimmed spectacles gave him a bookish air but he looked fit too. He was wearing corduroy trousers, a green checked shirt and a battered tweed jacket — the schoolmaster's weekend uniform.

'This is Antony Lucas,' Elise said. 'Antony, my daughter and son-in-law, Stephen and Cressida Crabshaw.'

Cressida laughed and advanced to shake hands. 'I prefer Cressida Weissman,' she said, 'certainly for professional purposes. Cressida Crabshaw's a bit of a mouthful, what with the alliteration.'

She was her mother's daughter, he saw. Although she lacked Elise's curves — flat-chested with boyish hips — her matte black hair hung like a heavy curtain to her bony shoulders and her blue eyes looked into his with a sparkle of mischief as her lips curved into a knowing smile.

Yes, he thought, you think you know it all and you know nothing, spoilt little rich girl.

He thought, *This is going to be so easy.*

'How do you do,' he said, rather formally.

She was dressed as casually as her husband, but much more stylishly. Her jeans fit her so that he wondered how she would find room for Sunday lunch. She'd tucked them into supple black leather boots which matched the black sweater he thought must be cashmere. Black wasn't her colour, he decided critically. No doubt she thought it 'artistic' but she would do better in the red shades favoured by her mother, a woman with more true style in her little finger.

He had come prepared to hate her. In his imagination her face had become that of Isobel — bovine and malicious — although physically two women could not have been less alike.

'Antony's joining us for lunch,' Elise said.

'Live locally, Antony?' Stephen advanced on him with a firm, masculine hand, pumping his up and down for a few hearty seconds.

'No, I live in London. I'm visiting Elise for the weekend.'

Cressida raised her eyebrows and gave her mother an amused look. Elise smiled distantly, held up Stephen's gift of wine and said, 'I'll just open this so it can breathe.'

Cressida followed her into the kitchen, shutting

the door behind her. She leaned back against it as Elise busied herself with the corkscrew. She could hear the murmur of voices from the sitting room as the two men made polite conversation. 'Don't look so worried, Mum,' she said. 'I'm not criticising. Dad's been dead a long time and no one expects you to spend the rest of your life like a nun.'

'It's not what you think,' Elise said crisply, easing the cork out of the bottle with a satisfying *plop*.

Her daughter clearly was not listening. 'So this is why you put us off last month with your "stomach ache", when you've got a digestion like cast iron. Mind you, I don't think I expected anyone quite so young and good looking, so —' she wagged a finger — 'you just take care, young lady. Still,' she snorted with laughter, 'good luck to you!'

Elise opened the oven and peered inside, releasing the seer and sizzle of prime meat. She took a Henckel eight-inch chopping knife from a wooden block on the counter and prodded a roast potato with it viciously. There were times when her child irritated her almost beyond endurance. Where did she get this sly coyness? Not from her or Joachim, surely; it must be a throwback.

She said, 'Kindly curb the wilder excesses of your imagination. Antony is not my lover — the idea is grotesque.'

It occurred to her that with Antony she had no baggage: no sleepless nights with a baby that would not be pacified, no memories of a more than usually tiresome adolescence. They had met as equals. She realised that Antony made her happy. Perhaps she was what they called a man's woman and should have had only sons.

And if he looked like his father in any way, then she would refuse to see it.

She straightened up, slamming the oven door, and concluded less hotly, 'He's just somebody I would like you to get to know.'

'Why?'

'You'll find out!'

She pushed the younger woman aside with ease and rejoined the men, saying, 'The roast's basting nicely. Twenty minutes, tops.'

Cressida stared after her for a moment, perplexed, before following her.

In the sitting room Stephen was proudly demonstrating his sons. Antony was on one knee on the floor, admiring their sleeping forms, offering only the odd word of encouragement to keep the proud father going.

Stephen had been born for marriage and fatherhood, Elise thought fondly, in a way that not every man was. He was serious, solid, sensible. He was popular at the College, with both staff and pupils, throwing himself into the school sports day and the amateur dramatic group with all the ardour of a true enthusiast.

She had sometimes wondered about people who left school, spent three years at university, then went straight back on the other side of the desk, as if they wanted to cling forever to that time that was so strangely called 'The best years of your life'.

Stephen had swiftly dispelled these doubts. He was an idealist, vaguely old Labour, clinging to the hope of a better world. At the age of thirty he had been ready for marriage and fatherhood and Cressida, a little disappointed at not getting a place at the Slade or the Royal College of Art, despite her name, half-hearted about her modest degree in English and History of Art from Surrey and the career prospects which it opened up for her, had fallen willingly into his strong arms.

Stephen believed in her talent as strongly as she did. He was proud of his artistic wife.

She joined the group cooing round the boys, who slept on oblivious to all the attention. She felt her heart swell with love as she looked down on their placid faces, their miniature lips puffing with each breath, emitting the faintest 'pop'. They were Joachim, known as Joe, and Benedict. Joe was eighteen minutes older than Ben.

'Don't be taken in by this scene of domestic bliss,' Cressida remarked to Antony. 'They were screaming non-stop from four a.m. till five minutes before we got here.'

'How old are they?'

'They were born a week before Easter,' Stephen said, 'just as school broke up, so that I could do the night shift for three weeks. Now how is that for timing?'

'Very organised, my daughter,' Elise said, 'just like her father.'

After allowing a few minutes of worship at the

twin cradles, Elise suggested letting the baby boys sleep in the quiet seclusion of the study and summoned Antony to help her lay the table.

Cressida pumped Antony for information all through the meal. She ate little, mostly sitting back in her chair with a glass of red wine cradled in both hands, her glittering eyes fixed on him, asking questions.

Always questions.

Antony told her politely that he lived in the unfashionable part of Barnes, near Hammersmith bridge, in a two-bedroomed mansion flat.

Yes, alone.

No, he'd never been married.

He was a solicitor in a small partnership in South Kensington; no, not a partner yet; oh, boring stuff, mostly wills and trusts.

No, he wasn't passionate about the law: it paid the bills.

Her manner was mildly flirtatious, testing the water again six months after the birth of her babies. Antony didn't respond in kind, being no more than tepidly friendly. Elise sighed inwardly: she couldn't put off telling Cressida that this man was her half brother and therefore out of bounds for flirting.

And yet she did put it off.

Elise was an excellent cook and Stephen ate steadily. Until he had satisfied his appetite, his sole contribution to the conversation was 'Why do we never have Yorkshire pudding at home?' A question which his wife answered with a roll of her eyes and a 'You'll get fat.'

When they'd finished the last mouthful of home-made apple crumble and custard, Antony volunteered to make coffee.

'I see he knows his way around the kitchen,' Cressida said, when his offer had been accepted and he'd departed on his errand.

'How hard can it be to find the kettle?' Stephen asked dryly.

When Antony returned with a silver tray, he distributed cups and saucers, laid out cream and sugar and placed the cafetière on the table for the coffee to draw. He resumed his seat next to Elise. There was a feeling of tension in the air.

She reached out and laid her hand over his. She felt his fingers tremble beneath hers and gave him an affectionate smile.

'Darlings,' she said. 'You've been asking yourself all through lunch who Antony is and what he's doing here, so the time has come for me to enlighten you.' She took a deep breath. 'Antony is my son. He was born thirty years ago, when I was eighteen, and single.'

Cressida cried, 'Mummy!' reverting to the childish appellation which had given way to the more plebeian 'Mum' some time during her adolescence. She looked suddenly very young.

'Let me finish, Cressie. Please. I gave Antony up for adoption the day he was born. A few weeks ago he sought me out. We have been getting to know each other and I want you both to welcome him into the family.'

Antony sat very still, staring at the starched linen napkin in his lap.

Stephen looked mildly surprised but interested. His eyes flickered over Antony and his mother, gauging the similarities that confirmed the close ties of blood. He smiled reassuringly at Elise and she responded gratefully.

Cressida found her voice and jumped to her feet. 'It's not possible!'

Stephen said, 'Cressie?'

'I'm sorry if this has come as a shock,' her mother said. 'I've been putting it off out of cowardice but you had to know some time.'

The young woman's face was red with pain and anger. 'How could you ...? How could you *not* ...? All these years.' She put her hands over her ears although no one else was speaking, shutting out some subspace din from her own brain. 'I won't believe it. I won't.'

The other three people at the dining table looked helplessly at her as she stood twisting her napkin into a rag in her fingers, screwing her face up as she tried not to cry.

'It's the money, isn't it?' She loomed over Antony, bitter contempt in her voice. 'That's what you're after.'

'Money?' Antony was genuinely surprised by this charge.

'You think you can get your hands on Mummy's

money by smarming round her, sucking up to her, well you can't because it was Daddy's money. *My* Daddy. Not yours. Whoever he might be.'

'Cressida!' Elise said. 'That's enough.'

Finally, feeling that words were inadequate, the young woman swept the cafetière over with her hand. The lid flew off, sending coffee gushing over the white cloth. The others leaped back from the scalding flood with exclamations of dismay, hurriedly scraping their chairs across the floor.

Cressida gulped, 'Come on, Stephen. Let's get out of here,' and made for the door.

Her husband got up to follow her. 'I'm sorry,' he mouthed at Elise.

Cressida turned in the doorway and addressed her mother as if there was no one else in the room.

'I shall never forgive you for this!'

And she left, followed by Stephen who was still grimacing silent apologies. They heard the back door slam a minute later.

'Some welcome,' Antony said.

'She'll be back.' Elise began calmly to gather up the sodden cloth.

'You seem very certain.'

'They've forgotten the babies.'

In the study next door a fierce wailing began, soon echoed by its twin, as some subliminal terror of abandonment woke the children.

Antony started to laugh.

* * *

Mr Hamilton made his way slowly along the corridor that led from the hotel reception to his room. He'd been given a suite on the ground floor because his legs were no longer up to a lot of stairs. He leaned on his cane, kept going by the thought of the bottle of brandy by his bed.

He recognised the girl: she had waited on him often enough, at breakfast as well as dinner. He thought he had heard one of the barmen call her Jenny. She came fast out of the steep and narrow staircase that led to the staff quarters, stopping abruptly on seeing him and flattening herself against the wall, the better to get out of his way.

She was out of uniform, off duty. Hamilton was old enough to have seen a hundred ridiculous fashions come and go — from flappers to the New Look; from hippies to girls with safety pins in their fleshy parts — but he thought she looked ludicrous in the baggy jeans that were too long for her, slit up both side seams so that they flapped as she walked, revealing a lining of floral print. Her midriff was bare under the sort of tight garment that women had worn as lingerie in earlier decades, not that he objected to *that*, though it was a pity she hadn't got more to display.

Her hair had been gelled into spikes.

He saw her lip curl and read her thoughts. Old age was disgusting to the young today. When he had been young he had been forced to show respect for his elders, to appreciate their superior wisdom, their experience; but the world changed so quickly now that yesterday's experience was useless, laughable. The young today lacked empathy, he thought, imagination: they could not conceive that they would ever be old and infirm.

She wasn't pretty in her grotesque clothes but she was young and fresh and he felt a stirring of lust along with the hatred she aroused in him. As he reached her he affected to stumble, lurching towards her so that she had no choice but to stick out a hand to steady him.

'Sorry,' he mumbled.

'You all right?'

He looked her in the eye. Hers were as blue as his had once been, and just as hard. 'Perhaps if you could lend me a hand, my dear.' He gestured. 'My room is there. Would you mind? Heh?'

Reluctantly she gave him her arm and he leaned heavily on her, smelling the clean warmth of her freckled skin. She was tall, taller than he in his shrunken dotage. He'd always liked tall girls, the length of their legs.

She hovered over him as he sank into his armchair with a sigh.

'You all right?' she said again.

Conversation, he thought, would not be her strong point, but he had never asked that of a woman. He reached into his inside pocket and took out his wallet.

'That's all right,' she said, half-heartedly backing away. 'You don't need to tip me.'

'I wasn't going to.' He removed five twenty-pound notes from the wallet and counted them out on the side table. 'I thought you might like to earn a little extra cash, Jenny, my dear. If you get my drift.?'

'I don't think I do, and my name's not Jenny.'

Jane, Joanne. As if he cared what her name was. He added two more twenties and a ten. It was probably more than she earned in a week.

'It must really piss you off to see all those rich buggers in the restaurant every night,' he said, 'spending a couple of hundred quid on dinner. Heh?' She shrugged. 'Spot of "room service",' he wheezed, 'from that pretty mouth of yours.'

She stared at him in disbelief. Then she said, 'Here's all you're getting from my mouth, you old bastard,' and spat, once, into his face.

She ran out of the room with her trouser bottoms flapping, slamming the door behind her.

Mr Hamilton began to laugh, a laugh that terminated in a fit of wheezing. Pulling a dirty linen handkerchief from his pocket, he wiped off the spittle and examined it critically.

Sick headache

When he was fourteen, his mother had come with him to a parents evening at his school one hot day in early July. Economics was the one subject that really interested him and the economics teacher had spoken of him in glowing terms.

His mother had pretended to be pleased, calling him her 'clever little boy' in that saccharine tone she could use when she wanted to, fussing over him in front of witnesses. She had ruffled his curls and he had been overcome with nausea, running from the room to vomit, not making it to the lavatories in time, messing the floor outside the headmaster's office.

'He's over-excited,' his mother had said fondly, her eyes, as they rested on him, promising unimagined horrors when she got him home. 'Excited at the prospect of our family holiday in Cornwall, enervated by the heat.'

The family holiday: the nightmare within a nightmare.

Antony hadn't been to Marlborough before and was impressed with the broad elegance of the High Street, its perpendicular churches serving as book ends. This was gracious living, he thought, just the setting for Cressida who had been born with a silver spoon in her mouth.

He was surprised at how busy it was, driving up and down for several minutes until he spotted a woman in a Volvo on her way out. He sat tapping on his steering wheel muttering 'For God's sake, woman, just put it in gear and drive'.

He didn't anticipate any difficulty in finding the house since he'd pumped Elise casually for directions, not mentioning that he intended to pay a call. Elise: he had tried Mum, Mother, Mummy, but they stuck in his throat; she had been equally uneasy with the names and had decreed that he should call her by her given name.

Her *adopted* name.

He had phoned her this morning, ostensibly to confirm their arrangements for the weekend; in fact, to make sure that she had no plans to be in Marlborough herself that day.

'What are you up to today?' he'd slipped in. 'Anything interesting?'

'Committee meeting at the Ashmolean,' she'd said. 'I was just going out of the door. It's a bit of a bore but they give us a good lunch.'

'In Oxford?'

'I'll make a day of it, spend a restful hour in the botanical gardens.'

Then he'd rung the office and pleaded one of his sick headaches.

He bought two hours on the machine. The bells of St Mary's were pealing joyously and he waited to cross the road while a wedding car drove slowly past, ribbons on the bonnet, a white bride in the back seat looking smugly out.

It was a warm day for October, so he slung his

jacket over his shoulder by his thumb and made his way along the north side of the street till he came to an alleyway between two shops, down which he could make out a vista of half-timbered houses.

He paused to admire his reflection in the window of a dress shop. He knew the effect he had on women and very few of them were immune. People said that women weren't as shallow as men, not so quick to run after a pretty face, but that hadn't been his experience. He'd been fifteen when they'd first started taking an interest: older women, in their thirties some of them, petting him, pretending that they were cooing over a sweet boy.

As if he couldn't see the rampant lust in their eyes.

He knew how to tantalise them, peering up at them from under his long, dark lashes like a whore. He knew how to make them beg.

He wrinkled his face in disgust, startling the shop assistant who'd been wondering if the gorgeous young man was coming in, hoping that he would, even if it meant he was buying a present for his wife.

Discomfited, she studied her magazine.

Antony turned down the alley and stopped at the third house on the left. Small, he thought, but pricey, with its central location and old-world charm. Schoolmasters weren't well paid, even at public schools, but Elise would have helped her daughter out. And Cressida didn't work, not really. He was prepared to bet that Elise gave her an allowance so that she could play at being an artist like her old man.

Had she talent, he wondered? Joachim Weissman had been the real thing — he could see that from the canvases at Alders End — but she could equally well have inherited her mother's talent for painting rather than her father's. Which would be galling for her. The children of artists, actors, authors and musicians seemed to take it for granted that they had the right to have their dynastic claims recognised and the path to fame smoothed for them.

There was no bell, so he raised the metal knocker in the shape of a dolphin and let it fall. He heard footsteps approaching, creaking on old wooden boards, and turned his back to the door, a casual passer-by who'd found himself, quite by accident, in the vicinity and thought he might as well knock, but if she was busy . . .

She said, 'Oh!'

He turned back, an innocent thing surprised.

She said, 'What do you want?' Her tone wasn't completely hostile.

'I was just having a look round Marlborough and I thought this was where you lived so . . .' He waved an airy hand. 'Of course, if you're working.' He made the slightest move that could possibly be interpreted as an attempt to leave in the hope that she would stop him, which she did.

She said grudgingly, 'You'd better come in.'

She *had* been painting, he supposed: she was wearing old jeans with oil paint, mostly reds and greens, on them, a tee shirt topped with a man's torn shirt, unbuttoned; her hair was covered with a scarf and she wore no make-up. She was barefoot and looked very young, too young to be a wife and mother.

'Quietly please.' She raised a finger to her lips as she led the way along the hall. 'I've just got the twins down for a nap.'

She pulled the scarf off as he followed her, running her hands quickly through her hair, tousling it. It was Elise's hair, darker than his own and not the same texture, straight where his was curly, matte where his was glossy. He wondered what his real father had looked like, whether he could get Elise to tell him that before he destroyed her life forever. He realised that Cressida was fussing with her hair in a way that was almost flirtatious, a fine-looking woman caught in a casual moment. She pulled off the torn, paint-smeared shirt and let it drop to the floor.

Women who wore their husband's old clothes; what was that about?

They were now in a sitting room that ran the length of the house, an airy oblong, the small panes of glass sparkling clean to maximise light. The floorboards were bare with a rug patterned in black and white geometric shapes and it was sparely furnished. Through the window he glimpsed a courtyard garden with tall shrubs in terracotta pots and a cast-iron table and chairs. He sat uninvited on a squashy black chair which sank low beneath his weight.

His half sister was looking at him helplessly. 'Do you want something? I mean coffee or whatever.'

'Some water?' he suggested.

She went into the nearby kitchen and returned with a full bottle of Evian water and two glasses on a wooden tray. She laid it on the floor and slumped down next to it, a few feet away from him, her legs crossed in the lotus position. He thought she would make an affectation of sitting on the floor, the perennial student.

'Do people call you Tony?' she asked.

'No one has ever called me Tony.' He unscrewed the cap and poured for them both.

'Look, I'm sorry,' she blurted out. 'I behaved badly.'

He smiled at her gently. 'It must have been an awful shock for you, Cressida.'

'If she'd only told me. I mean I thought we were close, closer than mothers and daughters usually are, more like sisters.'

In his observation that never worked out: the mother-and-daughter- more-like-sisters thing. It was a category error: your mother was your mother and not your confidante, nor your best friend, although she might be your worst enemy.

'She could have said,' Cressida muttered, and her pretty face was flushed. 'She could have told me she had a son and gave him up for adoption.'

'I think she wanted to keep it from your father,' he said. 'And by the time you were old enough to know the truth, I don't suppose she'd given me a thought for twenty years.'

'Oh, but that's impossible!' Cressida jumped up and

began to pace the width of the room. 'She was such a loving mother, so devoted. And she always said how she would have liked more children, how sad she was that it didn't happen. A woman doesn't just forget.'

'Time is a great healer.' How useful platitudes were. He reached out a hand and pulled her back down on the floor beside him. Anything to stop that wretched pacing.

'If I had to give up my twins, I'd just curl up and die.' Her face was solemn. She took a long swig of her water, then laughed, and the sound was Elise's laugh. 'But I always wanted a big brother.'

Unlike Isobel, he thought. 'Friends?' he said aloud.

'Friends.' She rose on her knees and put her arms confidently round him and he hugged her.

He inhaled the female scent of her hair.

It made him want to gag.

'What do your parents think?' she asked a few minutes later. 'I mean . . . you know.'

'My adoptive parents.'

'It must be difficult for them, or are they very understanding?'

Antony studied his fingernails, as if it was hard to find the words, as if it pained him. 'It doesn't arise, I'm afraid, since my parents died in a house fire a few years ago, along with my sister.'

She clapped her hand over her mouth. 'Oh, my God! I'm so sorry.'

'You weren't to know.' He stroked her arm. 'It's okay, Cressie.'

'Thank God you weren't there.'

'I was on a walking holiday in Ireland, otherwise I might well have been.'

What? The prison he hadn't set foot in for three years?

'Was the house burnt down?' she asked.

He injected great sadness into his voice. 'It was utterly destroyed. My childhood home. Razed to the ground, as they say.'

She giggled nervously, as people sometimes will at bad news. 'As a child I thought it was "raised" to the ground. I wondered why it made no sense but I didn't like to ask.'

'For fear of seeming foolish?'

'You understand about that?'

'Oh, yes.'

His father's fist slamming into the small of his back where the bruises wouldn't show. *You fool.*

She said, 'It was insured?'

'Of course.'

'But it's not the same. I mean, your childhood home.'

'No.'

'Your sister . . .'

'Isobel.'

'She was adopted too?'

'No,' he said after a short pause. 'She was their natural child.'

'Still,' Cressida said confidently, 'they'd have made no difference between you. I mean, they'd chosen you, hadn't they? That's what people always say about adopted children: that they're special, that their parents *chose* them.'

'That's what they say,' he agreed with a smile.

'What . . . what did they do?'

'My father was a barrister, at the Manchester bar. We had a big house in the country in Cheshire.'

'I hear that's very posh.' She said it with a laugh, the way southerners always spoke of anywhere in the north that had pretensions to gentility.

'The Surrey of the north. Mother didn't work. She kept house for us.'

'Just the four of you?'

'Just the four of us. I inherited everything which is why I'm not after Elise's money.'

'I . . . that was unforgivable. I don't know why that sprang into my mind. I suppose the truth is that I was afraid you would take her love from me and I felt so awkward about saying so that I said money instead of love and then I realised how stupid it sounded, how petty and greedy.'

'I won't take her love from you either.'

'Money is finite but love is infinite?' she suggested.

'Something like that.'

'But you — now you have nobody.'

He bent forward and kissed her quite hard on the lips, his hands tangling in her hair. For a few seconds she kept her mouth closed, then abruptly opened it to receive his probing tongue, the kiss deep.

He released her and said, 'Until now I had nobody.'

Somewhere, above them, a baby began to wail, joined almost immediately by a second, an identical, wailing.

Cressida jumped up, flustered, patting her rumpled hair into place. She looked as if she'd just got out of bed. She stared up the spiral staircase in the corner, then back at Antony. She ran up the first four steps, then stopped. She didn't look at him. 'I think you'd better go.' Her voice was cold and hard. She carried on up.

He rose and left the house without a word. Back in the alleyway, his thin lips curved into a smile. He had made a good start. He supposed he was going to have to have sex with the bloody woman at some point. He refused to call it making love. He'd always found sex a nasty, messy business, dirty and degrading.

He hated to be touched and needed all his self-control not to flinch away when Elise took his arm or kissed his cheek as she did so naturally, spontaneously.

* * *

'What name did you call me by?' he asked.

Elise said, 'What do you mean?'

'It was the Lucases who called me Antony — Antony Raymond McNeil Lucas.'

She laughed. 'McNeil?'

'A family name. They were very keen on tradition. But I wondered what name you gave me, in your heart . . .' He faltered at the look on her face. 'When you thought about me.'

'I didn't give you a name,' she said briskly. 'There seemed no point.'

He said, 'I see,' and changed the subject.

He had heard of women naming stillborn children — even miscarried children — but his mother had not deemed him worthy of a name.

* * *

Greg rang Elise to ask if she would like to come to dinner with him and Angie, maybe that weekend, although he hadn't yet quite figured out who would be doing the cooking.

'Greg, that would be lovely, but not this weekend. I'm literally off to the airport as we speak. Can I call you when I get back?'

'Airport?'

'I'm going to Vienna for a few days.'

'*Vienna*?'

'Is there an echo on the line?'

'Sorry!'

She laughed. 'I've been invited to the official unveiling of Rachel Whiteread's holocaust memorial on Wednesday.'

'Ah! I think I read something about that.'

'After all these years . . . I'm pretty sure Joachim would have refused to go — he'd never been back to Austria; he said there was nothing there for him any more — but they invited me and I thought, why not? So I'm making a little holiday of it. Maybe I'll go to Salzburg, see where he grew up. Maybe not.'

Her voice was suddenly weary. 'I could do with a break, to tell you the truth. Things have been a little *intense*.'

'Your daughter? How did that go?'

'Not good.'

'You okay, Elise?'

'Of course I am!'

For those in peril on the sea

Angelica hadn't yet adopted what Greg thought of as student hours, tumbling reluctantly out of bed at noon. She woke when his alarm went off at 7.00 but no longer got up with him, lingering in their warm bed for another hour or so, drinking tea and watching breakfast news on the portable TV.

That morning he had his usual boiled egg and toast soldiers sitting at the breakfast bar. A fierce storm had raged most of the night but had now burned itself out to give a cold but fine morning. He unbolted the kitchen door and stepped out in his slippers, walking backwards down the garden path till a more-or-less comprehensive view of the roof reassured him that his tiles were intact, his timbers safe from rot for a few more days at least.

He brewed a second pot of tea and poured a cup to take up to Angie shortly after 7.30. As he reached the top of the stairs he heard her say, 'Oh, my God!' and hurried into the bedroom to see what was amiss.

'Have you seen this?' she asked, gesturing at the screen where two presenters, a man and a woman, sat squeezed together behind a narrow desk, trying simultaneously to smile at the viewers and look grave at the news they had to impart.

'No. What?'

He hadn't had the radio on in the kitchen, enjoying the peace of the early morning before the hurly-burly of the day and another waspish meeting with DCI Krepski about Operation Cuckoo.

He handed her her tea and sat down on his side of the bed, looking at the TV where the picture had now given way to a location report. Angie hadn't answered his question but sat with her hands wrapped round the mug as if it was the only thing that could warm her.

Somewhere by the seaside, he thought, probably the south coast to judge by the pebbles on the beach. Gulls swooped through the air, raucous, and a thin rain was falling out of a white sky. It had all the bleakness of the English seaside resort out of season. A young woman in a beige raincoat stood talking to camera in the monotonous rhythms of the news reporter, emphasising words, apparently at random.

'It was at *about* 2 o'clock this *morning* that the *coast* guards saw the *distress* flare several *miles* out to *sea*,' she said, her voice earnest. 'The *lifeboat* was launched at *once* but arrived too *late* to help the Wyke *Duchess* and her sinister *cargo*. It was a *rough* night in Weymouth *Bay* last *night* and the little *fishing* boat was *scuppered* in heavy *seas*.'

'Were there any survivors, Janice?' the woman in the studio asked. The line wasn't good and there were a few seconds of dead air before the reporter responded.

'It is *believed* that one man was pulled *alive* from the *water*, Hannah, though barely *so*. He's in Weymouth *hospital* at the moment, under *heavy* police guard, and is *said* to be in a critical *condition*. He will, of *course*, be crucial in the *investigation* as to how so *many* would-be illegal *immigrants* met a watery *grave* a matter of *miles* from the end of their *long* journey.'

Angie sipped at her tea, not tasting it. Her face was sad. Greg glanced at her, then back at the screen as the studio presenter said, 'And now we're going over to police headquarters in Weymouth where Detective Chief Inspector Stan Krepski of the National Crime Squad is overseeing the investigation.'

Greg saw a tired-looking Krepski, also in a raincoat, navy blue in his case, his hair damp from the rain that fell steadily on the streets of Dorset. His name and rank flashed up on the screen in a caption as he stood outside the police station to make his statement to the waiting media. Drops fell on the lens of the camera, giving him a pock-marked look.

He seemed to be speaking without notes, his hands thrust deep into his pockets.

'The boat that sank off Fortuneswell last night was a fishing smack registered to a Nigel Driscoll of Wyke Regis. Mr Driscoll has not been seen since setting out yesterday morning, telling his family that he was going on a deep sea fishing trip. We must assume, at the moment, that his body went down with his boat, along with that of his brother Patrick.'

'Fortuneswell?' Angie remarked. 'They got that wrong.'

'It seems,' Krepski went on, 'that far from going

fishing, Mr Driscoll must have put in somewhere along the French coast near Cherbourg where he collected a party of men trying to make their way into the United Kingdom illegally. All but one of those men is now dead, drowned when the Wyke Duchess, no doubt overloaded for her size, capsized in rough seas.'

A middle-aged man with a bristly moustache called a question. 'Is the survivor under guard to stop him running away or for his own protection?'

'Both,' Krepski said tersely.

'Do you know the nationality of the men?'

'Not yet. The survivor is of Arab or north African appearance. We hope that when the boat is salvaged we may find papers giving us more details. Otherwise, the man in hospital is our only hope of learning more about this dreadful tragedy.'

'When do you expect to bring the boat up?'

'It's a difficult job but it will be done with all possible speed.'

Greg assumed that the meeting he had scheduled for this morning with Krepski would be cancelled or at least postponed.

The phone rang. Angie turned down the sound as he answered, hearing the news he had just anticipated.

'Yes, I saw it. Okay, I was expecting it. See you.'

'Why does the man in hospital need protection?' Angie asked him.

'If the people who organised this smuggling trip think he knows too much about them and will talk to the police, they may decide to kill him.'

'After all he's been through?'

'Let's say that they are not nice people.'

'I thought maybe they were trying to help refugees.'

Greg shook his head. 'They are business men, my darling, who help nobody but themselves.'

When he got to the police station he went into the recreation room, deserted at this time of day, and switched on the TV. It was, inevitably, tuned to a sports channel but a little trial and error soon located a 24-hour news service. With his meeting cancelled he had an hour to spare and this story interested him, though it was not on his turf.

Thank God.

Now the reporters had caught up with a tearful Mrs Nigel Driscoll: Adele, as the caption introduced her. She was younger than Greg had expected, not much over thirty, and clutched an infant, which was wearing only a disposable nappy and t-shirt, by one hand as she spoke with difficulty.

'People don't understand how hard it is for a fisherman to make a living, what with the quotas an' all. Sometimes Nige catches fish and has to chuck them back because he's over quota, just chuck 'em away even though most of them won't survive, when he could get good money for them at the restaurants. Throwing away perfectly good food. It's criminal.'

She looked around her, eyeing the reporters and cameramen, sure of their support. 'And you seen what they charge for a plate of cod in those seafood restaurants? And the Spaniards, and them, they take all the quotas and fishing's all Nige knows. It's all he's ever done and what his father did before him.'

She snivelled, apologised to her invisible audience, and wiped her nose with the back of her free hand. The child stared up at its mother with huge, vacant eyes, desperate to understand but not yet master of language.

'So I said to him, I said, "This is crazy, Nige. You can't go sneaking these Arabs and people into the country. You'll get in trouble" but he says it's that or sell the boat for half what it's worth, move to a town, get a job in an office.' She gazed vacantly across the sea outside her poor cottage. 'And that'd've killed us, especially Nige.'

But Nige had died anyway. Literally, not metaphorically.

'Pardon?' the woman said. The reporter repeated his question. She shrugged. 'This was the third time, I think. I don't really know. He didn't want me involved, see. Told me not to answer the phone even, though I said, "What if it's my mum with her heart?"'

The reporter brought her gently back to the point. 'Yes, we knew it was wrong but what choice did we have? He was a good sailor, Nigel, knew these waters like the back of his hand, but the storm last night. Well, you saw.'

The reporter asked another question and she said, 'Blame? I dunno who I blame. All I know is my husband's gone, and my brother-in-law, and the boat, and I don't suppose the insurance'll pay out, not if it was being used for something illegal. And Cherie left with no father.'

She indicated the child, which Greg had hitherto taken for a boy.

'He called me his duchess,' she said hollowly. 'I was the Wyke duchess. He named the boat after me'.

The camera dwelt on her empty face for a moment then a voice over said, 'This is Peter Tracey for Sky News, in Wyke Regis near Weymouth.'

'Iranian?' Krepski looked intently at Inspector Faber. 'Haven't had one of them for a while, Trevor.'

'Haven't had one at all, as I recall.'

'Don't suppose he speaks English?'

'Not so's you'd notice. Or if he does he isn't letting on.'

Krepski sighed. 'Do we have diplomatic relations with Iran?'

'Sure. Why not?'

'Weren't we at war with them over the Gulf a few years back?'

Faber said patiently, 'That was Iraq.'

'Oh! Get on to the embassy in London then, tell them to get someone down here pronto.'

'With respect —' Faber said. Krepski looked at him sharply. 'These men'll be dissidents, people who are opposed to the regime —'

'Rubbish! People who heard England was a soft touch, more like.'

'So the last person we want translating is someone from the embassy,' Trevor Faber persevered.

'Who then?'

'There are plenty of Iranian refugees in the country.' Krepski snorted but the inspector was used to his boss's little ways and talked on over him. 'Legitimate refugees, academics and so forth.'

'You've got six hours to find one,' Krepski said, 'then I'm going to the embassy.'

He was in a bad mood because the police doctor wouldn't let the wilting Adele Driscoll be questioned. She had been belatedly moved to a secret address when it was realised that her life might be at risk for the same reason that the survivor's life might be at risk.

He was inclined to think that she was telling the truth when she claimed to know nothing, but that wouldn't stop him from giving her a hard time to make sure, or protect her from a bullet through the head.

The man they'd fished from the water was out of danger, medically speaking, though weak, not merely from his near drowning but from weeks, possibly months of under-nourishment as he and his companions made their way with painful slowness across the continent of Europe in search of a new life.

Dr Balali was a short, plump, tidy-looking man with white hair and moustache. He might have been any age from thirty-five to sixty. He was a lecturer in Middle-Eastern history at Bristol university and had reached Weymouth within two hours of being contacted.

His manner was coldly polite, even mildly hostile. He inclined his head on introduction to the policemen but did not offer to shake hands, holding his firmly by his side.

The would-be refugee had been moved from intensive care into a private room where an armed policeman stood on guard at all times. The doctor was prepared to give them half an hour to question the boy and at six o'clock that evening Krepski and Faber gathered at his bedside with their interpreter.

The lighting in the room had been turned down to a permanent twilight and Krepski asked for it to be turned up. The guard explained that the light hurt the boy's eyes.

The DCI told him to wait outside.

Now that the patient was no longer wearing a breathing mask, Faber saw that he was young, about the age of his kid brother David, the baby of the family, who had just turned sixteen. He had a wisp of down on his upper lip where he was trying to grow a moustache, no doubt to make himself look older.

Trevor felt a surge of pity for him.

He lay on his back, his eyes fixed fearfully on the policemen. A drip on his right side delivered a saline solution smoothly into his skinny body. He had eaten some rice and a little clear soup, his stomach not ready for anything richer or heavier.

Dr Balali pulled up a chair next to the bed and

took the boy's left hand in his. He spoke to him for a few minutes in a low voice.

Krepski looked impatiently at Faber. Balali, intercepting the look, said, 'I am reassuring him, explaining that he must tell all he knows to the nice British policemen and that no harm will come to him.' He spoke to the boy again, this time with a questioning intonation.

'His name is Mohsen and he is fifteen years old.'

Krepski let out a tut of annoyance. The boy was a minor and ought, strictly speaking, to be questioned only when accompanied by a responsible adult. But it wouldn't exactly be easy to lay hands on his next of kin and the DCI decided that he had the authority to override the rule in an emergency.

They only had the boy's word for it that he was fifteen, in any case, and everyone knew what filthy liars these Arabs were.

'He comes from Mashhad, in the north of Iran, near the border with Turkmenistan.' The academic spoke again and listened. 'He set out from there in July. For four and a half months he has been on the road, sometimes left without food for days at a time, often in the dark.'

'Always overland?'

Balali asked and translated the reply. 'Yes, until they set out to sea from the coast of France last night. He was afraid of the sea, because he had never seen it before.'

'And with good reason, it seems,' Faber said.

'He was afraid that they were too many for the little fishing boat, but his companions told him not to be so foolish. They were excited because the end of their long journey was near.'

'He was afraid of the sea and yet he, apparently, was the only one who could swim,' Krepski said.

The boy spoke at length and his face was animated for the first time.

'There is a lake near his house,' Balali explained. 'He swam there from early childhood. He says he was the best swimmer in the village. But the sea was very different from the lake: the water tasted foul and the waves were high and it was cold, so cold, cold as hell.'

'*Cold* as hell?' Krepski queried.

'In many cultures hell is an icy place not the place of fire it is to you Anglo-Saxons. He struggled for a long time to stay afloat but he was exhausted and was about to give up and let the waters close over his head, when the lifeboat appeared out of nowhere and pulled him aboard.'

'Did he have family among the dead?' Faber asked. 'He does know the rest of his party are dead?'

'He knows.' Balali spoke to the boy and the men watched his face cloud over. 'He lost his father in the war when he was eighteen months old. He does not remember him.'

'The war?' Krepski asked.

The Iran-Iraq war. It took a terrible toll. He lost also two uncles. He says all the men on the boat were young, like him, none more than twenty.'

'Dear God!' Faber said.

Balali said soberly, 'You must understand that an

entire generation of men was wiped out in the war, like what you refer to as the First World War, which was really just a European skirmish.'

'I wouldn't call it *that* exactly,' Faber murmured.

'These boys were often the men of their families. It would be easier for them, too, to adapt to western life, to learn the language, if they were young. And it needed strength to make such a journey. He left behind his mother and two older sisters. They begged him to go, even though it took their life savings, even though they knew it meant they would never see him again or even know what had become of him.'

Faber thought of these women and girls, far away in a country, a culture, a way of life which he could barely imagine. He hoped that they would never know what had become of their sons and brothers but would continue to envisage them free and happy in the promised land of fields and forests, hills and lakes, of jobs and schools and doctors.

'What route did they take?' Krepski asked.

'He isn't sure. He was told beforehand that they would cross the border into Turkey, the only safe way out of the country. Then to Bulgaria and the former Yugoslavia, but he doesn't know if that was the route they took since he was shut up in a lorry in darkness for most of the time. That is why his eyes are so sensitive: it is the first time he has been in the light for more than a few minutes in many weeks.'

'Did he see where they set out from in France?' Faber asked.

'It was dark by the time they reached the coast and

they waited for two or three hours in a cottage near a sandy bay. They were offered food but he didn't like the look of it. He had heard that the French eat many pigs and feared there might be pig meat in it.'

'Then he can't have been *that* hungry,' Krepski murmured and Balali shot him an angry look.

'Why England?' Krepksi asked Balali in exasperation. The doctor had ordered them out of the boy's room when their half hour was up and they were standing in the corridor. 'Why here when there are so many nearer countries — places that don't require a sea trip.'

Balali smiled grimly. 'What do you want me to say, Chief Inspector? That the United Kingdom is the birthplace of modern democracy and so a land that all free souls reach out to? That it is famously tolerant, with its welfare benefits and its free education and health service —'

'Have you tried getting an operation on the NHS lately?' Krepski demanded.

'And its polite and honest policemen who do not beat up prisoners or lock them up without trial or torture them?' He shook his head. 'They come here to learn English and the Anglo-Saxon ways so they can go to America eventually. For that to them is the promised land, though the late and unlamented Ayatollah Khomeini called it the land of Satan.'

Family business

And so he grew cunning and bided his time. He learned his lines and movements like an actor in a long, long play, an interminable play, a soap opera, perhaps.

He was punished if he was bad and punished if he wasn't bad. He might as well be as bad as he could be.

After the sudden growth spurt of puberty, he saw that his father was not such a big man after all. He, Antony, was a late developer, shooting up to six feet tall at the age of fifteen, filling out in the chest and shoulders, no longer puny.

He joined the judo club at school, Tuesday and Thursday lunchtimes, not mentioning it at home.

His asthma improved: he grew out of it and no longer needed his inhalers regularly.

His day would come and they should expect no mercy.

Antony didn't go near Marlborough for more than a week. This was partly practical — it was half term and Stephen would be hanging around — and party tactical.

Give her time to stew.

He'd taken none of his annual leave that year, saving it for just such an eventuality, so two days before Halloween he poked his head round the door of his immediate superior, David Rhys Lloyd, to ask for a few days off.

'I shall need odd days here and there, over the next month or two,' he explained, 'maybe at short notice. Family business.'

Rhys Lloyd shrugged and said that was fine by him. He found Antony hard to talk to, hard to like. He was painstaking rather than inspired in his work, but he got the job done and the clients, even the men, liked him, which was most of the battle.

He lacked ambition, or he would have been a partner by now. Rhys Lloyd had come up the hard way — comprehensive school, red-brick university, iron out the Swansea accent, sheer guts — and found Antony Lucas, with his take-it-or-leave-it attitude to life, incomprehensible.

His parents had done him no favours, David thought, dying like that when he was twenty-four, leaving him with a comfortable inheritance. It was as if he had nothing to work for. He had his unmortgaged flat in Barnes, where no colleague had ever set foot, a new car — always the same make, model, even colour — every two years; his clothes were smart but unexciting.

Family business? It was news to David Rhys Lloyd that Antony Lucas had any family left.

He had watched female colleagues, from a partner to the usual gaggle of temporary secretaries, make a play for him over the years, always to come away empty handed. There were times when he thought that Lucas was an empty shell, a shop-window dummy.

Lights on, doors open, nobody home.

He would sit at office outings, nursing one glass of red wine before switching to mineral water, always in control.

There had to be something driving the man!

David, who had a vivid Celtic imagination, foresaw that one day Lucas would fail to turn up for work, without explanation. After a few days he would call the police and they would break into his flat and he would be hanging there in his bedroom, wearing nothing but a pair of women's stockings, with an orange in his mouth.

* * *

'Can I have a word, McFee? Heh?'

Mr Hamilton might be ancient but his voice carried across the foyer of the hotel like a Stentor.

The chef was leafing through the bookings for the restaurant that night. 'Can it wait, Mr H? Is it urgent?'

'I wanted a word about the staff, about the room service.'

'I'll catch you later,' the Scot said.

'Very well.' Mr Hamilton spun on his walking stick and began limping along the corridor towards his room.

McFee turned back to the red-headed girl who was on reception that morning. 'What's this name?' he demanded and, when she didn't answer, staring after the old man, 'Jen!'

'Sorry, Mr McFee.' She took the book from him

and peered at the scrawl. 'It's the Pritchards, that stockbroker and his wife from Leckhamstead. Regulars.'

* * *

Cressida looked paler when she opened the door this time, clutching her hand to the hollow of her throat at the sight of him. A little sigh broke from her tight lips, perhaps relief. He had a sudden image of her answering the door every time anyone knocked for the past ten days, hoping desperately that it was him, to be each time disappointed.

He stood with his head down, unthreatening, scuffing his feet on the doorstep like a naughty boy.

Then he looked up and gave her a radiant smile.

'I told you never to come back,' she said hoarsely.

'Actually, you didn't,' he pointed out. 'You merely told me to leave.'

'And that wasn't enough? You didn't get the message?' She was peering up and down the alleyway to see if anyone was watching. 'Stephen's mother has the twins this afternoon. She might come back at any second.'

'Then you can introduce us.'

She was shaking and he put out both hands to take her arms above the elbow, to steady and reassure. She was wearing a short-sleeved tee shirt and her skin felt cold to his touch, the flesh mottling under his fingers. He bent his head and pressed his lips to the sharp angle of her collar bone.

She jumped as if he'd scalded her.

Breaking free of his hands, she backed away before him. 'No,' she said, 'no,' but she didn't try to shut the door against him. She almost ran away down the corridor towards the sitting room. He closed the front door quietly behind him and clicked the latch up before following her.

'When are you expecting Mrs Crabshaw back with the twins?' he asked.

She hesitated then admitted, 'Oh, not for hours. She's taken them to her house in Swindon for the day. She often does.'

An unpaid nanny, in other words. You don't know you're born, he thought, with your husband and his mother dancing attention on you, making it easy for you.

They stood looking at each other for a moment then she almost fell forward into his arms, flinging her own round his neck. They kissed. She was fervent, frantic, biting his lips.

'Cressida,' he breathed into her shining hair. 'I've thought of nothing but you since my last visit.'

Which was true, in its way.

'I thought you were never coming back,' she gasped.

'Oh, I was always coming back.'

* * *

'Now what's the problem?' McFee asked an hour later. 'You're not satisfied with the room service, is that it? Everything comes straight from the kitchen and is the same as we eat in the dining room.'

'Oh, I've no complaints about the food,' Mr Hamilton said. 'I just wanted to arrange some extra services from your special staff. Heh?'

'I'm not with you,' the Scot said bluntly.

'From the ones you bring in at night by the lorry-load and keep up in the attic.'

McFee reddened to his hairline, though whether in embarrassment or anger it was hard to determine. He said coldly, 'I've no idea what you're talking about.'

'Oh, I think you do.'

The two men stood for a moment, their gazes locked. It was the Scot who looked away first.

'By the way,' Hamilton said. 'I didn't manage to get to the bank this week. Not as mobile as I once was. Wondered if you could let me have a bit of cash. Just add it to the bill, heh?'

McFee bit his lip till the blood came. 'See whoever's at reception. Say I said it was okay.'

* * *

Bag of bones, Antony thought dispassionately. Why didn't she put a little flesh on them? He supposed he had felt a few seconds of pleasure, a spasm, but now he wanted above all to wash himself thoroughly, to cleanse himself of her smell and her stickiness, but that wasn't what ardent lovers did.

'Cressida,' he murmured, as if he thought it poetry.

She lay curled away from him, on her right side, naked on the marital bed, the sheets and blankets scattered to the four corners of the room.

Blankets: he bet that was Stephen in full fogey mode.

He moved closer, fitting himself into the shape of her, and felt her flinch slightly. So this was how it was going to be: the urgent desire, the satisfaction; then the shame, the denial. He could play that game too.

'What have we done?' he sighed.

She didn't answer and as he reached over to nuzzle her face he felt cold tears on her cheek. They aroused no pity in him and he made no comment. The house was very quiet. As he lay there, he could make out the distant rumble of traffic in the High Street.

'And yet it's perfectly normal,' he said, after a while.

'Normal!' She spun onto her back, turning angry eyes on him. 'I've betrayed my husband and with my own brother.'

'Half brother.'

'You call that *normal*? Isn't it illegal?'

'Probably,' he said, 'but I won't tell anyone if you don't.'

Yet.

'We're attracted to people who resemble us,' he went on, 'down to the smallest details — the shape of the eyes, the length of the hands.' He laced her fingers in his, feeling the hard gold of her wedding ring with its attendant diamond solitaire.

He stooped to kiss her damp palm.

'It's a genetic thing,' he continued, his blue eyes boring into hers, a mirror image, holding her mesmerised. 'What could be more natural than that close relations, meeting for the first time in adulthood, should feel an overwhelming . . .'

He had rehearsed this speech and had meant to say 'love for each other' but the words choked him.

'An overwhelming desire for each other?' he concluded.

'What could be more *unnatural*?' She rose from the bed and began to gather up the clothes she'd dropped anyhow in the urgency of her passion. 'And we're not animals. We can resist our desires. We should have. We shall.' She held the pile of garments against her so he could no longer see her nakedness and almost ran into the bathroom to dress.

'You're irresistible,' he called after her.

He lay back with his arms behind his head, awaiting her return. He was mildly interested to see what she would say and do next. She would tell him to go, he thought, but she would not tell him never to return.

Candid camera

Trevor Faber attended post-mortems as seldom as possible. As always, he took a deep breath before entering the door into the cold interior. It was a pointless ritual since death by drowning wasn't contagious and he could hardly hold his breath for his entire visit.

People said drowning was a pleasant death, but how could they know? What could be pleasant about being unable to breathe?

A cadaver lay on the table in the centre of the room, its modesty protected by a sheet. The thin face was nut brown, but tinged with pink where the cold of the sea bed had done its work. The skin was roughened and pimpled like the flesh of a plucked chicken. A pinkish-white froth was visible in the slightly open mouth and one nostril.

Faber bent over for a closer look at the froth. He let his breath out slowly and drew another one. The dry cold seemed to pierce his lungs.

'I've seen that on drowned bodies before,' he commented. 'I think it suggests he was alive when he went into the water.'

'We're not looking for foul play,' Krepski grunted. 'Is this a murder enquiry, guv?'

The DCI shrugged. 'That's pretty much up to the Coroner but we'd better treat it as one till then. He walked round the table. 'How many have we got so far?'

'Six, including one of the Driscoll brothers. Nigel, we think.'

'Naturally. He was the captain so he went down with his boat.'

'He'd been a bit . . . nibbled.'

'He should just be grateful he's not facing manslaughter charges. The boy . . . what was his name?'

'Mohsen.'

'Said there were fifteen in his party.'

'Seventeen, including the Driscolls. The bodies we've got were brought up when the boat was salvaged. We assume the rest were swept overboard, or jumped like Mohsen. Their bodies are going to take longer to recover.'

And then someone would have to set off to Iran, assuming the authorities there were prepared to cooperate, with details of the DNA of the dead men, to try to establish who they were. Modern countries like the United Kingdom, where everyone was documented from the cradle to the grave, were not prepared to accept a handful of anonymous corpses in their records. The investigation would take months and would cost hundreds of thousands of pounds, if not millions, but no one would ever suggest that it was not worth doing.

Krepski looked at his watch 'Where is this bloody woman?'

On cue, a door opened at the other end of the

room and the pathologist appeared in her green scrubs. She was a plain, no-nonsense woman of forty who introduced herself unsmilingly as Dr Christine Merrylegs.

Faber thought that the name did not suit her.

'I'm ready to make a start,' she said, 'if you are. This is a long haul.'

Krepski said, 'Let's get it over with.'

'The body is that of a man of middle-eastern appearance, aged, at a rough estimate, between eighteen and twenty-three, a little undernourished but otherwise healthy.'

Dr Merrylegs was dictating as she began the first autopsy. She took the temperature of the body.

'Bodies cool twice as quickly in water as in air,' she explained to the two detectives 'and stabilise at the temperature of the water within twelve hours. That makes time of death even more difficult to hazard than usual.'

'The working hypothesis is that it was within half an hour of the distress flare being sent up,' Faber said. 'Say 2.30 yesterday morning.'

'Nothing I can see conflicts with that. There is some evidence of head injury which is likely to be post-mortem.' She turned to Krepski who had been standing like a stone statue since the start of the procedure, watching and listening, saying nothing. 'If the body was bobbing about in a boat for several hours after death, then that's to be expected.'

'No possibility it was done before he went into the water?' Faber asked.

'Unlikely, I'd say, although it is more difficult to distinguish the two in a case of drowning. Ante-mortem injuries will bleed but the water washes the evidence away; while post-mortem injuries bleed more than usual because of the high fluidity level of the body.'

'Then what makes you so sure?' Faber asked.

Krepski shot him a sharp look: their job was hard enough without complicating the case with foul play and he, for one, was prepared to take the woman's word for it.

'You see the pattern of the bruising.' Dr Merrylegs swept her hand down the corpse's face. 'Nose, fore-head, chin — the prominent points of the face. He would have been lying prone in the water, with his head lower than the rest of him, and those are the vulnerable parts.'

Faber nodded, satisfied.

The doctor wiped the foam from the man's lips and nose then pressed down on the chest wall. Another slick of froth formed at once. 'This certainly suggests that he was alive at the time of immersion,' she said.

'That's not really in doubt,' Krepski said impatiently. 'Can we get decent fingerprints off him?'

'Maceration of the skin following immersion begins on the palms, finger pads and the soles of the feet,' Dr Merrylegs said. 'Obtaining prints will be a delicate operation but we'll do our best.'

She pulled off the sheet, leaving the young man naked. This was the hardest bit for Faber to watch: the sheer helplessness of the victim. He looked so small and pathetic, so young. His penis was curled like a caramel snail on his thigh, a small scar behind the head where his circumcision had been clumsily performed. Faber wondered if that had troubled him. If so, it would do so no more.

The two policemen watched as the pathologist opened the corpse with a long slit from breastbone to pubis. Faber took a half step back, anticipating the stink of rotting flesh, but there was nothing.

She gave him a half smile. 'Salt water slows the rate of putrefaction.'

She made the cross incision and lifted a mass of organs out of the body cavity. The lungs looked grey and doughy and bloated.

Nope, Faber decided, *this* was the hardest bit to watch.

He made an excuse and left the room.

* * *

'I sometimes think I married too young,' Cressida said, 'started a family before I was ready. I mean, who, these days, marries at twenty-two? It's absurd.'

She was sitting cross-legged on the bed, naked. Her could see the black bush between her legs, the pink fleshy lips within. To think that men paid good money to look at that in magazines.

He smiled tenderly. 'Why did you?'

'It seemed right at the time. I suppose it always does. But now I see women my age — older — free, single, having fun. And I'm knee-deep in nappies and baby formula. I can't run out for a newspaper without getting out the double buggy, making sure the twins are warm enough and taking them with me.'

She moved easily forward onto her stomach, kicking her legs in the air above her. Her face was close to his thigh and her tongue snaked out and licked his flesh. He squirmed, which she took for encouragement.

And,' she said, 'Stephen doesn't see me as a woman any more, but as a mother. And who wants to fuck a mother?'

She looked a challenge at him and he dutifully said, 'I do!'

It was his third such clandestine visit in little more than a week. Today there had been no talk of guilt and shame. Of the unnatural and the abnormal. Of the illegal.

'Stephen's a lovely man,' she said, 'but he's so . . .

'Boring?'

'No!' She hit him with the pillow. 'He's sensible and decent and honest.'

'Well, don't worry your head, my darling.' He sat up and took her in his arms. 'Because I am none of those things.'

She giggled. Let her not claim later that she hadn't been warned.

He said, 'Have you told him I've been here, to see you?'

'God, no!'

'I meant the first time. I thought you might have told him we'd made our peace, after that tantrum you threw at Alders End that Sunday.'

'No.'

'And your mother?' He took care to say 'your mother' and not 'our mother'. It was not yet time to remind her that she was breaking one of the harshest taboos of civilisation.

She shook her head, burying her face in his manly chest with its tangle of dark fuzz. Her words were muffled. 'We haven't spoken about that incident at all.'

He grinned. 'Now why was that, I wonder?'

She inhaled his subtle scent without reply.

* * *

'Have you any Nurofen?' Elise asked. 'I've can feel my period cramps starting. Roll on menopause, I say.'

'In my bag.'

Elise picked up her daughter's capacious leather handbag without ceremony and began to rootle through it. Laughing, she pulled out a slim plastic object and held it up.

'A mobile phone?'

Cressida blushed. 'Everyone has one these days.'

'I don't. Seriously, darling, you're at home most of the day and anyone who wants you can reach you there.'

'Oh, well, they cost practically nothing and one

might as well have one for emergencies. What if I was out with the twins and one of them was taken ill and we were miles from anywhere?'

'I suppose it's possible.' Elise put the tiny thing back and carried on searching for pain relief. 'You'd better let me have the number.'

'I'd rather you didn't mention it to Stephen.'

Her mother looked at her in surprise. 'He's hardly going to object, is he? It's your money, after all.'

'Oh, you know what an old fogey he is.'

* * *

'I hope you're comfortable here,' Faber said.

Adele Driscoll glanced round the anonymous room without interest, as if comfort and discomfort no longer had a role to play in her life, as if she no longer knew the difference. It was a box of a room with cream walls and carpet, a plain blue sofa and armchair grouped round the TV. A shelf held paperback books and board games, a pack of dog-eared playing cards.

There was no telephone.

A door stood open into the hall, one into the galley kitchen; the last, opposite, gave onto the bedroom where her daughter was sleeping. The window showed chimneys and satellite dishes and sky.

In a dead voice, she asked, 'How long will I have to stay here?'

'Until the rest of the smuggling ring is rounded up, I'm afraid.'

That got a reaction. 'But that could be weeks.'

More likely months, Faber thought, or years. He sat down on the sofa next to her and laid a hand on her shoulder. She was wearing a cardigan which had been washed so often that the wool had matted into little balls. His frugal mother had cardigans like that. He restrained himself from plucking them off. Her hair smelled dirty and the blond gave way to brown at the roots. She must have been a nice looking woman once.

'What about Nigel's funeral,' she said, 'and Patrick's?' She lifted tearful eyes to him. 'I must say goodbye. And me mum. She's not well.'

'It wouldn't be safe for you, Adele. You must see that.'

'But I don't know anything.'

'They don't know that.'

'Who are *they*?'

'That's what we're hoping you will tell us.'

They both jumped. Krepski had appeared in the doorway from the hall, silent as a panther on his rubber soles. It was a gift that Faber admired in such a big man. He moved forward and took the armchair, pulling it round so that it faced the sofa instead of the TV.

'I want you to tell me everything you remember, Mrs Driscoll. That way you'll be able to go home the sooner.'

'I've told you a hundred times: I didn't even answer the phone. He told me not to.'

'But you must have some idea where the illegals went to from Nigel's boat.'

'A van,' she said after a pause for thought. 'A lorry.'

'Which?'

'I don't know! Between the two, like a small removal van.'

'Closed or with windows?'

'I only saw it once. It was dark.'

'Think.'

She threw Krepski a hostile look and Faber said, 'Take your time.'

Finally, she said, 'No windows.'

'Good. Now we're getting somewhere. This van came to your cottage?'

'No!' The idea seemed an affront. 'The boathouse. Nigel kept them in the boathouse. I didn't want them in my house. They might be diseased and I had Cherie to think about. I told Nige. I said, "You'll catch something from them dirty Arabs", but he just laughed.'

She choked back tears at the memory of Nigel and his laughter, the thing she had first noticed about him.

'How long would they stay in the boathouse?' Krepski asked.

'A few hours. A day. No more.'

'And then the van came?'

'In the night. Two, three a.m. Nigel told me to stay in bed and I did.'

'And you never even looked out the window, I suppose?'

'Once,' she admitted. 'Like I say. I saw this van.'

'What colour was it?'

'Dark.'

'Brown? Black? Dark blue?'

'I don't know.'

'How many men, apart from Nigel?'

She said reluctantly, 'Two.'

'Describe them for me.'

'It was dark.'

The DCI's voice rose. 'Think!'

Hers rose louder. 'It was dark!'

'Mum!' The little girl began to wail in the adjoining room, wakened and frightened by her mother's shouting. Adele Driscoll sprang up and left the room. She brought the crying child back with her and dumped her on the sofa next to Faber. He retreated.

Krepski stood up, as if the wailing child was driving him away. He nodded to his inspector who joined him.

'We'll be back,' Krepski said. 'Have a good think, if you ever want to leave this place.' He looked round in distaste, then walked out, shutting the front door hard behind him.

'Steady on, Stan.' Faber ran to catch him up.

'You're not usually so soft. She's nothing but the wife of a criminal.'

'Widow. A criminal who drowned in his own boat at the age of 35.'

'And whose fault was that?'

Faber didn't answer because, like Adele herself, he didn't know who to blame. He followed his boss through the lobby. They made sure that the front door locked behind them. Across the street two men sat in a plain blue saloon car. One, in the driver's seat, was slumped down with his eyes closed. The other, alert, nodded to the two men.

'Let's hope "they" don't find her,' Trevor said with a shudder.

'It might be more helpful if they do.'

* * *

The next time he came Antony brought a digital camera with him and took some candid shots of her. She protested, holding her hands up to cover her face. He pulled them down, wrestling with her across the bed. It seemed to excite her and he was obliged to have sex with her for a second time.

Exhausted, she made no further objection as he snapped her this way and that, pushing his camera into her intimate places. Would Stephen recognise his wife's most intimate parts, he wondered, from half a dozen others, in a game show perhaps, and those timid little breasts?

'There.' He showed her the pictures on the small display window, one by one. 'I shall print those off and keep them with me when we're apart.'

'I hope you're going to keep them in a safe place.'

'A very safe place.'

'Speaking of which, it's reckless of us to go on meeting here. Yesterday, Stephen came home suddenly in the middle of the afternoon. He had an unexpected free period and decided to pop back for tea. It's barely fifteen minutes walk.'

'Then we shall find somewhere else to meet.'

Cressida, what a bloody stupid, pretentious name. It suited her, though, as she had betrayed her husband and her little game of happy families with the first good-looking man who crooked his finger.

* * *

Giacomo McFee walked into Hamilton's room without knocking that evening, followed by a tall woman in her late twenties, thin to the point of boniness. She had a handsome face with strong features, a large nose and well-fleshed lips. Her hair fell straight and loose to her shoulders, bleached to the colour of wheat but with three inches of black root.

Her clothes were cheap and did not fit her well but she had a dignity about her which gave her grace.

'Come in, do,' Mr Hamilton said with heavy sarcasm. He was standing in front of the wardrobe admiring his reflection in the mirror. He ran his hand over his bald head as if to smooth the bumps.

'This is Maria,' McFee said.

Hamilton turned and looked her up and down. 'She's a bit skinny.'

The woman looked down her nose at him, her black eyes flashing with contempt. She turned to McFee.

'This is joke? Yes?'

'No joke,' McFee said. 'You might as well get used to it. I'll be back for you in half an hour —'

'An hour,' Hamilton protested. 'It takes me half an hour to get going these days. Heh?'

McFee's mouth twisted with distaste. 'An hour. Not a minute longer.' To the woman, he said, 'Don't leave the room till I come back for you. Understood?' She looked puzzled and he repeated the words more slowly, pointing at her and then at the floor with his finger.

'You. Stay. Here. Wait for me. Understood?'

'I understood.'

The chef left the room, shutting the door behind him. Outside he stopped and grimaced at the white panelled wood. He wasn't a pimp and the old man had better watch his step.

Anatomy lesson

'Sorted out your problem in Weymouth?' Greg asked Krepski politely.

'Sorted it out? Ask me again in a year's time.'

'Oh, God. Was he really still going to be seeing this man regularly a year from now? Five years from now? Could he stand it?

'I've pretty much handed it over to the Dorset police,' the DCI was saying, 'but Trevor's down there still, liaising.'

'What about the survivor?' Barbara asked.

'Still recuperating. After that he'll be held at a centre for a bit till we can deport him.'

'You're sending him back to Iran?' Monroe stared in disbelief. 'After all he's been through?'

'What else are we supposed to do?' Krepski snapped. 'Pat him on the head for being so bloody clever, give him a council house and the dole and let him stay here forever?'

'But won't he be punished for trying to flee the country?' Greg asked.

As if Krepski cared. 'That's not my problem. Frankly, the more this sort of thing happens, the better.'

The three Newbury officers stared at him, stunned.

'In what way, sir?' Barbara asked.

Krepski spread his hands, annoyed at having to state the obvious. 'Word gets back and the next bunch of illegals think twice about it.'

'And what about the Driscoll brothers?' Greg said coldly.

'Serves them right too. They knew what they were letting themselves in for, getting involved in smuggling.'

'And that's a capital crime now, is it?'

'Maybe it should be. These people are worse than murderers, in my book; they're undermining our way of life.'

'And Adele Driscoll, and the baby? Did they deserve to lose their husband and father?'

'It's not my problem,' the DCI said again. 'Now can we get on?'

Monroe lingered after Barbara had left to see Krepski out. Greg said, 'Something on your mind, Tim?'

'I don't think Krepski's the right man for this job.'

'I'm inclined to agree, but it's not my decision.'

'If you spoke to someone high up at the NCS, though, went over his head. I'm sure his superiors haven't been treated to his views the way we have.'

'I wouldn't be so sure. It's the sort of thing you hear in the pub every day now.'

'It's not as if he would be demoted or anything. The NCS have dozens of projects going at any one time. Just ask for him to be moved sideways. There must be someone owes you a favour.'

Greg got up. 'I'll think about it.'

'Sir —'

'I said I'll think about it.

* * *

'Would you like to look at my work?' Cressida asked.

No.

'That would be wonderful! I'd been hoping you'd suggest it, but I didn't like to ask. It's such a personal thing for an artist.'

'Oh, well.' She blushed. 'One must get used to people viewing it.'

She led the way to a brick outhouse that protruded into the courtyard garden like a massive carbuncle. 'An old privy,' she said with a laugh, as she unfastened the padlock that secured the door.

Apt, Antony thought, since her 'work' was probably shit.

Inside, the bare bricks had been whitewashed, making the cramped space look larger, while a skylight had been cut into the roof, sprinkled with rotting leaves from a neighbour's clematis.

'The house is a bit small,' she said, 'now that we have the boys. It would make more sense if Mum made Alders End over to me. I could use Daddy's studio then. And there's the tax point of view too. Death duties.'

'Inheritance tax.'

'Assuming she lives another . . . is it seven years?'

He nodded. 'She's still a young woman, bound to live another seven years.'

'But it doesn't seem to occur to her and I don't like to ask.'

'Further for Stephen to get to school,' he pointed out.

'There is that, I suppose. Of course, if someone else were to raise the subject with her, some disinterested party . . .'

He pretended not to understand the hint. No doubt she'd be delighted if Elise made the paintings over to her too, and the rest of her capital. People did it all the time to save tax. An accountant who did business with his firm referred to it as the King Lear Syndrome. He was sure that Elise had more sense and would cling fiercely to her financial independence.

He scrutinised the room intently for something to do.

The only furniture was a tall stool standing in the middle of the wooden floor in front of an easel. On the easel was a half-finished canvas, a male nude, turned away from the onlooker, his face fixed on some distant point.

Competent enough, he thought, moving to stand in front of it, but this was no Tinker Girl. There was a spark lacking, an inspiration. This was the work of a painstaking student. She probably had the man turned away because she couldn't do mouths. He made noises of awe and delight and watched her lap it up.

'Stephen?' he asked.

She looked hurt. 'It's you! That's why I hid the face, so it should be our secret.'

He looked more closely, the way he avoided looking at himself in a mirror. How grotesque the human body was: this elongated biped with its too-big head, its sloping shoulders, its ape-like arms swinging, hairy.

'Wow!' he said and she threw him a look of such unbridled adoration that he had to turn away, brushing past her to inspect the rest of the wasted canvases. She favoured the human form, he saw. Of the pictures that littered the place he could see no landscapes, abstracts or still lives.

He remarked on it.

'Um.' She nodded as if he'd had a great revelation. 'People. I'm a people person.'

'Oh, yes!' he said. 'So am I.'

'We've got a lot in common. We're alike.'

'Yes,' he said. 'We are.'

They were very alike: the difference was that he knew himself to be a monster while she, she believed herself to be a fundamentally good and decent person.

And this monstrous egoism comes from you, Elise. It must do, mustn't it, unless it was there in both our fathers?

It's in you, somewhere.

On the back wall hung two posters. One was the famous Da Vinci picture of a naked man spreadeagled in a cosmic circle; the other a detailed anatomical drawing. Antony went to stand in front of this latter, intrigued. This was the unadorned man, skinned, stripped of the face he showed to the world; this was the heaving mass of tissue that held itself so dear, that thought it had a soul.

White skeleton, red blood, sinews and muscles in shades of blue.

'Isn't the human body incredible?' Cressida joined him and slipped her arm round his waist under his jacket. 'So simple and yet so complicated. We complain when we're ill, and yet it's a miracle that it all works so perfectly for most of the time. I can stand and look at this for hours.'

Antony was barely listening to her babble. He raised a hand to the picture, tracing the line from the pulse in the neck to the bulging muscle of the heart, safe behind the bars of its white cage of ribs.

'The heart,' Cressida murmured, laying her head on his shoulder. 'So powerful and yet so fragile.'

He wished she would stop saying 'and yet'; it sounded so phoney.

* * *

Justin Greif swaggered into the dining room at Boxford Hall with his fiancée Philippa Cole. It was eight o'clock on a Wednesday night and the place was heaving with the wealthy and influential of the Thames Valley. Although he was an undersized man in a pair of unflattering specs that made his brown eyes comically huge, Greif was not short of confidence and he expected to be greeted with cries of joy.

Nor was he disappointed, since Giacomo McFee said, 'Nice to see you again, Mr Greif, Miss Cole,' which was as close to unbridled joy as the Scotsman was ever likely to get.

Greif punched him lightly on the arm and said, 'Did you put that champagne on ice like I said, Giacomo?'

'Oh yes. It's all ready for you.' McFee looked with a quiet distaste at the hand on his arm, then gestured to one of his waiters and added, 'Tom, here, will take care of you.'

'Only it's a special occasion,' Philippa said eagerly. She had seen McFee on *Richard and Judy* which meant that he was famous. She held out her left hand to show him the single vast diamond on her ring finger and simpered. She was a large woman, taller than her man and of athletic build, and simpering didn't suit her.

'Jolly good.' McFee turned away to greet the next arrivals with, 'I was just about to give your table away, Mr Jackson. You're late!'

By twenty past nine, Justin and Philippa's celebration was not going as planned. Half way through their puddings their voices began to rise to a low screech and fellow diners turned to stare at them as waiters glanced uneasily at each other and wondered whether to send for McFee who had now retired to his office to count his money.

'Don't you understand,' Justin was shouting, 'I have to protect myself from gold-diggers.'

'I am not a gold-digger!'

'Then sign the bloody pre-nup and prove it, you stupid shiksa bint.'

'Jewish pig!'

'Jewish pig? Where's the logic in that? Jews don't keep pigs.'

Philippa had been to Sunday school every week for eight years and she knew better. She yelled triumphantly, 'Then what about the Gadarene swine, Mr Knowall, where did they come from?'

Justin was rendered speechless by this and even more so when Philippa picked up her plate and pushed the better part of a bread and butter pudding into his mouth, half choking him.

He jumped up with several spoonfuls of *crème anglaise* running down his chin and spat out the remnants onto the tablecloth. He scraped back his chair, and flung the melting remains of his own *assiette de sorbets* wildly at his fiancée. It almost missed her, catching the top of her fair hair and dripping down her neck onto the dress she had bought for the occasion.

She gave a scream of rage and flung herself at him. She had played netball for Hampshire in her late teens — goal attack — and found the table no obstacle. It collapsed, depositing its contents on top of Justin who was now pinned painfully to the floor by the woman he intended to spend the rest of his life with.

The waiters leaped on the pair and tried to separate them, only to find that they had joined forces against the new assailants. A wine waiter staggered back, clutching a bleeding nose, and crashed into another table, sending that flying and breaking a window.

The rest of the diners watched the floor show in a trance-like state, doing nothing, except for one timid-looking woman who drew out a mobile phone and whisperingly called the police.

In his usual corner, Mr Hamilton laughed till the tears formed puddles in the wrinkles of his ancient cheeks.

By the time PCs Whittaker and Clements responded to the 999 call fifteen minutes later the diners had ascertained the reason for the quarrel and were taking sides.

A fat woman in a too-tight dress was wagging her finger in Justin's face and saying, 'If you really love someone you don't even think about money.' She turned to her skinny and rather cowed-looking husband. 'Isn't that right, Bruce?'

'Yes, dear.'

A ratty little man in a too-large suit took her to task. 'He's worked hard for his money. Why should he have to give it up just because his marriage doesn't work out.'

'And she's contributed nothing, I suppose?'

'You don't know anything about it, you fat cow.'

'Bruce!'

'You can't talk to my wife like that.'

'And whose army's going to stop me?'

McFee had emerged from his office to see what the racket was about and stood staring in disbelief at the wreckage of his dining room. When the two uniformed constables entered the room his eyes filled with the rage which his employees knew only too well.

He was clearly audible over the existing din as he bellowed, 'Who called the *polis*?'

The staff denied it vigorously as the chef turned his furious black stare on each of them in turn. Then he strode into the gang of customers huddling round Greif and his fiancée. They immediately fell silent.

He demanded, 'Which of you bastards called the *polis*?'

The timid woman glanced round, seeking support. There was no reason for her to confess, but McFee's eyes seemed to hypnotise her. She nervously raised her hand.

The Scot jabbed her in the chest with his finger. 'You! Yer barred.'

She gave a little squeak of terror.

Her middle-aged companion put a comforting arm round her. 'It's all right, Rosemary.' To McFee he added, 'Don't worry. We shan't be coming back and don't even think of charging us for tonight's little fiasco.'

They would have liked to storm out but were forced to pick their way carefully through the slippery debris of spoilt food and the obstacles of broken furniture, only to find PC Chris Clements blocking their way.

'I shall need a statement, sir.'

'The chief constable is a personal friend of mine,' the man snapped.

Clements, used to this dubious claim, answered demurely. 'I'm sure the chief'd be delighted to see you doing your civic duty, sir.'

'So long as you're quick about it,' the man said, more amenably. 'Can't you see my wife is upset?'

'If you could wait over here —'

'Now just a minute,' McFee said. 'This is all a mistake. Everything's under control here, lads, and you're not needed.'

'Under control?' PC Whittaker raised his eyebrows as he surveyed the chaotic scene. 'What's it like when it's out of control?'

'I can deal with any trouble,' the chef persevered. 'I'm sorry if your time's been wasted, but I'd like you to leave my premises now.'

'Not so fast.' Whittaker was a tall man and strongly built. He had natural authority and wasn't afraid of some tuppenny-halfpenny cook, even if he did appear on TV. 'This is a public place and a public order offence has been committed, not to mention criminal damage.'

He surveyed the room and spotted the wine waiter who was still nursing his battered nose, blood dripping steadily onto his white shirt. He pointed. 'And there's been an assault. I'm going nowhere till I'm satisfied as to exactly what went on here tonight, and neither is anyone else.'

McFee stood glaring at him for a moment, but Whittaker stared impassively back and folded his arms across his chest in a gesture of no surrender. The chef changed tack and gave him a wolfish grin. He put one arm round Whittaker's shoulders and pulled him a little apart.

'I'm sure we can come to some arrangement,' he murmured.

The constable bristled. 'Meaning what, exactly?'

'I can sort this out. Really. Nobody's hurt — Roddy suffers from nose bleeds all the time — and the mess isn't half as bad as it looks. I'm sure you've got more important things to deal with —'

'Not at all, sir. It's a pleasure.'

'Meanwhile, it would make me very happy if you and your lovely girlfriend would be my guests for dinner one night.' He glanced across at Clements. 'And your colleague too, of course.'

'My wife and I don't like our food messed about with,' Whittaker growled.

The chef turned away in disgust, shrugged and said, 'Then get on with it!' He pointed at Justin and Philippa. 'Those are the gobshites that started it all.'

Justin and Philippa were holding hands and gazing lovingly into each other's eyes, oblivious of the chaos they had wrought.

* * *

Cressida lay on her side at the edge of the bed. She was pretending to be asleep but her eyes were open. She watched the display on the clock radio change, its red light flipping seamlessly from 10:59 to 11:00.

In the bathroom Stephen was gargling. Even in
the early days of their love she had never found this
an alluring sound, but at least his breath smelled
sweet.

11:04.

He padded into the room, switching off the light
in the hall, humming a soft tune. They left the bedroom door open, the better to hear the twins in the
night. She lay very still, aware of familiar sounds as
he removed his tartan dressing gown and hung it on
the hook behind the door, kicking off his slippers
and arranging them, toe to toe, by the bed.

The little habits which had once seemed so
charming.

He pulled back the covers on his side and sat
down heavily, making the mattress rock. She felt
him leaning over her and wanted to scream. His lips
brushed her cheek.

'I know you're not asleep,' he said. His voice was
teasing, flirtatious. He was pressing close against
her and she could feel his erection bobbing between
her buttocks, seeking a path through her clamped
thighs.

'Mmm?' She turned over on her back and did an
imitation of a woman who's just been rudely wakened. 'What? What time is it?'

'I know you weren't asleep?' he repeated.
'Nobody sleeps that quietly. They move and mutter
and fidget. Only psychopaths sleep perfectly still
like that.'

That wasn't true, she thought. Antony had once

dropped off to sleep for a few minutes after their love making and she had watched him tenderly as he lay like a warm and exquisite statue in her bed.

'So tired,' she murmured.

She was wearing an old nightgown she had found at the back of the airing cupboard. It was shabby and shapeless and had been washed to the colour of sludge. It should be a passion killer if anything was, but it didn't seem to put Stephen off. His hand slid up under it, gliding over her belly to caress the breasts that had shrunk back to nothing within a month of the birth after she gave up breast-feeding as a bad job.

She wriggled, trying to evade his hand. 'Not tonight, Stephen.'

He withdrew his hand at once and turned over so that he, too, was lying on his back, a foot of cold mattress between them.

'Sorry,' he muttered.

'No, I'm sorry.'

'Only it's been a while.'

'I'm tired,' she said again.

'You're always tired these days.'

'The twins —'

'But it's always me who gets up for the twins!' He clicked off the bedside lamp and rolled onto his side, facing away from her. He tugged the bedclothes with him so that she was left without enough covering.

She sighed and tugged them back. There was a brief tussle. 'I wake up too,' she pointed out.

He didn't answer and soon she heard the deep, regular breathing which told her that he was asleep.

She lay awake, staring into the darkness.

11:09.

* * *

'And do you know what they were rowing about?' Barbara said the following morning. 'He wanted her to sign a pre-nuptial agreement and she wasn't keen. Can you believe it?'

'What happened to "For richer, for poorer",' Greg asked. But as a divorcee himself he wasn't, he reflected, in the best position to cast the first stone. 'So what happened?'

'Andy and Chris arrested this couple of lovebirds who started the trouble. They've been released on police bail and told to present themselves at the station again this afternoon, preferably sober.'

'So, is the wedding off?'

'Apparently not. Andy says they were like a pair of little birds in their nests by the time he got them home, cooing endearments at each other till he wanted to throw up.'

Greg groaned. 'I despair of couples like that.'

'Funny thing,' Barbara said. 'Well, not funny really.'

'What?'

'When they got home they found they'd been burgled.'

'What? Where do they live?'

'The Old Rectory in Alderbright.'

'Another one!'

'Looks like the same man,' Barbara agreed.

'But surely they had an alarm, big place like that?'

She shook her head. 'They only moved in two months ago, still got the builders in.'

'Much taken?'

'Portable stuff: jewellery, trinkets, cash. Some petty vandalism: sofas slashed, crockery smashed. The usual pattern.'

'Will you do something for me, Babs? Will you ask them if they have their gardening done by a bloke called Silas Weatherby.'

'Weatherby? Okay. Now?'

'If you will.'

'I'll give them a ring.' She left.

Greg became aware that Monroe had been unusually silent.

'You all right, Maril — Tim?' he asked.

'Eh?'

Greg repeated the question.

'Oh, yes. Sorry. I was talking to Krepski this morning.'

'Anything new?'

Monroe slowly shook his head, then burst out, 'I don't like the way he talks about the immigrants, sir. I know they've no right to be here but he talks about them like they were *animals*. Especially the women.'

Greg winced in sympathy. 'With no papers and little English, prostitution is often the only way they can make a living,' he said.

'But he talks like all Slav women are tarts.' He hesitated. 'My wife is from Slovenia, you see.'

'Really? I thought her name was Kate.'

'Kveta, Kate to her English friends. Sir, have you thought any more about what I said the other day?'

'I have indeed. I'm sorry, Tim, but I think I'd be sticking my nose in where it doesn't belong if I made a complaint about Krepski.'

This clearly came as a blow to Monroe. After a moment, he said, 'One of these days I'm gonna shove his words right down his throat.'

Greg could think of nothing to say to this and was glad when Barbara came back into the room.

'Negative,' she said.

'Sure? Only he lives practically next door.'

'They use a firm of contractors: Greenscapes of Newbury.'

'Okay,' Greg said, 'it was just a thought.'

He was disappointed, but when he heard later that day that McFee had asked for the charges against Greif and Cole to be dropped, he was more than disappointed. He was very cross indeed.

So was Andy Whittaker, who had come into the station especially to deal with his arrest, since he wasn't on duty until ten.

'I went through all this with him last night,' he complained. 'He was annoyed that we'd been called at all and wanted to deal with it himself but I told him it was a criminal matter.'

'He's been paid off,' Barbara said. 'You know who this bloke Greif is?' Both men looked blank and she sighed and raised her eyes to heaven. Patiently, she explained. 'Greif Haulage. You must have seen the vans and lorries about the place: blue with the wording in darker blue. He's got a big chunk of the market round here.'

'That's him?' Greg laughed. 'The first time I saw one I read it as "grief haulage" — thought it was some new breed of undertaker.'

'He's worth millions,' Barbara said. 'Hence the pre-nup.'

'How old is this bloke?' Greg asked.

'Twenty-eight, twenty-nine.'

Greg made a noise like 'pah!'; it was half envy and half disgust.

'The other one tried to bribe me and Chris to leave,' Whittaker said. 'The Scotch chef.'

Greg's ears prickled like a spaniel's. 'Bribe!'

'Offered us a free meal in that poncy restaurant of his. If that wasn't a bribe then what was it?'

'I'd call that a bribe,' Greg agreed.

'We told him to where to stick it, naturally.'

'It's understandable,' Barbara protested. 'Posh restaurant, negative publicity. I'm not excusing it but to call it a bribe . . .'

Greg got up from his desk. 'I'm going to talk to McFee and take a look round the place.'

'You, sir?' Barbara said.

'Yes, sir. Me, sir.'

'It's a pretty minor matter,' she objected, following him out of the room. 'I can go, if you like.'

'I don't think it is minor, Babs. People don't buy

their way out of trouble under our legal system; this isn't a banana republic. Besides, where do illegal immigrants get taken on for starvation wages?'

'Sweat shops, cleaning firms . . . cafés and restaurants.'

'Precisely. Anyway.' He grinned to prove he was joking. 'If he was prepared to offer Whittaker and Clements a free meal, who knows how much he'll try to bribe a superintendent!'

Proof error

Why had he left it so long to seek her out, his birth mother?
After the deaths of his adopted family he had hoped to find,
if not happiness, then a certain peace but, as the years
went by, that peace had seemed as elusive as ever and he
had realised that his work was not yet done.

It had taken him a year to track her down, a task made
harder by the fact that she had changed not only her surname, as might be expected, but her first name too.

There had been times when he'd been close to throwing
in the towel, or, rather, to hiring a professional, a private
detective to do the job for him. But he didn't want to leave
a trail. He wasn't sure what he intended to do to his
'mother' when he found her but he didn't want her name
ringing a bell with some retired copper later.

All he had to start with was a birth certificate, the original one, confided to him only after a session of coun-
selling at which he told many lies.

'I'm thinking of marrying, starting a family of my
own. Thank you. She's a lovely girl. We're very happy.
Anyway, I had a sudden longing to know where I came
from, to learn more of the heritage I'll be handing down to
my children. Lots of people do? Really? Yes, I can imagine.'

Fortunately the woman had been middle-aged, plump,
plain and long-married and had responded to his mild flir-
tation as to a god.

Mother's name: Elsie Mary Riley. Father's name: not given; no surprise there. An address in Clapham which had not, thirty years ago, been fashionable. He had gone there, checked it out. You never knew: it might have been her parents' house and she might still be living there.

But life was never that simple.

Long hours at St Catherine's house, poring over the marriage registers for every year from the date of his birth onward. Too many bloody Elsie Rileys, each of whom had to be eliminated.

As it were.

He would have passed over Elise Riley without stopping had his speed-reading eye not misread the first name, like a proof reader who sees what he expects to see. He noticed the discrepancy only when he'd paid for the certificate. And then he wondered. And then he probed. And then he found that her date of birth was the same as his mother's.

Now he had the address where she'd been living at the time of her marriage twenty-eight years before. Again, he took the trouble to visit the flat in Kensington; again, he was predictably disappointed, although the local newsagent told him that the Weissmans had moved to the country ten years ago.

He didn't know where: to a Londoner the country is the country and is where people go when they're tired of life.

But Elise Weissman was not a common name, not like Elsie Riley. She might have divorced, of course, remarried and changed her name again, but he felt he was due a bit of luck after all these months.

And he got it.

The Internet made such researches easier. Indeed, it

made them possible. It was the stalker's friend. He worked his way through the entries on the electoral register. Almost everyone was on that, even if their telephone number was ex-directory, even if they never bothered to vote.

He started in London, in case the bucolic idyll had proved short-lived, then pushed out gradually through the smarter counties: Surrey, Sussex, Bucks, Kent. He drew a blank each time.

But in Berkshire he found her, the solitary Elise Weissman.

He wrote a carefully drafted letter. He'd been working on that letter for the whole year of his search, rereading it every time he felt like giving up, marvelling at the skill of its composition.

It began This is a very difficult letter to write, and perhaps also difficult for you to read.

The reply had come ten days later. So, she had hesitated, he thought. It was short but positive. She asked him to come and see her.

Few women of Elise's age walked by themselves in the Savernake Forest, but it never occurred to her to be afraid. Yes, it was strangely remote — a medieval relic in this valley of software houses and Internet companies — and there had been murders committed here over the years, but she knew the woods from her adolescence and she felt inviolable amid the autumn leaves.

She left her car at the quieter end of the forest, just west of Bedwyn Common, giving a half smile to the old biddy who was stationed, as always, at an upstairs window of one of a cluster of houses. She got the usual suspicious look in exchange. Clearly a woman alone in such a fancy car was no better than she should be.

If ever Elise needed an alibi . . .

Most visitors parked near the main roads: the A4 or the A346. People who chose the secluded parts often had something to hide and she had more than once come across an illicit couple, struggling back into their clothes in the illusory privacy of a steamed-up car.

She would walk past, pretending not to notice, whistling a little tune. Once out of sight, she would smile indulgently at these youngsters, too desperate with passion to care about their undignified discomfort. Usually there was a second car parked nearby, the lovers having met by arrangement, far from the unsuspicious eyes of deceived spouses.

She imagined them emerging furtively from the trysting car, straightening their office clothes — it was often a lunch-hour rendezvous — exchanging the slightly embarrassed looks of those whose lusts had been efficiently satisfied and who could not now remember why the matter had seemed so urgent twenty minutes ago. Then a hurried final kiss and the revving of engines in opposite directions.

She had never seen a condom discarded in the woods; you got a nice class of adulterer in the Savernake Forest. Elise laughed inwardly at her thoughts. She was glad that that period of her life was over, that she had peaceful widowhood to look forward to, calm of mind, all passion spent.

She was a grandmother and, of all the roles she had played in her life, this one was the best.

She walked fast, kicking the fallen leaves up with her boots. It had been a dry autumn and the ground crackled beneath her feet. Bellini ran ahead of her, doubling back every few minutes to make sure she was following, darting off to sniff out interesting smells, quietly content.

Elise too felt quietly content. Christmas was only a month away and this year there would be the twins to share it with her at Alders End. True, they were too young to understand, to enjoy the tree she would trim for them, the delicate wooden crib that was a memento of a trip she and Joachim had made to Bethlehem ten years ago, fulfilling at last that old Jewish pledge: 'Next year in Jerusalem'.

Making a Jewish pilgrimage and buying a nativity crib. That had satisfied both their beliefs, or lack thereof. You didn't need to be a Christian to enjoy the skilfully carved ox and ass, the tiny manger which she filled with fresh straw each advent, the blank-faced baby.

The presents that she and the children and Sheila Crabshaw showered upon the twins would be more for their own pleasure than that of the youngsters, but such pleasure should not be underestimated.

She had made her peace with Cressida, who was not one to bear a grudge. Stephen, as always, had been the peacemaker: dear, calm, sensible Stephen whom she loved like her true son.

Her son. This year, for the first time, Antony would be with them for Christmas. She could not have anticipated this new emotional trauma, the polite letter arriving unheralded one August day, blowing a cold wind through her cosy life. If she had known in advance she would have been fearful, angry at the digging up of feelings she had thought long buried, but she was glad she had agreed to meet her son, however much she might have resented him thirty years ago.

He was not to blame for all she had suffered and, over the last few weeks, she had felt something very like love for him growing inside her.

She joined the Grand Avenue, heading northwest, the old roman road a few yards away to her right. She wanted a long walk today, despite the chill in the air. She reached the crossroads where eight paths met, nodding a greeting to another dog walker, such a familiar face that he was almost an old friend, although she knew nothing about him, not even his name.

She turned due west towards Cadley.

She saw the two cars from some distance away: a white VW Golf and a blue Citroen, side by side under a massive dying oak, its leafless branches stark against the sky. She shook her head in silent laughter: to be young, to ignore the November cold in the heat of your desire.

It was not an urgency she had known. After the

birth of Antony she had been wary of men for a long time. Joachim had been the second man to possess her — the second and the last — and he had been old enough to prefer the pleasures of deferment, of a leisurely love making that might go on all afternoon and far into the evening.

He had given her so much and not merely the material comfort he had to offer. He had taught her about art and music, books and architecture, developing her intellect and her taste like a doting father. She had given him true affection in return, but she had never been insanely, desperately, helplessly in love and, on the whole, she was glad to have been spared that madness.

The Citroen was the same model and colour as Cressida's, but she knew that her daughter wasn't much of a one for country walks, preferring the ergonomic cleanliness of the gym, where she was free of the vagaries of the weather, the mud and wildlife, all the things that made walking worthwhile.

It was a popular car among young wives.

She glanced round for Bellini and saw the little dog waiting patiently at the far side of a patch of mud which she, Elise, had strode through without heeding it. Sighing, she turned back, picked the dog up and tucked her under her arm. The terrier nestled into her, pushing her damp nose into her mistress's quilted jacket.

Perhaps she should invite Gregory Summers for Christmas dinner, along with the mysterious Angie whom she had yet to meet. Dear Greg, she thought with affection. How good it had been to see him again after all these years, to remember —

The back door of the Golf opened and Antony got out, neat as ever in jeans and a sleek Guernsey. After she'd got over her astonishment she opened her mouth to shout to him, but then she saw Cressida emerge after him. Even from this distance, Elise could see that her face was flushed and her hair dishevelled as she fumbled with the zip of her own tight jeans, leaning forward the better to fasten it.

She stood frozen in the shadow of a beech tree, watching the scene unfold before her as if in slow motion. Her grip on Bellini tightened until the little dog gave a whimper of protest. Elise placed a gloved hand over her muzzle to silence her.

In the distant tableau Antony and Cressida stood kissing, his hands invisible in her beautiful hair. They drew apart and seemed to be gazing into each other's eyes, although she couldn't tell if they were speaking. Finally, Cressida broke reluctantly away and got into her own car. Antony leaned in at the driver's window for a few last words, a final exchange of tenderness.

Elise saw her daughter kiss her own fingers and press them to the mouth of her lover, her brother. It was a gesture she had watched her make with her father as a child, later with Stephen: affectionate, intimate, supremely confident in its certainty that she was adored.

Soon she heard the engine fire.

She began to run, Bellini still clutched in her arms. She didn't know where she was going, only that it was away from here, preferably into another universe where this horror wasn't happening. Her eyes blinded by tears, she fought her way along footpaths that were barely passable and into the undergrowth itself. Branches scratched at her face and once she tripped on a tree root and almost fell.

She stopped only when her breath deserted her.

She realised that she was thoroughly lost. She stood in a small clearing, gasping for air, a stitch in her side and a pain in her lungs. To think that she'd prided herself on how fit she was for a woman of nearly fifty. Bellini was struggling and she dropped her unceremoniously to the ground.

When she felt able to walk on, she made her way through the trees, trying to discern some glimpse of the sun, to give her an idea of direction. For the first time in her life the dense forest made her afraid. In a world turned inside out, she could rely on none of the old certainties.

Finally, with a sigh of relief, she came out at King George's Column, rising incongruously, tall and slender against the skyline.

Now it was only a short walk back to her car.

Relief robbed her of the adrenaline that had kept her going and she sank down on the plinth and laid her head on her arms. She felt as if her brain were boiling over like a neglected pan of pasta.

Bellini stood butting her rhythmically in the calf with her head.

'Excuse me.'

She made no response to the voice above her until a tentative hand touched her shoulder.

'Are you all right?'

She glanced up to see the old man she had nodded to earlier, his retired greyhound standing at his side, looking snootily down its long nose at her. He took a mobile phone from the pocket of his cagoule and held it up triumphantly.

'Do you need help? The police?'

She began to sob uncontrollably.

* * *

Christmas day, Antony thought as he drove along the M4 at a shade under ninety miles an hour, keeping an eye out for patrol cars. How he had hated that time of year in the Lucas's home; it had been worse than the summer holidays, if that was possible.

This would be the best Christmas ever, with not only Cressida, Stephen and Elise present, but Stephen's mother too. That would be the moment, after lunch, all of them sated with rich food and fuddled with drink, to produce the photographs, to throw them on the table like the gauntlet of challenge.

There might be a fight, he thought with glee, between him and Stephen. He would fight a lot dirtier than decent, honest Steve.

Above all, he saw in his mind's eye Elise's face,

his mother's ashen features, as she watched her perfect little world collapse around her.

Revenge was the sweetest thing in life.

It was the *only* thing.

A very English riot

'Seen you before?' McFee grunted when Greg introduced himself.

'I dined here a few weeks ago as the guest of Mr Hamilton,' Greg reminded him.

'Oh, aye. I remember now.' His thin lips pressed together, as if he'd have ejected Greg on sight that night had he known him to be *polis*.

'Is he still staying here?'

'Oh, aye,' the Scot said again, rather gloomily. 'He's taken root in the Garden Suite.'

Greg decided that it wasn't necessary for him to pay his respects to the old man. 'So, I believe you had a bit of trouble here last night?' he said. The dining room had been restored to its usual civilised state in a remarkably short space of time, although the broken window was boarded up. 'Judging by the scene my people described,' Greg added, 'it must have taken you all night to clear up.'

'It wasn't so bad. We just cleared everything out, pretty much hosed the place down.' He followed Greg's eye to the window. 'Glazier's on his way.'

'Only it seems you want the charges against Mr Greif and his fiancée dropped.'

'He's a good customer. Local. Regular.'

'But the damage must run into thousands.'

McFee shrugged. 'Look, Superintendent, man to

man, Greif's paid for the damage and a bit extra, a good bit extra. Far as I'm concerned, that's the end of the matter.'

Whittaker had mentioned that McFee had banned the customer who called the police from his restaurant; yet he was prepared to let what Greif had done go. A strange sense of priorities, Greg thought.

He said, 'But, as the constables explained to you last night, several arrestable offences were committed. I don't feel inclined to let Mr Greif get away with criminal damage and assault just because he's got a lot of money in the bank.'

'There was no assault.'

'A bloody nose, I heard.'

'Roddy Duncan? The man's a bleeder. High blood pressure. Stands up too fast and he's off like a tap. No one touched him. Ask him. He'll tell you himself.'

'I daresay he will.'

'Look, it was a wee row that got out of hand. Let's not turn it into the great train robbery, eh?'

Greg acted like a man who knew when he was beaten. He said rather lamely, 'It had better not happen again, that's all I can say. This sort of thing can cost you your licence.'

'Splendid.' McFee was all bonhomie now he thought he had won. 'Can I offer you a drink before you go, Superintendent?'

'No thanks, and I'm not going just yet because I'd like to take a look at your kitchens.'

McFee was stunned. 'You what!'

'You are opening tonight?'

'Yes, but you're not Environmental Health.'

'No, but I'd like to take a quick look, all the same.'

'You got a search warrant?'

Greg laughed as if it was the best joke he'd heard all week. 'I'm not *searching* for anything, Mr McFee. I've always been fascinated by top-class restaurants, how such a complicated set-up runs like clockwork. Having had such an excellent dinner here, I'd be really fascinated to have a look behind the scenes.'

The chef was mollified by Greg's best butter; besides, he knew a quid pro quo when he heard one.

He said curtly, 'This way.'

The kitchens were larger than Greg had expected and not so hot, with double doors standing open to a walled courtyard through which he could glimpse some beds of herbs and a lot of dustbins. The old kitchen garden, he supposed, when this had been a private house — one mad old man ministered to by a score of servants.

The staff seemed to snap to attention when McFee entered the room and Greg half expected to hear someone shout, 'Captain on the bridge.'

It was a noisy place — chopping, sizzling, bubbling — and Greg breathed in so many different delicious smells he feared collapse by sensory overload. Half a dozen people were working non stop, although it was still several hours till dinner.

'This is my deputy,' the Scot was saying, 'Barney Duff.'

The man who did the actual cooking, Greg inferred. He saw a happy, rosy face looking up at him from under a chef's hat. Up, because Duff was about five foot two and as round as an apple. He would never do on TV where people didn't like to be reminded that there was a connection between eating well and storing subcutaneous fat.

'How do you do,' he said.

'Do you mind if I don't shake hands?' Duff held up his own which were covered in flour. Sheet after sheet of pastry, as thin as muslin, lay before him on a marble board.

'Oh, not at all,' Greg said hastily. He was reminded, for no particular reason, of a friend of his mother's who had once commented that it was amazing how clean her hands were after she'd been kneading pastry. She'd later offered him a slice of cold apple pie and adolescent greed had vied with squeamishness until greed won.

He glanced back at McFee. 'That'll be fine, thank you, Mr McFee.

But the chef was not to be dismissed so lightly. He retired to the side of the room, leaned against the wall between two massive refrigerators — one for cooked and one for raw food — and folded his arms across his chest.

'Are you Environmental Health?' Duff enquired anxiously, 'only we had an inspection last month —'

'Just an interested amateur,' Greg assured him.

'Amateur chef?'

'More of an amateur eater.'

Duff looked puzzled and said politely, 'Well, make yourself at home.'

Greg walked round the various banks of stoves and preparation areas, aware all the time of McFee's eyes on him, scorching a hole in his jacket. He inspected the stockpot which was simmering with a dark broth. He could see split bones with their brown marrow jelly, whole carrots and baby turnips, celery, fresh herbs: a big improvement on the Oxo cube.

Nearby, a young man was chopping leeks into slivers, his wickedly- bladed knife moving so quickly that it was a blur. Greg hesitated to speak to him in case he disrupted his concentration and caused a blood bath with bits of finger added to the mix.

The youth finished, sweeping the last of his greeny-white slices into a bowl that was already brimming with them, and wiped his face with a damp cloth. Like all the staff, except Duff, he wore a hairnet. In his case it was covering what must be shoulder-length dark hair of a faintly greasy consistency.

He took a ladle and skimmed the top of the stockpot.

'Hot work,' Greg remarked. 'You been here long?'

'Only three months,' he said in a strong Welsh accent. He grinned at Greg. 'Still on the menial tasks. Do the leeks because I'm Welsh, see. Joke.'

'Do you like the work?'

'Impossibly long and anti-social hours for a minimum wage — what's not to like? You thinking of joining us, then?'

'Why does anyone do it?'

The lad lowered his voice and flickered his hazel eyes towards McFee. 'To be him one day, see. Posh hotel, fame, money.' He grinned lecherously. 'And all the girls you can eat.'

'I suppose the place is a goldmine?'

He shrugged. 'I stay in the kitchen and leave the accounts to people who can add up. But overheads are high. Lot of wastage.'

Greg moved on. A well-rounded Asian boy was washing lettuce with the thoroughness of someone about to perform an operation on it.

'Good afternoon,' Greg said.

''Ow do,' the boy replied in broad Yorkshire.

'They seem to keep you busy here, Mr . . .'

His eyes glittered with mischief. 'Venkatacha-lapathy.' Greg blinked and he added, 'I suggest you call me Pran.'

'Thank you. Hoping to make a career in catering, Pran?'

'Me family owns a chain of curry houses in West Yorkshire,' the lad explained cheerfully, 'and I want to reposition them at the higher end of the market, once I've got the experience under me belt, like.'

'Reposition?'

'Question of margins,' he explained, with a look in his eye akin to that of an evangelical preacher confronted with the town trollop. 'Cheap place, bog-standard ingredients, low profits; posh place, slightly dearer ingredients, much higher prices. Retire to a bungalow in Harrogate at forty-five. Only logical, innit?'

'Good luck,' Greg said, moving on.

'Better class of clientele too,' the young man called after him. ''Stead of bolshy kids with lager coming out their ears calling me Abdul.'

Another man was skinning chicken breasts and hammering them flat for rolling and stuffing; a second was peeling potatoes as if he had spent his whole life doing it. Both were local, or as good as: one from Abingdon, one from Aylesbury.

Finally, he spoke to the only woman, a skinny twenty-something, blonde under a hairnet which somehow managed not to detract from her ethereal beauty, framing her face like that of a Florentine Madonna. She was making *petits fours* from the richest, darkest chocolate Greg had ever seen. Following his covetous eye, she laughed and gave him a piece.

'Lovely,' he said thickly, reluctant to swallow it and put an end to the gustatory ecstasy.

In a pretty French accent, she said. 'You're welcome.'

'A man's world then?' he said.

'*Comment*?'

He repeated the remark more slowly.

She said, 'I see. Yes. Women do not like to be shouted at so much, I think, but my skin is thick.' She had to mean metaphorically since her skin was almost translucent from where he was standing.

Finally he nodded to McFee and said, 'Thank you. Most interesting.'

'Happy?' McFee said coldly.

'Delirious.' Before the Scot could stop him Greg

walked out through the double doors and into the courtyard. He stood looking at the back of the Hall while McFee hastened to join him.

'How many rooms do you let?' he asked.

'Thirty, including two suites.'

'I hadn't realised the place was so big.'

'It's based loosely on the chateau at Cheverney,' McFee volunteered.

There was a central house, two storeys high, flanked by two three- storey wings, the third floor a bank of tiny windows nestling under a mansard roof.

'Guest rooms too?' Greg asked, pointing to these latter.

'Just attics. Storage. Staff accommodation.'

'Do they all live in?'

'Almost all. It's part of the pay, you might say, a free room and all you can eat, which is why this minimum wage is such a stupid idea, because it doesn't take that into account.' This was clearly a sore point. 'Do you know how much my wages bill has gone up in the last —'

'Not a police matter,' Greg said, 'fortunately.' He plucked a sprig of rosemary from a bush and chewed it. It blended well with the lingering taste of cocoa bean. 'I am most grateful, Mr McFee and I won't take up any more of your time.'

He offered the man his hand. The chef looked as if he would have liked to refuse it, then took it and quickly released it.

So McFee wasn't using illegal labour in his

kitchens, Greg thought as he drove back to the station.

Shame.

* * *

Well, this brought back memories.

The place had once been a household name, dividing families in their hotly held opinions like a civil war.

Greenham Common air base at the south-eastern edge of Newbury, scene of so much trouble during the eighties as protesters camped for years on end to campaign against the American Cruise missiles that were based here, ready to be fired at Moscow at a moment's notice and precipitate the final battle.

They had endured great hardship: living in tents, without washing facilities or lavatories, cooking over open fires, teaching ragged children who should have been at school. They had left husbands, boyfriends, parents, jobs and university courses because they wanted those children to have a future, not a mushroom cloud and a nuclear winter.

They had been some of the most reviled people in the country, perhaps for one reason above all, that they were women: irresponsible women who had left their rightful place by the fireside; anarchists and lesbians.

How the world had changed in little more than ten years: few people could have foreseen that the collapse of Communism would be so sudden and so total. The nuclear enemy was no longer the all-powerful Soviet Union, reduced to an impoverished and crime-strewn federation of independent states, but a collection of unpredictable egomaniacs, mostly in the middle east.

The missiles had gone home a long time ago but, curiously, the last of the peace protestors had left only recently.

For some of them, perhaps, it had become a way of life.

'So this is it.' Angie loosened her seat belt as Greg's car came to a halt by the perimeter wire not far from the main gate. 'What a desolate place.'

'You've never been here?' he asked in surprise.

'I kept meaning to come and take a look, but I never got round to it. You know how it is.'

So it had become a place for sightseers, he thought, a piece of history, where once it had been the destination of pilgrims. He said, 'Don't fancy spending a winter here myself. Do you?' It looked particularly bleak today on an overcast morning in November. Recent heavy rain had created a series of dirty lakes inside the perimeter.

'Several winters more like,' Angie said.

For there was more trouble fermenting at Greenham, as if the place was destined never again to know peace. It was the uniformed branch who had been called on to deal with it, but Greg had decided to take a look for himself, since it was tangentially related to Operation Cuckoo.

Not that he confused asylum seekers with illegal immigrants, even if the tabloid press did.

Angie had come along for the ride.

The Home Secretary had recently announced that a series of holding camps were to be set up across the country to house would-be refugees until their cases could be properly examined and a decision made. It was clearly not fair that the channel ports should bear the brunt of the trouble and expense of caring for them and the burden must be spread.

Greenham was to be one such camp and, since decisions about the fate of refugees took years, they could look forward to a long stay in the Berkshire countryside.

Gregory Summers could see them in his mind's eye: men, women, children of all ages, all colours, all shapes of face. They would walk the confines of their cramped world, slightly bewildered, yes, but secure in the knowledge that they didn't face death or torture, not today.

The Council objected that it had been hoping to reclaim the land by persuading local farmers to graze it again, but the Home Office replied that they needed only part of the large expanse and that there was room for both cows and people. Pre-fab dormitories had been delivered late one night and sited at the eastern end of the camp. New fencing had gone up, making a compound about four acres in size, something like a POW camp out of *The Great Escape*.

Fait accompli.

The announcement had provoked two — equally savage — reactions: the Not In My Back Yard contingent had organised a protest against the taxpayers of

Newbury having a lot of scrounging, workshy foreigners dumped on their doorstep; while those who objected to asylum seekers being herded into camps like criminals wanted to put *their* point of view to the authorities.

Both had arranged their rallies for noon on Sunday. It would be like the meeting of matter and anti-matter which, if Greg had understood old episodes of *Star Trek* correctly, would cause a reaction which would make a Cruise missile look like a firecracker.

Chief Superintendent Barkiss had hastily authorised overtime for the demonstrations on Friday night and every spare man had been drafted in.

It was half past eleven and only the most enthusiastic of the protestors had turned up so far. Two girls aged about eight or nine, supervised by an eager-faced man in a bobble hat, held a banner between them which read 'Close the Nazi death camp' while a trio of teenage boys with close-cropped hair and big boots held up placards which read 'Keep beggars off our streets'.

'They do themselves no favours by exaggerating,' he commented.

'Keeping them in a camp like this means housing, feeding and clothing them,' Angie pointed out, 'and educating the children. Why not let them work?'

'In case they disappear and are never seen again.'

'So what, if they can support themselves?'

He could see why people tried to bypass the bureaucracy by illegal means. If he had a choice of spending years in a camp like this, waiting for a court decision that was often little short of arbitrary, or taking his chance on a small fishing boat in the English Channel in a storm, he might risk the latter.

At the moment the two groups were content to glare at each other, awaiting reinforcements, while the policemen sat in their vans, keeping an uneasy eye on the situation, fingering their riot shields and batons.

Three uniformed officers, a sergeant and two constables, had got out to stretch their legs and make a minor show of force. The sergeant peeled off and headed towards Greg's car. The superintendent, who had ignored the designated parking areas, wound his window down.

'Have to ask you to move — Oh! Sorry, sir. Didn't recognise you there for a moment.' A big man, he loomed into the car. 'Morning, Mrs Summers.'

'All right, Dave?'

'You could be a bit close here, sir,' the young man warned, 'if there's trouble.'

'Don't worry, Trafford. I'll keep out of harm's way. Good luck.'

'Thank you, sir.'

Dave Trafford rejoined his colleagues who were watching the exchange with interest.

'Do you think it's true,' one of them whispered behind his hand, 'what they're saying about Mr Summers and his daughter-in-law?'

Trafford shrugged loftily, too grand for the gossip of mere constables. 'Why not? They're both single.'

'Yeah, but it's a bit yeuky, if you ask me.'

'I don't think anyone did.'

Protestors were arriving in dribs and drabs: by car, on foot, on bicycles. Greg amused himself by trying to guess on sight which contingent the new-comers belonged to.

First was a man of about sixty, fit-looking in tweeds and a military-style moustache. He drove a vintage Rover, polished to a high sheen, with per-sonalised number plates.

'Nimby,' Greg said. 'Retired Major.'

They watched as the 'major' shook hands with the man in the bobble hat and kissed both the little girls soundly.

'Duh! Strike one,' Angie said.

Next was a straggle-haired woman in a Citroen 2CV, dressed in what seemed to be hippie clothes, drooping things circa 1972.

'Anti Nazi,' he said confidently.

She took a placard from her boot. It read starkly, 'Send them home.'

'Strike two!'

This was harder than it looked. 'What do you think?' he asked.

'A plague on both their houses.' She didn't mind Shakespeare so long as it had Leonardo DiCaprio in it.

Two young women who couldn't have been more than twenty, but who already had infants in pushchairs, held banners which read, 'England for the English'.

'A deep-seated, atavistic fear of the stranger,' Angie murmured.

'I can see that psychology course of yours is going to come in handy.'

'Sod you,' she said amiably. 'I'm just a beginner.'

There were now about forty people, divided almost equally between pros and antis, except that both lots were opposed to the camp, though for different reasons. This might occur to them at some point or it might not.

A mass of dark clouds filled the sky above the airbase. It began to drizzle, then to rain in good earnest, a fresh wind spitting it into the faces of the protestors. They turned their collars up and looked exasperated. A few women produced umbrellas and some took refuge in their cars.

'That'll cool their ardour,' Greg said.

The policemen paced up and down looking mildly bored, their thick uniforms impervious to rain. One of the anti Nazis produced a brazier from the back of an ancient Dormobile and his colleagues clustered round it, rubbing their hands. After a few minutes a couple of Nimbies wandered over to join them. One of them was carrying a dozen cans of lager which he quickly broached and soon they were all laughing and joking together.

Two men from opposing sides swopped banners and howled with mirth as they posed for photographs. Somebody had a ghetto blaster and soon Spiller were pouring out as people jumped up and down to the music with little jerky movements. It had turned into a regular party, with everyone forgetting why they had come, rather like a funeral wake.

Sergeant Dave Trafford, looking vaguely disgusted at this lack of action, kicked a pebble viciously into the wire.

'A very *English* protest,' Angie remarked. 'Perhaps we should let a refugee stay if they can explain what happened here this morning.'

'Better deport me then because I'm buggered if I can.' Greg heard his stomach rumble. He'd lingered in bed with the papers and not bothered with breakfast.

Angie cupped her hand to her ear. 'Was that thunder I heard?'

He started the engine. 'Can I press you to a pub lunch, ma'am?'

She refastened her seat belt. 'Consider me pressed.'

Come into my parlour

'Elise?'

She said evenly, 'Antony.'

'I just rang to say I'll be a bit late down on Friday night.'

'No problem.'

'I'll be there at nine o'clock, ten at the outside. Don't bother about feeding me. I'll get something here.'

'Very well.'

'You sound a bit faint,' he said. 'Are you all right?'

'Perfectly.'

'It must be my mobile. Needs recharging. See you Friday.'

'See you.'

They hung up.

Antony parked in the drive next to his mother's Lotus, lining his VW Golf up with her car in perfect parallel. He was a neat man, because in his childhood any hint of untidiness had earned him the severest punishment, whereas Isobel's room could look like the village hall at the end of a particularly trying rummage sale and nobody said a word.

He might have rebelled against the conditioning in adulthood, but the roots went too deep.

To his surprise the house was in darkness. He

checked his watch and saw that it was twenty to ten, well within the parameters specified. He took his weekend bag from the boot, along with a bunch of yellow carnations that he'd picked up at the Heston service station, and looked uncertainly about him.

There was no moon and he was struck by how dark it was in the country. Alders End was cut off from the village by a good fifty yards of empty road, beyond the scope of its street lighting. It had been like this in Cheshire, at the Lucas's house, and there had been nights in his teens when he'd sneaked out, climbing down the iron drainpipe from the bathroom, to relish the silence of the darkness.

After years in the twenty-four hour brightness of Hammersmith, it made him nervous. It was almost sinister.

Elise must be in, surely, if her car was here. He walked up to the porch and was about to pull the bell when it occurred to him to try the door. It was unlocked. Nothing unusual about that. Even after dark Elise often didn't bother to lock up till she went to bed.

He pushed the door open and went in. 'Hello?'

Nothing. Not even the noise of that wretched dog.

'Elise?'

Nothing.

He felt a moment of panic but forced himself to be calm. There was a perfectly reasonable explanation: his mother had slipped out to walk an impatient

and incontinent Bellini and left the door on the latch
for him.

For some reason it hadn't occurred to him to
switch the light on. He did so now and the hall
brightened into its familiar contours: the old cream
of the walls with the dark wood of the stairs and
skirting, the chessboard of black and white flagstones. He put down his case and laid the flowers on
the oak half table that stood against the side wall.
The house was warm and he peeled off his jacket
and hung it on the newel post.

He walked forward slowly, putting his head
round the open doors that led off the hallway: the
study, the dining room, the downstairs cloakroom
with its old-fashioned lavatory pan and high flush.

He thought that he heard something, a distant
whining, coming from upstairs.

Bellini?

Finally he walked into the sitting room at the
back of the house, clicking on the overhead light,
illuminating Joachim Weissman's most personal
pieces, the ones he could never bear to part with. So
he had not stumbled on the aftermath of a burglary.
He took the scene in briefly: no sign of a struggle, of
chaos. There had been a fire in the grate at some time
that day and the coals still glowed red-white. A
paperback book lay abandoned face down on Elise's
favourite armchair. He picked it up. She was half
way through a chapter.

The Marie Celeste must have been something like
this.

He called again. 'Hello?'

Listened.

Nothing.

He passed into the kitchen and fumbled with the light switch inside the door. It clicked but nothing happened. He clicked it futilely off and on again. The bulb must have blown. Some light entered the room from behind him and the fittings and appliances loomed like ill-assorted giants: a Welsh dresser, the Aga, an American-style fridge the size of a boxroom.

He took two steps into the kitchen before he sensed movement behind him.

Something slipped over his head and round his throat: a garrotte, narrow, flexible and strong, not rope, not string, more like a thin wire. His hands reached up in automatic panic, trying to get his fingers into the gap between noose and neck but it was already too tight and his nails scrabbled at it helplessly. His field of vision went black about the edges and the shadowy room began to sway and swirl around him.

He could hear breathing: soft, calm breathing in his ear as his assailant maintained his grip, ratcheting up the tension in the wire, squeezing the life out of him.

Or *her* grip. Because, in a moment of perfect clarity, he knew who it was who was trying to kill him.

And why.

He fought for his own breath. A moment ago he would have said that his life meant nothing to him but now he struggled desperately to hang on to it. The panic of his childhood asthma attacks came upon him again and he slumped to the floor, toppling backwards against her legs.

The sudden movement took her by surprise and the noose loosened for an instant. He got two fingers of his right hand inside it and survival seemed a possibility after all.

Then he was free, not knowing how. The piece of picture wire that had been choking the life from him dropped to the floor beside him and he heard his mother's voice — it seemed like miles above his head — exclaim in muted annoyance.

'I can't do it. Damn me! I can't do it.'

Her footsteps pounded away into the next room.

He gasped for breath but now a full blown asthma attack had seized him, the first since he had left 'home' ten years ago. He rolled on his side, into the foetal position, trying to keep calm, to take shallow breaths, not the deep breaths that instinct dictated and which tore into his scarred lungs.

He found the wind to call feebly, 'Mother!'

She was at his side in an instant, a pair of shapely legs in tan nylon. 'Antony?'

'Inhaler,' he wheezed. 'Jacket pocket. Hall.'

She ran off and returned in half a minute with the inhaler in its blue plastic container. He struggled to sit up and she helped him, putting her arm round his shoulders as he gasped the drug deep into his lungs.

Once. Twice.

After half a minute he was breathing more easily,

his head cradled against her shoulder. He was aware of sweat running down his face from his hairline. He felt damp all over and feared for a moment that he had soiled himself, the way he invariably did when he was locked in the cupboard under the sink.

The sink. The kitchen. The worst place in the house.

'Must get out of here,' he murmured.

She helped him into the sitting room and he sank on the rug in front of the hearth, still wheezing, and rolled over on his back. He slipped his thumb into his mouth and began to suck vigorously. She kneeled at his side. He could see her face now, a mixture of concern and fear.

He summoned up the breath to ask 'Why?'

'I could ask you the same question. Why? Why have you set out to destroy my daughter's life? Your own *sister*.'

'Because it seemed the best way to hurt you.'

'God damn you to hell, Antony!'

'Too late,' he said. 'I have been in hell all my life.'

She looked at him curiously. 'How so?'

'Water?' he said.

She fetched him a glass. He drank it in one draught and held it out for more. She refilled it and he sipped more slowly.

'Tell me,' she said.

He told her.

She stayed kneeling like a penitent, her back straight. He spoke slowly at first, then gained fluency as his asthma attack passed and air returned to his lungs. He told her about the Lucases, about the beautiful house in Cheshire that had been a cruel prison to him, about the beatings, the humiliations, about Isobel. After the first revelations, she hung her head, her gaze fixed on the rug. Once or twice she closed her tearless eyes and emitted a little moan of pain.

When he had finished there was a long moment when neither of them spoke, the ticking of the grandfather clock loud in their ears. Finally, she said, 'I will not add insult to injury by saying that I'm sorry.'

'Why didn't you abort me?' he said bitterly. 'Thirty years ago you could have murdered me and the law wouldn't have lifted a finger to stop you. So why didn't you spare me the horror of my life?'

The question was clearly rhetorical but she answered it anyway. 'That would have been the logical thing to do, I suppose, but it simply never occurred to me. My Catholic upbringing may have had something to do with it. I thought you would be all right, that the people who took you would want you and love you.'

She cried out, 'Why did they adopt you if they didn't want a son to love? It makes no sense.'

'No,' he agreed. He had long given up trying to make sense of it.

He rubbed his neck gingerly. His throat was sore inside where the wire had bitten and he could feel the striation on his neck. The full import of what she had tried to do came home to him.

'I'd never have thought you had it in you,' he said with a little laugh.

'Don't let this veneer fool you, Antony, this gracious, middle-aged lady with her expensive clothes and her glamorous car. Somewhere underneath is the real Elsie Riley: the tinker girl who's not afraid of anything.'

'Ah, yes! The Tinker Girl.'

'You should have looked harder at that painting.' She leaned back on her heels. 'What are you going to do?'

'Do?'

'Call the police? Accuse me of attempted murder?'

He hadn't thought of it. He shook his head slowly. In a strange way, he respected her for acting, for not wasting words in reproach, for not taking refuge in tears and hysteria like a woman.

'Could you really have killed me?' he asked.

She said soberly, 'I think I have demonstrated that I could not. I disappoint myself.'

'How would you have disposed of my body?'

'I hadn't thought that far ahead,' she admitted. 'I wanted you dead and I could live with the consequences. I am not afraid to take responsibility for my actions. I thought only of protecting Cressida.'

'She wouldn't have thanked you for it.'

'No doubt she's besotted, but she would have got over it.'

'How did you know about me and her? Did *she* tell you?'

'Hardly!'

'So how did you know?'

'Does it matter?'

'I suppose not.'

'But it is over, Antony. It's *finished*. Do you hear me?'

'I hear you.' He rose unsteadily to his feet and sank onto the sofa, burying his head in his hands. He felt exhausted. It could all have been over by now if she hadn't relented, consciousness fled; he could have been in rest eternal.

He felt a pang of regret.

'Let's get you to bed,' she said. 'You can have one of the sleeping powders Joachim used to take. He bought them in the States; talk about knock-out drops.' She saw the flicker of fear in his face. 'Don't worry. I won't try to kill you again. The moment has passed. You can lock and bolt your door from the inside, if you like.'

She helped him upstairs to the spare room, pausing only to release a cross Bellini from her imprisonment behind the stout oak door. She helped Antony strip off his damp clothes till he stood naked before her, so thin and white that he filled her with pity. The sheets felt cold as she turned back the quilt but he climbed inside and pulled them up to his chin so that only his nose and eyes peered out, an animal that had gone to ground. His things were spread out to dry on the old-fashioned radiator that took up half the wall.

She rummaged in the medicine cabinet in her

bathroom, as the dog danced round her heels, and brought her son a gaudy box, filled with red sachets of white powder, and a glass of water. He sat up and examined the box, reading the instructions with care then mixed up a powder and drank the tasteless substance in one gulp.

'I'll go now,' she said, 'and let you rest. Lock the door behind me.'

He held out a hand to stop her, propped against the pillows, pale and tired like a sickly child. 'Even to attempt it, Elise? Your own son? The child of a man you must have . . .' He wanted to say 'loved' but he had never known what that word meant. 'You must have cared for,' he concluded lamely.

She walked across to the window and laid her hot cheek against the pane. Her voice was steady, but low.

'You were born after your father raped me.'

In a small, desolate voice he said, 'No wonder you didn't want me.'

'I couldn't stand the sight of you. They said, "It's a boy" and I screamed, "Take it away, take it away".' She stayed leaning against the window for a moment then reached a decision. She pressed her lips to his forehead and left him to his rest.

As Elise came into the house a little later, the first thing she saw was the bunch of carnations on the hall table, drying in their cellophane. She couldn't leave innocent flowers to die so she took them to the scullery and arranged them in a glass vase and placed them in the exact centre of the dining room table.

She left her muddy shoes in the boot cupboard under the stairs and ran up in her stockinged feet. Listening carefully at Antony's door she could hear no sound. She tried the door knob, just as an experiment, and found it locked. He was taking no chances.

His revelations had been terrible and yet there was a small part of her that despised him. He was a victim and she had worked so hard all her life not to be a victim.

To her surprise she fell into a deep and undisturbed sleep that lasted for more than nine hours. When she awoke Antony had gone.

So it is finished, she thought, and I have survived.

A result

'It was 1970,' Angie said. 'It's not like it was the fifties or something.'

Ah, yes, the fifties, Greg thought, that unimaginably distant era.

Hunched over her laptop, she groaned and rubbed her left shoulder. He came to stand behind her and began rhythmically to massage her tired muscles with his thumbs.

'Ooh, that's better,' she said.

'We shall have to get a second phone line put in if you're going to spend all this time on the Internet,' he said, peering over her shoulder. 'What if the station wants to contact me urgently?'

'They'll get hold of you. They always do.'

'True. What are you doing?'

'Talking to a professor of psychology at Princeton.'

'Ah, he *says* he's a professor of psychology from Princeton; he's just as likely to be a cowboy from Montana.'

'It's a she.'

'So he claims.' She laughed. He said, 'What are you talking about?'

'Puerperal psychosis and the latest series of *Frasier*.'

'It must be a woman then. I've noticed that only women can think about two things at once.'

'The superior sex.' She drifted back to her original train of thought. 'It was only six years later my mum had me and she never even thought of having me adopted, just dragged me up as best she could.'

'You've been dragged up really nicely,' he said and kissed the top of her head.

'Thanks. So she could have kept him, your mate, if she'd wanted to.'

'I suppose it's a very personal decision.'

'I suppose it is.'

She bent her head back and their lips met, upside down. They fitted together just as well that way.

A message popped up on the screen. 'Tallulah? U there?'

'Tallulah?' he queried.

'No one uses their real name in chat rooms.' She typed in 'No!' and logged off.

* * *

In the back corridor of Boxford Hall a grandfather clock struck midnight, its chimes slow and sonorous.

There was no one to hear it. In the restaurant a wedding reception was continuing far into the night, although the bride and groom were long gone, sneaking off to their secret honeymoon destination which was, as everybody knew, the Bahamas. Weary staff were impressed by the amount of champagne that was being drunk by the lingering guests.

One of the bridesmaids was sitting weeping

alone on the stairs, her pink-meringue dress crumpled. She had been promised a shag with the best man but he'd disappeared upstairs with the bride's mother.

In the Garden Suite at the end of the corridor, an old man sat slumped in his armchair behind a locked door. His wrinkled face had collapsed into his large collection of chins and his eyes were open. He wore nothing but slippers and a dressing gown, which gaped indecently at the front.

A bottle of brandy stood on the table at his side, three-quarters empty. His walking stick lay on the floor some distance from him, where it had rolled, and an overturned tumbler had spilled its amber contents on the cream carpet.

A few minutes earlier his expression in death had been one of rage and disbelief; now his features had relaxed into nothingness.

* * *

When Greg reached the station the following morning he was greeted by an exuberant Barbara. She was prancing round his office like a footballer who's just scored the winning goal in the world cup final.

'Result!' she yelled when she saw him. 'Result, result, result!'

Her enthusiasm was contagious and he grinned at her. 'So we got a result? At what exactly.'

'We've got our burglar. Picked up in Hoe Benham last night. The house has a silent alarm — no box, no wires, but when the back door was forced a light came on at the security firm in Newbury. We caught the Weatherby kid red-handed, high-tailing it through the back door with a pocketful of rings and a diamond necklace.'

'Ha!' And to think that he'd been prepared to believe Dickon Weatherby when he said he was starting afresh. He must be getting soft in his old age. 'Where is he?'

'He?' Barbara's face was puzzled. 'I'm talking about Jennet Weatherby. She's had a good night's sleep and is waiting for us in the interview room.'

Now it was Greg's turn to look puzzled.

He recognised the girl at once: the red-headed waitress from Boxford Hall.

'She had access to the restaurant bookings,' Barbara explained, 'and she knew — or could find out — where the customers lived, so on her night off she went and burgled their houses.'

And it was, Greg thought, as simple as that.

Or maybe not. 'Didn't we pick up the link: that they were all out at the Hall the night they got done?'

'They weren't. She's not daft, our Jennet. Ignorant, ill-educated, but not stupid. She overheard their conversations too, while she was serving them, talk of how they'd be away shooting in Scotland that weekend, or at a wedding in Yorkshire, or nipping off to Saint Moritz for a few days.'

'Not daft at all,' Greg said. 'Let's see what she has to say for herself.'

Jennet Weatherby was resigned. She knew there was no way she was going to talk her way out of being found in a strange house with the booty in her pocket. She'd been caught in the act and she was too proud to bluster. She sat hunched in her chair in the interview room. She was dressed all in black — her burglar's outfit: sweat pants tucked into socks above boots, a polo neck jersey and a sleeveless fleece jacket with breast and side pockets. They had taken from her a chisel and a pair of pliers when they arrested her.

'Are you sure you don't want a solicitor?' Barbara said, sitting down opposite her.

'He's on your side, isn't he?'

'Absolutely not. He would be on your side. That's the whole point.'

Jennet looked at her as if she were stupid. 'He's still one of you, though, isn't he? Lawyer, doctor, policeman, judge. People who talk nicely and wear suits and live in big houses.'

'No solicitor then,' Greg said. He sat down next to his colleague.

She turned deliberately away from Barbara and spoke only to Greg from then on. 'I want to make a deal,' she said.

'A deal?' Greg raised his eyebrows. 'You've been watching too much television, young lady.'

'There's things you don't know about Boxford Hall, things I reckon you'd like to know.'

'I'm listening.'

'Have we got a deal?'

He sighed. 'I can't make these charges of burglary go away, Jennet. I'm not Harry Potter and I can't wave my magic wand.'

'They're busting with money, these people. Do you know how much it costs to eat at the Hall?'

'Roughly.'

'Saturday night I waited on a table of eight people. Okay, they were knocking back the booze but their bill came to more than a thousand quid. More than a grand! It's immoral, that's what it is, spending that much on a meal.'

'But not illegal,' Greg said mildly. 'And somehow I don't think that argument is going to go down very well in court.'

'No, and why? 'Cause the judges and magistrates and lawyers are all rich bastards who can afford to eat there too.'

She had, Greg conceded mentally, a point, if only a small one.

'Look,' she said, cards on table. 'It's my first offence, okay? The judge'll postpone sentencing till he's got reports from the Social and that's when you can put a word in for me.'

'You know the ropes then.'

'Bloody hell! The number of times I've been to court with Dick over the years, I could run one of them places with my eyes shut.'

'How old are you?' Greg asked.

'Nineteen. Why?'

'All right, I'll put in a word for you.' He didn't happen to think that a girl's life should be wrecked at that tender age, although something told him that Jennet Weatherby was already beyond redemption.

'So what about McFee?' he went on.

'He brings girls in, hides them in the attic.'

Greg glanced sideways at Barbara who had gone very still, as if she was afraid that a sudden movement might scare Jennet's information away like a shy gazelle.

'The staff quarters?' he asked.

Jennet shook her head, leaning forward to sketch an invisible plan on the table with her index finger. 'The wings are three storeys but the middle bit of the Hall's only two floors, right?'

Greg followed the swift movement of her hand, conjuring the image of Boxford Hall into his mind's eye. 'Right.'

'But there's a big space under the roof of the middle bit, like a secret chamber, and that's where he keeps them.'

Greg thought about it. It made perfect sense that paranoid old Lord Boxford should have incorporated a hiding place into his chateau.

'You can get into it from the staff corridor on our side,' Jennet explained, 'the right hand side as you look at the building. It ends in an wood-panelled wall but there's a way to open it. I don't know how, though.'

Greg said, 'Girls?'

'Girls, women. Some of them are as old as thirty.'

'That old? And they can still get up the stairs?'

'Eh?'

'Nothing. Go on.'

'Foreigners. Men occasionally, but usually it's girls.'

'What sort of foreigners?'

She shrugged. 'I dunno. I can hear them jabbering sometimes, through the wall. Gibberish.'

'Asians? Arabs?'

'Not usually. White, but foreign.'

'Eastern Europeans? Slavs?'

She brightened. 'Yeah. Yeah, I reckon it could be. My dad says they come here to take our jobs and stuff because England's so much better than their countries.'

'Does he. How do they get there?'

'They come in trucks in the middle of the night. They only stay a few days, each lot, before they're moved on, a week max. Then the room's left empty for a bit, till the next lot. So you gotta go at the right time. It was empty for almost a month recently. That's unusual.'

Waiting for a boatload of Iranian boys who never showed up, Greg wondered. Aloud, he said, 'And is it empty now?'

'New lot been there two or three days. And I heard McFee on the phone yesterday morning. He didn't know I was there and he said, "We move them Saturday, just before dawn".'

'He could have been talking about anything.'

'Except he was mad when he turned round and saw me in the doorway. He shouted at me what was I doing skulking about like that. I was bringing him his morning coffee, like always, and I acted like I just got there, like I never heard nothing and he calmed down.'

Saturday: that gave them three days. 'Do the rest of the staff know about this?'

'No one's mentioned it to me. People walk round with their eyes closed half the time. Only there's not many of us sleep in the north wing, see, more in the south wing and I'm the one with the end room, nearest the secret one.'

'And you haven't spoken to anyone at the Hall about it?'

She sneered. 'Why would I? A secret's not a secret if you've told it, and then it's worthless.'

As she stood up to leave the interview room, he saw again how tall she was, and as thin as a grey-hound. He gauged her feet at a size eight, medium for a man but big for a woman.

He said, 'Did you ever think of burgling Lady Weissman?'

She was wary. 'Bit close to home, that, what with Dad working there.'

'Answer me, girl!'

She stood for a moment, visibly thinking. 'I went there one night, check the place out, see how easy it'd be to break in, but she saw me and that bloody dog started barking. Don't like places with dogs, even stupid yappy ones, so I gave it up as a bad job. Anyway, there's not much there worth nicking; she's got no good jewellery, nothing.'

She shook her head in disgust at the idiocy of a wealthy woman who didn't spend her spare cash on diamond necklaces.

Greg said, 'But wasn't she kind to you — Lady Weissman — when you were a kid? Dickon said something about Christmas parties for the village children.'

Jennet stared at him. 'So what?'

'All right. Take her to the charge room please, Sergeant.' He lowered his voice. 'I'll get on the phone to the NCS. Bring her up to my office after you've charged her.'

He didn't want McFee to know that Jennet had been arrested.

Greg handed Jennet the phone and said, 'Make it good.'

'I will.' She punched some numbers into the pad. It rang only twice before somebody answered, the modulated twittering of the corporate receptionist. Jennet placed one finger inelegantly into her right nostril and spoke thickly into the receiver.

'That you, Sandra? Michelle, sorry. It's Jen. Look, I've got this bloody flu that's going around . . . What? Yeah, just on my night off too. So, anyway, I'm gonna hole up at my dad's for a few days, so can you tell — ? No, you're right, no point in spreading it about. Do I? Yeah, I'm all bunged up. Soon as I get off the line I'm going to bed with a hot toddy. Okay, see you.'

She hung up. Greg mimed applause. She took a small bow.

'You should be on the stage,' he said.

'If you mean I'm a bloody good liar, just say so.'

Charity begins at home

Greg was surprised later that morning when his secretary, Susan Habib, said that Piers Hamilton was on the telephone. He'd never known Piers to phone him at work before.

But which Piers was it, come to that? He picked up the receiver and punched a button to make the connection. 'Summers.'

'Gregory, I was wondering if you'd heard about Great-uncle Piers?'

Well, that answered that question. He said, 'Heard what?'

'He was found dead in his hotel room this morning.'

'Oh!' The death was surprising, in its way, though it could hardly be described as premature. 'My sincere condolences, Piers.'

'I thought they might have reported it to you.'

'To me? Why?'

'Not you personally, with you being the great panjandrum, but, well, sudden death . . .'

Great Panjandrum Summers: that had superintendent beat any day.

'Are you trying to tell me it's suspicious?' Greg asked.

'God, no! The doctor reckoned it was a stroke. Seems he had his usual four-course dinner in the hotel, then bought a bottle of best brandy from the bar and retired to his room about ten. He was probably dead by midnight. It would have been quick, no time to call for help. Still, it was sudden.'

'But the doctor signed the death certificate?'

'Eventually. He ummed and erred a bit as he didn't know Unc and hadn't been treating him. He talked about getting on to his GP in Chelsea but I explained that Uncle Piers hadn't seen a doctor in years, didn't believe in them, and in view of the fact that he was ninety-six, the doc finally signed.'

'Good.' It definitely wasn't Greg's problem. 'How did they know to get hold of you?'

'They found his passport in the bureau, with his wallet and such like. You know that bit at the back where you say who to contact in case of emergency? My name and address were there. I'm not technically his next of kin — that'd be Dad and Uncle Angus — but it seems that I'll do in the circumstances.'

'Well, if there's anything I can do to help, mate.'

'I just wanted to tell someone, I suppose. He'd been there all my life, always looking about a hundred and fifty, so I naturally assumed he'd live for ever. You know what they say about how only the good die young, by which maxim Great-uncle Piers' demise is definitely premature. I may have to bury him with a clove of garlic and a stake through his heart.'

'Have you told the rest of the family?' Greg knew that Piers' parents had disowned him when they'd found out he was gay.

'I'll put an announcement in the *Times*,' Piers said, 'then they can come to the funeral if they like. Or not.' He sighed. 'I was fond of him, you know. He could be difficult but, like he said, we were the black sheep of the Hamiltons, him and me, and now it's a flock of one. Suppose I'd better try to get hold of his solicitor, see if he was bullshitting all those years when he said I was his heir.'

'And where were you last night between the hours of ten and midnight, sir?' Greg said in his most pompous, PC-Plod voice.

Piers laughed. 'Don't think it had never crossed my mind but, as it happens, I was taking photos at an eighteenth birthday bash in Great Shefford all evening. Quite fancied the birthday boy.'

'Piers!'

'Don't worry. His little girlfriend was keeping a close eye on him.'

* * *

David Rhys Lloyd stood in the doorway of Antony's office feeling foolish: the sheer emptiness of his junior's massive desk felt like a reproach. There was one file open in the very centre of the table and the younger man sat with his dark head bent over it, motionless, seemingly unaware of his boss's presence.

Something had gone badly wrong with the office heating and calls to the managing agents over the past three days had done nothing to reduce the temperature from its tropical misery. Naturally, the windows didn't open. David had stripped down to shirt sleeves, losing his tie the moment he walked in the door every morning.

He was surprised and somewhat dismayed to see that Antony Lucas was impervious to the heat, sitting in full office attire: suit with jacket and waistcoat, Jermyn Street shirt with gold cufflinks, carefully knotted tie.

He'd always said he was a cold fish.

David cleared his throat and Antony looked up without surprise, turning his blank blue eyes on him in patient query.

'Got the Pemberton file?' David asked.

'Yes.' Antony rose and went to the filing cabinet with its fake wood front, chose a drawer without hesitation and plucked the relevant file out without needing to look.

He held it out but David raised hands in denial.

'You going to be about for the next few weeks?' he asked. 'Got your family business sorted?'

Antony thought about it. 'My family business is apparently concluded.'

'Only old man Pemberton wants to make a new will which will involve a pretty complicated trust. I wondered if you'd like to handle it.'

Antony said, 'No problem.' He sat down at his desk again and bent his head over his work. David took it as his dismissal and turned to go but Antony called him back. 'By the way, I've lost my mobile somewhere —'

'Have you tried phoning it?'

'Of course. It's dead. Probably lying under a ton of mouldering leaves in a wood somewhere. Anyway, I've got a new one. He took a reporter's pad from a drawer in his desk and scribbled a number on it. 'You can call me on this now.'

'Fine.' David left. He told himself that he must have been dreaming when he thought he saw Antony Lucas sucking his thumb over his papers.

* * *

At one o'clock Greg drove to the Savemore supermarket a couple of miles from the police station to get the week's groceries. Life had been easier when Angie worked here and brought a few items home every day, but, much as he disliked this chore, he was glad that she had finally taken another path in her life.

He considered himself a methodical shopper, making a detailed list after interrogating the fridge and kitchen cupboards, arranging it in order according to the layout of the store, driven to fury when, every six months or so, the goods were shuffled about, apparently at random.

Today the layout was familiar and he began to drift along the aisles with his trolley, feeling his brain turn to jelly as he went.

Jelly? He didn't need jelly. Who did? He had read recently that jelly was Britain's favourite pudding but if God had wanted people to eat jelly he wouldn't have invented tiramisu.

Tiramisu? Good idea. Why wasn't that on his list?

He bought things that were quick to cook but nutritious: pizza, ten minutes in the oven; microwavable pasta; chops to grill. Vegetables and salad were ready chopped and washed. He picked up a bag of apples because he was too lazy to think of a more interesting fruit. He only wished that there weren't so many varieties to choose from: in his youth apples had been eaters or cookers, red or green, and that was it.

Finally he checked his list to see if he had forgotten anything. At the bottom, in Angie's large, square hand, was written 'tampons'. His ex-wife Diane would have cut her own throat before she asked him to buy her tampons, but then he never did the shopping in those far off days. He left his trolley and made for the toiletries, grabbing the first packet he saw. Too bad if they were the wrong size. Did they even have sizes?

He buried them underneath his lamb chops.

After fifteen minutes he took his place at what he hoped would be the shortest check-out queue — only two customers ahead of him — and determined to be patient, although there were times when he wanted to yell 'Let me through: I'm a policeman'.

He was next to the express till and level with a man of about sixty-five, his well-lined face framed with a mane of white hair, his clothes shabby and slightly old-fashioned. In his basket were a few cheap items: tins of meat and macaroni cheese,

Savemore own-brand baked beans at eight pence a can, a slab of soapy Cheddar.

Greg caught his eye and gave him a half smile of complicity, receiving a bewildered stare in return.

As the queue shuffled forward, inevitably faster than Greg's own, the old man felt in the pockets of his threadbare overcoat and produced some printed slips. Greg recognised them, although he had never actually seen them in the flesh, as vouchers, issued to asylum seekers instead of cash to ensure that they bought food and didn't waste tax payer's money on worthless beads and wampum.

Behind the old man was a hard-faced woman. She looked about Angie's age but was dressed in the uniform of the rising young executive: black suit with unnecessarily short skirt, crisp white blouse, the latest mobile phone strapped to her belt. She couldn't seem to keep still, hopping from foot to foot, craning forward to see why the queue wasn't moving faster, tutting loudly. She was holding nothing but a three-pack of tights and Greg glanced involuntarily down at her legs. There was a big ladder up the side of the right one, disappearing under her hem.

After a moment, she leaned forward and poked the old man hard between the shoulders. 'Perhaps you'd like to start unloading your basket,' she said in a loud voice.

'Please?' the old man said.

She made incomprehensible gestures. 'It'll speed things up.'

'Please?'

'Oh, for God's sake!' The woman snatched the basket from the man's hands and began to unload his groceries onto the conveyer belt. 'Here!' she said. 'You've got nine items.'

'Please?'

'This is the eight items or less check-out.'

Fewer, Greg thought pedantically. Eight items or *fewer*.

'You are in the wrong queue,' the young woman enunciated slowly.

'Just let him pay for his stuff.' Another — older — woman behind the first said impatiently. 'Now that he's unloaded it.'

'*He's* unloaded it?'

'I haven't got all bloody day.'

'Pay!' The first woman snatched the vouchers triumphantly out of the old man's hand. 'You call this paying? He's just one of those scroungers, an illegal immigrant. This is my taxes.'

Both women glared at the old man who said 'Please' helplessly and pawed at his vouchers, trying in vain to retrieve them from the strong fingers of the woman in the suit.

Greg had had enough. 'He's an asylum seeker,' he said, 'not an illegal immigrant. Give him back his vouchers.'

The first woman stared at him rudely, as if he, like the old man, were a lower form of life. 'What business is it of yours?' she demanded.

Greg took out his warrant card and flourished it

in her face, rather more aggressively that was his habit.

She recoiled and said, 'Oh!'

'Now, perhaps you'd like to give this gentleman back his property before I mistake you for a thief.'

The woman returned the vouchers with a bad grace. 'The sooner they shut them up in those camps the better,' she muttered. 'It's not like we don't have problems of our own.'

'Charity begins at home,' the second woman sniffed.

'Is there a problem here?'

Greg recognised the assistant manager, a man still young enough to be a martyr to acne. He seemed to be wearing the same cheap polyester suit and hideous tie he'd had on the last time Greg had seen him. His name badge identified him as Mr J. Linden.

'I think we've sorted things out now, thanks.' He held up his warrant card again.

'Mr Summers!' The lad said. 'Didn't recognise you for a moment, sir. You're Angie's dad, yeah?'

Greg gritted his teeth. 'Dad-in-law.'

'Oh, yeah. Right.'

The assistant at the express check-out had rung up the old man's pitiful goods and said, 'Three pounds, eighty-nine please.'

He gave her all the vouchers and she sighed, sorted through them, took one for five pounds and put it in the till, which she then closed.

'What about his change?' Greg asked.

'We don't give change for vouchers,' the assistant

manager said cheerfully, handing the old man a plastic carrier bag without looking at him. 'Government policy.'

'Really? I must buy shares in supermarkets.'

'Quite right,' the second woman said, 'or they'll just spend the change on drink.'

Greg gave her a withering look.

He felt himself poked in the ribs at that point and turned round. He saw a harassed looking man with a toddler clinging to each trouser leg and a younger child in the trolley seat.

He said, 'Please mate, I haven't got all day.'

Greg realised that the queue ahead of him had cleared. He hurriedly shovelled his groceries onto the conveyor belt, piling them haphazardly into bags at the other end and wielding his credit card.

As he left the shop, weighed down with four carrier bags, the old man was waiting, holding his solitary one.

'Please,' he said, holding out his right hand.

'Please what?' Was he begging? Greg stopped and put down his bags. One of them promptly keeled over, depositing a box of eight Tampax Super and some apples on the ground. 'Can I help you?'

He looked baffled then nodded back at the store, thrusting forward his hand. 'You good man. Please.'

'Oh, I see! You're welcome.' Greg shook hands with him, retrieved his groceries and made for his car. He just had time to drive home, stuff the food in the fridge and be in the magistrates court by 2.15. As he'd asked for a special sitting, in camera, for Jennet Weatherby, it wouldn't do to be late.

After a few yards, he turned back and called, 'Good luck.'

The old man stood there, as if he might stand there for all time. Then the Savemore courtesy bus drew up and, when it was gone, so was he.

Greg fastened his seat belt and started the engine, then switched it off again. He glanced at his watch and grimaced.

He caught up with Linden in his ugly, cluttered office, cut out of the corner of the loading bay by three pieces of wobbly hardwood. He stuck his head round the door.

'You taking on staff?' he asked.

Linden gave him a surprised look. 'Police work getting too stressful for you, Mr Summers?'

'It's for a young man, eighteen, no qualifications.'

'Well, that's no problem as such. We have plenty of unskilled workers: shelf stackers, trolley dollies, packers and carriers.' He nodded out of his plastic window to the loading bay. 'Unloading deliveries. Turnover's high so I can always make room for someone.'

'He has a juvenile record.'

'Oh!' The young man flushed. 'We don't... Sorry. Company policy.'

'Even as a personal favour for me. And Angie.'

'Well . . .' Linden stared at his blank computer screen as if seeking inspiration.

'Go on. It's the best way to help keep a basically decent boy on the straight and narrow.'

'All right.' Linden sighed. 'Tell him to come and see me and I'll see what I can do.'

Greg was panting when he arrived at Newbury magistrates court that afternoon. Dickon Weatherby had turned up to support his sister, returning the favour of many years. Greg went over to speak to him. The boy, recognising him, nodded without rancour.

'Must run in the family,' he remarked. 'Just when I decide to go straight, Jen starts breaking and entering. We're like one of them weather vane things — you know? — where the little man and the little woman can't be out at the same time.'

'Bad luck on you, Dickon. I'm sorry.'

'Bad luck on Dad,' he said glumly. 'He knew I were a bad lot but he always thought the sun shone out of Jen. First, he said he didn't want to see her no more, but I talked him round. I mean, she's family. We're all she's got.'

'You do understand that you and your father mustn't talk about this to anyone for the moment.'

'Well, we don't want to boast about it!'

'If anyone asks then Jennet's in bed with flu.'

His sister was remanded on bail to face trial at the crown court at a date to be determined. One condition was that she was to live at her father's house in Alderbright, to which she agreed. If everything went according to plan on Saturday, there would probably be no job for her to go back to at Boxford Hall.

Dickon paid the bail and they left the court together, his arm round her shoulder. His cropped hair had grown since Greg had last seen him and the two auburn manes shimmered in the winter sun, a pair of fox cubs.

They went to stand by the bus stop. It would be a long wait for a bus to Alderbright. He called to them. 'You want a lift?'

Dickon got in next to him in the front; Jennet sprawled across the back seat until he told her to put her seatbelt on.

'So what you gonna do if I don't?' she asked with a sneer. 'Arrest me?'

'You can always wait for the bus,' he said mildly.

'Yeah?' She leaned forward between the front seats. 'But then somebody might see me, Mr Summers, somebody from the Hall and —'

'All right, all right.'

She slumped back and put her booted feet up on the upholstery. Greg decided to ignore her antics. 'You interested in a job, Dickon?' he asked, as he pulled out of the car park. The boy stared eagerly at him. 'You know the Savemore supermarket on the trading estate?'

'I know.'

'If you go tomorrow and ask for a Mr Linden, tell him I sent you, he'll give you a job.'

'Straight up?'

'It's not a bookshop but it's a start. You'll get

experience of working regularly: discipline, punctuality, being polite to customers. Then, when you're ready to move on, you've got a bit of a work record and a reference. You can get there, can you?'

'I got a bike. He knows about my record?'

'He knows. He probably won't mention it so you needn't either.'

'That's brilliant.'

'Don't let me down because he's doing this as a favour to me.'

'I won't. I'm dead grateful.'

'Yeah.' Jennet's voice was full of sarcasm. He could see her hostile eyes in his rear-view mirror. 'We're grateful for any little crumb, people like us Weatherbys. All the crap jobs no one else wants to do: waitressing, shelf stacking, bloody gardening.'

* * *

Cressida rang Antony's mobile number for the hundredth time.

Still nothing.

She curled herself in a foetal position and sobbed. Next door one of the twins began to cry.

She ignored the sound.

* * *

'You're a faster worker than I gave you credit for.'

Greg drained his glass of white wine and looked down at his superior officer quizzically. Down, because Chief Superintendent Jim Barkiss was five foot eight — if he held himself very upright.

He said, 'Sorry, sir?'

'Only here you are, arriving at a fundraiser as Lady Weissman's date just a couple of weeks after I asked you to call on her. I mean, if she was already a friend of yours then you'd surely have said so at the time.'

Those who knew Barkiss well knew that his open, honest face hid a strange inscrutablility. He had to have heard the canteen gossip about Greg and Angie but he had never broached the subject. Now he seemed to be implying a warmer relationship between him and Elise than in fact existed, standing with his eyebrows raised, waiting for Greg's response.

'We were at school together,' he explained. 'Only with her moving away and changing her name I didn't realise who she was at first.'

'Really? You mean she comes from round here?'

'Born and bred. We grew up like brother and sister.'

'I won't bother to congratulate you on your conquest then.'

'It's honestly not like that.'

'Good.'

Both men turned to look at the subject of their conversation. As secretary of Friends of the Refugee, Elise had gathered all the names and faces of Newbury at this fundraiser: actors, writers, singers, captains of industry and a director of British Airways.

Greg would not normally have been invited into such august company but an embossed invitation had arrived in the post with Elise's own 'Do please come' in her elegant hand in the corner, so he had written his cheque for fifty pounds and dug out the best suit again. The day before the event she had rung and asked if he would act as her escort for the evening. All eyes had been upon them when they arrived.

Barkiss finally expanded on his last comment. 'She's quite something. I'd have been bloody peeved if I'd been forced to envy you.'

'Yes,' he agreed. 'She is. Quite something.' Greg felt again the admiration of his first glimpse of the grown-up Elise in Hungerford High Street. It wasn't just that she was beautiful and elegant. Her blue eyes blazed with intelligence and her manner with vivacity as she moved among the guests, flirting with one, talking earnestly with another. He was fairly certain that he had no sexual interest in her, nor she in him.

Apart from anything else, he loved Angie.

'Bizarre affairs, these fundraisers,' Barkiss commented. 'I mean, you pay through the nose for a couple of glasses of wine and some canapés, not to mention a new dress for the missus and probably a taxi home. Stand around talking to a lot of people you wouldn't cross the street to meet. Why don't we just write out a cheque and stay home with *Eastenders*?'

Elise, who had been moving ever nearer, overheard this last remark. She tapped Barkiss sharply on the arm. 'Because charity is like justice, James, it must not only be done, it must be seen to be done.'

Mrs CS Barkiss, seeing her husband in conversation with the attractive and wealthy widow, was making her way towards them. Barkiss said, 'Uh, oh! I'm for it now,' and made off to intercept her.

Greg and Elise laughed together.

He liked Edna Barkiss. A plain, shapeless woman, she had a dark sense of humour which she revealed only to those who knew her well and would not be shocked by it. She had abandoned a career in law to be a wife and mother and had lived contentedly with that decision.

Barkiss's comment about the new dress was a joke since she was wearing the same outfit that Greg had seen her in at every social event for the last two years. Edna was no shopper and her husband's pretence that she spent all his salary, along with his make believe that she was a jealous dragon, was the sort of long-standing raillery that marks out the most successful unions.

Elise laid her hand on his arm and said, 'I must circulate. Catch you later.'

In a few minutes he found himself next to Edna as they refilled their wine glasses. They exchanged cordial greetings and talked about the new Human Rights legislation, a topic on which she was far more knowledgeable than he, making him wonder if there wasn't a corner of her that regretted the career.

'Off to Portugal soon?' he asked, when they had exhausted human rights.

'I shall be a golf widow when Jim retires.'

'Maybe you should take it up yourself.'

'Maybe. If you can't beat them . . . How well do you know Elise Weissman?' she asked suddenly. He explained how it was that he knew her both intimately and not at all. She stood digesting his story, ruminating it. She did look a little like a ruminant, he thought, not unkindly: a sheep with brains. 'Do people change?' she asked finally. 'Do they have a fundamental nature which is fixed at birth?'

'I don't know.'

'They say that leopards don't change their spots and yet . . .'

He thought of Dickon Weatherby who was, he hoped, embarking on a new journey in life. 'Perhaps if the change in circumstances is great enough.'

'The trauma?'

'It doesn't have to be traumatic. What makes you say that?'

'Just a feeling I sometimes get, when I'm with Elise Weissman, a sense of a soul that has known trouble. I'm a little psychic, you know.'

'Get away!' he said, startled. She had to be joking. Didn't she? Edna Barkiss, psychic? Plain, sensible Edna?

She laughed, a little embarrassed. 'I've had too much of this chardonnay, Gregory. Do me a favour and forget I said that.'

As she walked away, he realised that she hadn't been joking.

* * *

Antony closed the Pemberton file and placed it on his desk, lining the bottom up exactly with the bevelled edge of the wood. He folded his arms and sank his head on his chest in thought. His thumb sneaked up into his mouth without his being aware of it.

Sir Jeremy Pemberton's trust was straightforward enough for someone as steeped in trust law as Antony; it was the sheer size of it that irritated him. Upwards of seventy-five million pounds was to be held for the benefit, essentially, of his one surviving child and three grandchildren, along with great-grandchildren as yet unborn, undreamed of.

Large sums of tax would be avoided or postponed by this means.

It occurred to him that it might be amusing to make a botch of the trust so that, when Pemberton was dust and it was too late to remedy the situation, it could be declared null and void after a lengthy and expensive court battle, allowing the government to swoop on Sir Jeremy's millions with cries of glee.

Antony had inherited three hundred thousand pounds from the death of his adopted family, after tax. Not that he had been named in his parents' wills but with Isobel, their legatee, dying with them and intestate, he had been left the sole heir.

It was small change to Pemberton, small change to Elise. He thought about the pictures on her wall at Alders End. His knowledge of art was hazy but he'd seen a report in the *Telegraph* just a fortnight ago of a

Joachim Weissman selling for three million dollars in the States.

He had looked up Weissman's will at the Probate Registry. He had left his estate to his 'beloved wife Elise', absolutely, everything but two hundred and fifteen thousand pounds which went straight to Cressida to take best advantage of the nil-rate tax band prevailing two years earlier.

He had been well advised by his lawyers.

The value of the estate for Probate had been a little under six million pounds and, as a solicitor, Antony knew that that would most likely be an under-estimate.

'Rich old Jew,' Antony murmured. How often his father had come home after a bad day in court, spitting venom and blaming his own shortcomings on the 'Jewish Mafia'.

He pounded his fist on the table.

She owed him. Apart from anything else, the bloody woman had tried to kill him.

'No,' he said through gritted teeth. 'No, Elise. It is *not* finished.'

He came unannounced, a week before Christmas. It had been dark for hours and he could see, in the bay window of the dining room, a Christmas tree. He pressed his nose to the panes like an urchin out of Dickens, a beggar boy excluded forever from the bounty within. The tree sparkled, not with anything so vulgar as tinsel or fairy lights but with tiny threads of gold and silver that reflected the light from the hall. Beyond the tree, on the table, there were presents, seemingly dozens of them, exquisitely wrapped and ribboned, the papers shining, also gold and silver.

He found the front door locked, and made his way round the back, letting himself in through the kitchen. He could hear music playing in the adjacent sitting room: Brahms, he thought, although music meant little to him. What could music say to a man with no soul?

He moved forward into the doorway and she turned and looked steadily at him. She raised her hand with the remote control and silenced the CD player with a flick of her finger. A log fire burned in the grate, crackling as the bark caught.

In his mind's eye he saw the Lucas house as it dissolved, almost melted, in the flames. He felt the searing heat and the unimaginable pain of being roasted alive.

Isobel's screams . . .

'I thought we agreed,' she said, interrupting his thoughts.

'*You* agreed. I've changed my mind about going to the police. I had a word with a colleague who specialises in criminal law. It seems that attempted murder is almost as bad as the real thing: it carries a potential life sentence. How do you fancy spending the next ten or fifteen years in prison, Elise?'

'Show me your evidence. It's your word against mine.'

'True, but if I make a complaint then the police will have to look into it. It might get out. In fact, I'm sure it would. What would all your smart friends say to that, Elise, your arty set? "There's no smoke without fire."'

'You clearly don't know my smart friends,' she said with a smile. 'They're the biggest crooks in the land. They would be disappointed in me, true, but only because I made a hash of it. Publish and be damned, Antony.'

He had expected her to stand firm, so he had back-up.

'And then there are these.' He passed her the thin folder he'd been holding under his arm. 'I thought you should be the first to see them.'

She glanced up at him before opening it, then examined the top picture. She closed her eyes with a long sigh. Soon, though, she re-opened them and began to leaf through the collection of ten or twelve pictures, 10x8" glossies printed on a good quality colour printer.

He had done them at the office one evening.

As well as the ones of Cressida, naked and lewd, there were others he had done with a timer device, pictures of them both, merged at the sweating loins. Cressida's head was flung back in a gesture of ecstasy, but still recognisable.

Elise shut the file again, her face empty of emotion. 'I have never been much interested in pornography.'

She held the folder out to him.

'Keep it,' he said, 'I have copies. I thought I might put them on the Internet, create a little website for them. This sort of thing's very popular. Oh, and I shall e-mail them to Stephen's headmaster — a side of one of his master's wives he won't have seen before, or so I imagine.'

'How do I know these pictures are genuine?'

'You have the evidence of your own eyes.'

'Ah, but have I? I'm an intelligent woman, Antony, I read the papers. I know that you can do almost anything with digital photos these days.'

'Yes,' he said with a smile. 'You're right: you can. As it happens, these are the real thing but, you know, it wouldn't much matter if they weren't. They would do the same damage. Now, isn't that interesting? Still say "Publish and be damned", Elise?'

She knew when she was beaten. She said, 'What do you want?'

'Tinker Girl.'

She drew in a sharp breath. She had not been expecting this particular demand and was astonished by how much it hurt. 'Why that, of all things?'

'Because it's valuable and because I know how much losing it will mean to you. Give me the painting and I shall go and you will never hear from me again.'

She said, 'I must think about it.'

'All right, but don't take too long.'

* * *

'So who came to the funeral?' Greg asked.

Piers shook his head sadly. 'No one. I mean, there was only me from the family. Giacomo McFee came along, though, which I thought was nice of him.'

'Your uncle was a good customer.'

'Sure, but not any longer.'

Greg couldn't tell if Piers minded that no one from the family had come. If his parents had come, if they had spoken after fourteen years, there might have been the chance of reconciliation.

He cleared his throat. 'I'm sorry I didn't make it myself. With the chief-super off golfing in Portugal it's hard to get away from my desk.'

'You only met him once,' Piers said with a shrug.

'But he made a big impression.'

Jumping the gun

Somehow Greg didn't think McFee was the type to go quietly.

Krepski agreed, which was why he had a score of men waiting in four vans when they met. It was two hours before dawn on the twentieth of December. Four of the officers, including the DCI himself, were authorised for firearms and had been issued with Smith & Wesson .38 snub-nosed handguns.

Not even six o'clock, Greg thought, stifling a yawn, as his car lurched to a halt. His alarm had gone off at 4.55. Angie had turned over, eyed the digital display, murmured, 'You *cannot* be serious,' and gone back to sleep.

He had enjoyed the brief drive along empty roads under a starlit sky.

On the main road between Newbury and Hungerford was a hamlet called Halfway with a pub called the Halfway Inn. This had always struck Greg as vaguely indecent but he was probably just a dirty old man. When Barbara had been unable to find anywhere sensible for such a large number of police officers to rendezvous in Boxford, he had suggested the pub car-park, which was only a couple of miles from the hotel and had the added merit of being an equally short distance from his house.

The marked vehicles waited in a circle in the back

part of the car-park, out of view of the main road. Greg got out of his car shivering and blowing on his hands, to make his way to the lead van. He found Krepski there and the two men exchanged cool greetings.

Greg had been told that he need not come on this raid, in a way that made it clear that his presence was not desired.

'You can come if you like, of course,' the man from the NCS had said, 'but —'

'I do like.'

This was his turf and he didn't want another dog pissing on it.

'Any word?' he asked now.

'I've got four men hidden out in the grounds. They'll call the minute there's any sign of action.'

Krepski was kitted out like a man on an SAS raid and was wearing a bullet proof vest. He offered one to Greg, who hesitated.

'Illegal immigration is big business,' Krepski growled. 'Which would you rather — look foolish or take a bullet through the heart?'

Greg took the vest and fastened it on with some difficulty, not wanting to ask for help. Monroe had just joined them; it was the first time the superintendent had seen him without a suit and he looked almost intimidating in combat trousers, climbing boots and a black leather blouson.

He looked wide awake too.

'Used to getting up at all hours with my baby daughter,' he laughed, by way of explanation. His eyes were bright with excitement and Greg thought that perhaps he'd been wrong when he thought Marilyn destined for a life shuffling paper behind a desk. He could now see a well-developed musculature in the chest and shoulders of the younger man.

Barbara's neat little hatchback flew in from the A4 a moment later. She and Tim accepted vests without demur, although Barbara found hers a poor fit. 'Not designed to fit round tits,' Krepski remarked and got a crushing look for his pains.

Greg realised that he had never seen Krepski look so happy, not even with his boat load of dead Iranians. Like Monroe, he was lit up with excitement as another man might be lit up by beer.

Wasn't it for moments like these that they'd all joined the police force in the first place?

'Halfway in?' he heard one of the constables guffaw. 'Sounds like your sex life, Dennis.'

'Sod you.'

Krepski's mobile rang — oddly, the tune was *Für Elise* — and he shushed his men as he answered it. He listened intently for a few minutes, asking no questions, then said, 'We're on our way. ETA in ten minutes. Keep out of sight.' He disconnected.

He went off to talk to the men in the other vans. Greg could see the pale face of Trevor Faber leaning out of the passenger window of the second one. When Krepski returned he said tersely to his own driver, 'We're off. Side lights only.'

The four vans left the car-park by the back entrance and turned left, making their way silently through the village of Hoe Benham, the perfectly-tuned engines purring in convoy. A lone milkman watched them go, turning to look after them till a bottle slipped from his chilled hand to shatter on the pavement, making him swear.

Greg heard a distinct *whump* as a member of the local fauna met a premature end under their front wheels. Probably a pheasant since the silly creatures showed no road sense at all, spending the autumn gathered in conversation in the middle of the road like a parliament of fowls.

They turned right opposite the Bell Inn, pulling south on the road that followed the river Lambourn all the way to Newbury. After half a mile they turned right into the private drive that led to the Hall, proceeding slowly over the speed bumps.

The handsome building loomed in the darkness ahead of them, a giant unlit Christmas tree standing stark against its frontage. It had been a cloudless night, frosty, but the stars were fading with the approach of daylight. Greg had never really understood about the darkest hour being just before dawn; until now.

The lead van came to a halt and the driver whispered something to Krepski who was riding shotgun beside him. Greg craned forward to hear but the DCI leaned back and muttered, 'Vehicles ahead, sir! It's as we thought.' He spoke to the driver again. 'I want to hear, Connors.'

'Sir!'

The convey waited, their engines switched off,

almost as if they were holding their breath. Greg heard a door slam in the distance, another shut with more circumspection, sound carrying clearly on the night air.

'They're moving them,' Krepski said gleefully. 'They're only bloody moving them tonight.'

'As Jennet Weatherby said,' Greg pointed out.

Krepski's lip curled. 'Lying's bred into girls like her.'

Jennet hadn't taken to Krepski either, since he had tried to bully her and she was not going to be bullied. After five minutes with him she had refused to speak to him further and communicated only with Greg. She had referred to him as Crapski, a memory which now made Greg smile.

'There's no other way out of here by road, is there?' Krepski was saying.

'No, only on foot across the fields to Alderbright.'

'We take the blokes in the vans first, put them out of action, leave a couple of men to keep an eye on them, then we go in. Wait.'

Krepski slid his door open and slipped out. He stopped for a matter of seconds at the other three vans, giving orders. Greg glanced at Monroe who shrugged. Maybe they had underestimated Krepski; he seemed like a man who knew what he was doing.

He was back. 'Right,' he said. 'We can have speed or we can have stealth, so I've gone for speed, surprise.'

All four engines fired as he spoke and the police vehicles hurtled up the remaining 200 yards of drive, jolting over the last few speed bumps till Greg was sure his spine must be sticking out of the top of his head. They slithered to a halt on the gravel, forming a ring round the two windowless vans that stood backed up to the side door of the Hall, their tailgates open.

Their headlights blazed on as one.

Krepski was out in an instant and Greg jumped after him. He wasn't going to miss any of this.

The DCI called softly but clearly, 'Armed police. Don't move.'

There were two men with each van, caught like rabbits in the glare of the undipped beams. One held up his hands at once. Two stood bewildered. The fourth attempted to run but the men from Krepski's advance surveillance team materialised from the shadows and brought him down before he'd gone twenty yards. Greg heard the noise of his face scraping painfully across the gravel and winced in sympathy. He was roughly dragged up, cuffed and returned.

The vans were dark blue with wording on the side in a darker shade, italic, very tasteful. Once more Greg's eye read them as 'grief haulage'.

It all made sense now and Justin Greif had a lot of grief coming to him.

Meanwhile, Krepski had inspected the vans and found them empty.

'You —' he pointed to the four constables who'd been hidden out in the grounds, 'stay here and deal with this lot. Everyone else inside with me.'

Greg laid a hand on his arm. 'The man who runs this haulage business lives at the Old Rectory in Alderbright. I think we need to pick him up at once in case anyone manages to get a warning to him.'

'Good thinking. Trevor?'

'Sir?'

'Take three men and pick up — what's his name?'

'Justin Greif,' Greg supplied.

'At the Old Rectory in Alderbright.'

Faber went off without a word, signalling silently to three constables to follow him.

'Let's go,' Krepski said to Greg.

The side door of the hotel stood open. Jennet had drawn them a detailed plan and Krepski led the way along the corridor of the north wing to the back stairs.

'What the hell —?' McFee appeared from nowhere, without his chef's whites for once, nondescript in jeans and a sweatshirt. He recognised Greg. 'You again!'

'McFee,' Greg told Krepski.

'Arrest him,' Krepski barked out.

Two men stayed to do that while the rest followed their leaders up the stairs to the old servant's quarters. Greg noticed the words 'Garden Suite' on a white wooden door next to the stairwell and wondered why they rang a bell.

Members of staff poked quizzical faces out of their rooms. Those who were on breakfast duty were already dressed; others wore pyjamas or, in the case of plump Pran, nothing but a towel wrapped round his loins. A half-naked woman peered out from behind him and Greg realised with a slight shock that it was the ethereally beautiful French girl.

Recognising Greg, the young Indian-Yorkshireman said, 'Bloody Norah, for an 'orrible moment I thought you were me dad!'

To each, Krepski said, 'Police operation. Please stay in your rooms for your own safety, ladies and gentlemen.' Those who were slow to comply with this polite request were bundled unceremoniously back inside.

The wall at the end of the hallway looked solid to Greg: plain wood panelling, unexpected in servants quarters, perhaps, but not so much so as to draw attention to itself. Krepski fiddled with it for a few minutes, running his hands over the wood, looking for knotholes, a hidden spring, muttering the occasional curse as his search proved fruitless.

'Life's too short,' he said finally and signalled to one of his men who came forward bearing an axe and began to attack the panelling. It was hollow and was demolished to splinters in less than two minutes.

Greg became aware of gasping and muttering from the other side, all in a language he didn't recognise, let alone understand. Beyond the splintered wood there was darkness.

He followed Krepski through the gap into the secret room and the muttering stopped. Greg could smell the fear — even above the scent of unwashed bodies, unlaundered clothes — and part of him enjoyed it. He groped around on the wall till he located a light switch and illuminated a single bare bulb dangling by a long wire from the roof.

They all blinked.

It was a long and narrow room, its ceilings sloping almost to the floor. There were no windows, just a couple of skylights, no more than a foot square, both covered with a blind. Camp beds had been crammed into every available space, most of them strewn with the pitiful belongings of the women who were living there.

Two dozen of them, Greg calculated. They stood watching the policemen with frozen faces, many of them clutching each other in terror. One fell to her knees and began to wail what might have been prayers, her hands clasped imploringly together.

The place was dusty and airless and there was an unpleasant smell.

Krepski opened his mouth to speak but, from somewhere in front of the hotel, came the unmistakable sound of a single gunshot.

Krepski went white, then purple and rushed out of the room.

Greg took charge. 'You stay here,' he said to Monroe and Barbara. 'Get the women ready to leave.' As an afterthought, he added, 'There's no need to frighten them.'

Krepski was already halfway down the stairs when Greg caught up with him. He had drawn his own pistol and covered the last few yards across the foyer to the front door by pressing himself against the walls. Greg kept in his shadow, fingering his bullet-proof vest dubiously.

Suddenly the bulky thing didn't seem half bulky enough, and surely any sensible guman would aim for the brain, lodged only behind a flimsy carapace of flesh and skull.

In the porch were two young constables. One stood with his gun limp in his hand, looking slightly dazed.

'What happened?' Krepski snapped when he was satisfied that no one was in immediate danger. He holstered his own gun and Greg let out a little sigh of relief.

The young men looked uncomfortably at each other. 'The Scotsman got away,' one said finally.

'What!'

'I told you he wouldn't go quietly,' Greg remarked.

'What was that shot we heard?'

The constable with the drawn gun gulped. He looked barely old enough to shave and Krepski cut an alarming figure in his combat fatigues. 'I fired over his head, guv. I thought it might scare him into . . . surrendering.'

His boss's voice was quietly vehement. 'Have you gone raving mad?'

'Sir!'

'You fire your gun if your life is in immediate danger, or a colleague's life or a civilian's, *and under no other circumstances*.'

'Yes, sir.'

'Which bit of that didn't you understand, Dexter?' The boy made no attempt to answer this rhetorical question and Krepski said, 'Give me your gun.' He handed it over. Krepski looked uncertain what to do with it, then thrust it at Greg who was too surprised not to take it. 'I'm cancelling your firearms certificate, as of now, and don't even think of reapplying. Not ever.'

'No, sir.'

Greg was also not sure what to do with the holster, so he strapped it on. He'd often wondered what it would feel like. The pistol was smaller than he'd expected, a steel and aluminium revolver with a short barrel. It weighed practically nothing and yet it felt heavy at his side.

Krepski was still berating his underling. 'There'll have to be an enquiry into this.'

'Yes, sir.'

'Which way did McFee go?' Greg cut in.

They pointed.

'You.' Krepski poked Constable Dexter in the chest. 'Wait in the van. You're no longer part of this operation. You.' His colleague. 'Get after McFee.' To Greg. 'Where did you say that footpath leads?'

'Alderbright, where Faber's gone.'

'You've got the van drivers properly secure at least?'

'Sir.'

'Then four of you take a van and try and head him off. Call Inspector Faber and see if he can help.'

As they set off he called after them, 'And if you catch him, don't bloody shoot him!'

From somewhere above them a patrician voice boomed out. 'I say! Can you keep it down out there? People are trying to sleep.'

Most of the women were being led downstairs by the time they got back to the hidden attic. Two or three lingered, still gathering their meagre belongings under the patient eyes of the police officers.

The woman who'd fallen on her knees was still sobbing hysterically and was being gently carried out by two enormous policemen who spoke soothingly to her. Since it was clear that she didn't understand a word it hardly mattered what they said.

'Mary had a little lamb,' one murmured gently.

'Hickory dickory dock,' the second added reassuringly.

Greg stared after them and shook his head in disbelief.

'No trouble, apart from her,' Barbara said. 'It's almost as if they're relieved — Christ!' She'd noticed Greg's holster. 'Since when have you been authorised for firearms, guv?'

'I'm looking after it for a friend.' He sniffed the air. 'What *is* that awful smell?'

'Take a wild guess.'

One corner of the secret room was screened by a couple of sheets hung over an old wooden clothes horse. Greg followed Krepski to examine it and realised immediately that this was where the unpleasant odour was coming from. Behind the makeshift screen were four metal buckets, a basin of dirty water, a towel and a roll of hard lavatory paper.

Krepski deliberately kicked one of the buckets over, loosing a stream of acrid yellow liquid to trickle between the bare floorboards.

'Was that really necessary?' Greg asked.

Krepski ignored the question, his face still grim from the shooting incident. He came out waving a hand in front of his nose.

'What a shithole,' he said.

'You think this is a shithole?' A petite, rather pretty young woman with curly brown hair answered him in fluent English. 'Where we came from, that is the shithole.'

'And who are you?' Krepski asked. He swaggered up and loomed over her, hands on hips. She was a skinny woman, but then they all looked underfed. Krepski was huge in comparison and she took a step back, pressing up against her bed which screeched away across the floor on its metal legs. She was clutching a plastic carrier bag to her chest, a few words written on it in Cyrillic script. A yellow nylon sweater spilled from the top, an incongruously cheerful colour.

She found her voice. 'My name is Seskia and I wish to claim asylum.'

'You're too late, love,' Krepski sneered. 'You have to claim at your port of entry, *on* entry, or not at all.'

'But there are exceptions,' she said calmly, 'and I wish to claim anyway.'

Krepski's voice rose. 'I said you're too late, you stupid tart. Comprendez? Don't you get it? These islands are overcrowded already. *We don't want you here.'*

His eyes slid insolently up and down her body.

She flushed with shame but stood her ground. 'I wish you would speak to me with more respect. In my country I was an English teacher —'

'Then you should have stayed there, instead of coming here whoring.' He laughed without merriment. 'But that's what you Slav women like, isn't it? Just can't get enough —'

Greg hardly knew what happened next as it was all over in a matter of seconds. Monroe seemed to fly at Krepski, clearing two or three of the camp beds like a steeplechaser, and sending him slamming into the rear wall. The clothes horse collapsed into a dozen pieces of splintered wood and one of the grubby sheets wrapped itself round the two men as if it were their shroud.

Greg, Barbara and Seskia took an automatic step back and stood, transfixed, while Monroe punched Krepski repeatedly in the face. Neither man uttered a word, merely grunts of pain or triumph, which gave an odd effect, as if the fight was happening behind sound-proofed glass. They slid down into the pool of urine that had been upset earlier.

Blood streamed from Krepski's face and onto his bulletproof vest.

They disentangled themselves, reducing the thin cotton of the sheet to rags. Monroe stood shakily up, looking as if the fight had finally gone out of him, but Krepski staggered to his feet and ran at his adversary, head down, catching him full in the solar plexus.

Monroe, though winded, grabbed the other man by the hair and tugged at it, making him gasp with pain. Then he spun round and drove Krepski's head hard into the wall.

Seskia looked from Greg to Barbara in confusion. Barbara said, 'I'll take the little one.'

'Okay.'

Greg seized the dazed Krepski from behind as Barbara got Monroe in an armlock. Struggling with him she stepped back into one of the buckets.

'Shit!' she exclaimed.

'Most aptly put,' Seskia said as Barbara gingerly lifted her boot out of the mess.

'That's enough.' Greg had his arm round Krepski's throat and the DCI's face was getting redder and redder. Blood dribbled down his chin and onto Greg's sleeve. A single molar — dark with amalgam fillings, its roots crimson — fell from his mouth and clattered to the floor.

'I said enough, Stan. Can you hear me?'

The man finally stopped struggling and Greg relaxed his grip. Krepski hung his head, sucking air into his lungs like a pump, his eyes trying to focus. Barbara released Monroe and he sank to the floor, panting and rubbing his abdomen where his adversary had head-butted him.

Greg examined the wall where Krepski's bullet

head had left a visible dent in the plaster. 'Are you hurt?' he asked. 'I mean really hurt. Ambulance hurt?'

The DCI shook his head, still unable to speak.

'Look at my boots!' Barbara wailed. 'They're ruined and they're practically new.'

Seskia handed her a threadbare towel. Barbara nodded her thanks and, sitting on the nearest bed, used it wipe off the worst of the damage.

'I'll have you for this,' Krepski hissed at Monroe, his voice thick with his own blood. He seized the nearest remnant of sheeting and began to stanch the flow from his nose and mouth, making unpleasant snorting noises. 'You're bloody mad. I'll have you busted down to constable for this, or in prison.' He gestured at Greg and Barbara. 'I have witnesses.'

After a moment's pause, Greg said, 'I didn't see what happened. Did you, Sergeant Carey?'

'It was all too quick,' Barbara agreed.

'No speak Eengleesh,' Seskia added.

Krepski straightened up and stared at Greg. 'And you'll swear to that on oath, will you, *sir*? Swear you didn't see Monroe attack me for no reason?'

'I don't think it'll come to that,' Greg said calmly. 'I don't think you'll want your senior officers to hear the way you spoke to our prisoners, or the sort of things you've been saying about immigrants ever since this operation started. If there's a formal hearing the press might get to hear about you. In fact, I think I can guarantee it.'

Krepski turned and slammed his fist against the wall, making a second dent. He was obviously thinking hard.

'Whose side are you on?' he asked finally.

'The side of decency and reason,' Greg snapped.

Krepski scrabbled about for his tooth, stuck it in his pocket and walked away, clambering through the hole in the wall and trudging wearily along the corridor, his shoulders slumped in defeat. Greg went back to the primitive lavatory and spoke sharply to Tim Monroe.

'My office — this afternoon — two o'clock.'

'Sir.'

'Go and wait in one of the vans. And clean yourself up, man. You stink of piss!'

Of the refugees only Seskia remained in the room now. Greg took her gently by the elbow. 'Come along. Time to go.'

She took a last look round the room. 'I am not so sorry to leave this place. Or am I?'

He said, 'At least you're still alive, love, and not mouldering at the bottom of the sea.'

As they descended the stairs, she said, 'Please, what is hickory, dickory dock?'

Trevor Faber's van drew up as they left the building and the inspector jumped down lithely from the passenger door before it had come to a full halt. 'No one home *chez* Greif,' he began, then he caught sight of his boss and his mouth fell open. 'What the hell happened to you, Stan?'

Krepski brushed past him without answering and got into the van. The bleeding had stopped but his face and clothes were covered in blood and urine. He looked like an extra from a slasher movie, the unnamed man who dies before the opening credits.

Or, since it was the festive season, a gigantic robin redbreast.

Greg unfastened his gun holster, looked at it for a moment and handed it to Trevor Faber who took it in surprise.

'Whose is this?'

'Yours.'

'Mine?'

'The NCS's. Greif not at home, you say?'

'The house is in darkness. We knocked loud enough to wake the dead.'

'Okay. I'll get some of my people to keep an eye on the place till he shows up.'

'*If* he shows up.'

'I don't think anyone had time to warn him. He's probably gone skiing for Christmas. I don't imagine he gets personally involved in the dirty work, anyway. Any sign of McFee?'

Faber shook his head dispiritedly. 'Gone to ground like an old fox but the men are hanging on till full light to make another search of the fields and footpaths. Can you let us have a dog handler?'

'Sure. I'll see to that the moment I get into the station.'

'Cheers.'

Krepski loomed out of the passenger window and yelled, 'Trevor!'

'What happened to him?' Faber whispered to Greg. 'He may be stupid but he's usually got the sense to duck a punch.'

'Didn't see this one coming,' Greg said.

'Trevor!'

'All right!'

By tacit consent Greg and Barbara got into a different van from Krepski. Greg didn't see where Monroe had got to and, at that moment, he didn't much care. He tore his bullet-proof vest off and hurled it to the floor, then walked away to the front of the van. All the seats there were taken up by immigrants and the constables who were keeping an eye on them. They looked at him curiously.

Barbara joined him and put her hand on his shoulder. 'We did a good night's work, Greg,' she murmured in his ear. 'We did what we set out to do, give or take a missing celebrity chef.'

He tried to put it in perspective. 'I suppose.' He glanced at the women they had taken into custody, eight of them sitting silently in the van. Some had their heads bowed; some gazed into space, their faces immobilised by fear; the praying woman was still shamelessly weeping. 'Since obviously these poor women would have brought the country to its knees.'

She wrinkled her nose. 'Though I don't think I'm ever going to wear these boots again.'

He sighed. 'Wasn't it Napoleon who said, "Next

to a battle lost there's nothing half so melancholy as a battle won"?' Barbara bestowed on him the small smile she reserved for his barmier moments. He shrugged mentally; it was a man thing, and not something that women understood.

As they climbed out of the van at the Halfway Inn, he remembered why the words Garden Suite had seemed familiar. He said to Barbara, 'I'm going to apply to have Mr Hamilton's body exhumed.'

She was used to his incomprehensible pronouncements and asked patiently, 'And who might he be?'

'An old man who was staying at the hotel, died suddenly a couple of weeks ago. He was staying in the Garden Suite which is at the foot of those stairs they took the women up and down. Old people aren't good sleepers and there's a chance he saw or heard something that may have cost him his life. In view of tonight's events, I think we should make absolutely sure that nobody helped him on his way.'

Acting DCI Monroe presented himself punctually in Greg's office at two o'clock that afternoon He had managed to change his clothes though the ones he'd borrowed were not a good fit. He'd also showered and rinsed his hair; it was still damp and clung to his head in tendrils, giving him a woebegone look.

He was walking a little stiffly but the superintendent didn't invite him to sit and he stood more or less at attention throughout the interview.

Greg folded his arms, leaned back in his chair and regarded his junior officer for a moment. 'I won't lie under oath for you,' he said in the end, 'but I hope it won't come to that.'

'I know I was stupid —'

'You can say that again!'

'Thank you for sticking up for me, sir, for putting Krepski off making a complaint.'

'Let's hope I was successful.'

'I guess we were all overwrought, what with that gunshot. It rattled me, I don't mind telling you. I hate guns.'

'The only people armed and dangerous were Krepski's own men,' Greg pointed out.

'I didn't know that at the time, sir.'

Greg had been thinking hard all day about what he had best do with Monroe. 'I want you to apply to transfer back to your old post,' he said, 'with immediate effect.'

Monroe was shattered. 'I've only been here a month, sir. It's going to look bizarre for me to give up a temporary promotion so soon.'

'I don't care what you tell them. Say you need to be based nearer home with the new baby, if you like.'

'That'll look good on my CV: "he has to be home early to change nappies".'

'Better than "He made a vicious and unprovoked assault on a fellow officer".'

'You clearly didn't think it was unprovoked, sir.'

'I'm not debating it with you, Inspector. What

you did was inexcusable and you probably deserve to be kicked out of the force.'

'I spoke to you, though, weeks ago. I told you you should ask for Krepski to be taken off this operation before something went badly wrong.'

'But nothing did go wrong,' Greg pointed out, 'except for you going off your head like that. We arrested twenty-five illegal immigrants and put a stop to the activities of McFee and Greif. What with the death of the Driscoll brothers, that's one route into the country closed off for good.

'Still,' he relented, 'I feel partly responsible for what happened, which is why I'm letting you off so lightly. This is my best offer, Tim.'

'Thank you, sir.'

'Dismissed.'

There would be other Driscoll brothers, of course, other Greifs and McFees. What motivated them? In the case of the fishermen it seemed to be a simple and understandable urge for survival and their grisly fate would not deter other desperate men.

But Justin Greif? Giacomo McFee? Both, apparently, wealthy men, successful in their chosen careers, respected in their communities, who had now thrown away everything they had worked for. Was it mere greed or something yet to be unearthed: an expensive drug habit or horrendous gambling debts?

Time, he hoped, would tell.

Which reminded him: he picked up the telephone

and asked Susan to get him the Coroner's office. It was time to set in motion the exhumation of Mr Hamilton. He was not looking forward to telling Piers that he was planning to dig up his uncle before his grave had even settled, and he hoped to God that he wouldn't end up having to check his friend's alibi.

But at least then they would know the truth about his death.

And the cases Greg hated most were the ones where he never really got to the truth.

The right tool for the job

On the morning of December the 23rd Elise rang
Antony at his office.

'You win,' she said. 'The portrait's yours.'

He had been expecting capitulation but he didn't
gloat. All he said was, 'I'll collect it this evening.'

'Come around ten. I'll have it ready for you.'

'No ambushes this time, Elise. Fool me once,
shame on you. Fool me twice, shame on me.'

'No ambushes.'

Elise examined the Henckel knives as she hadn't
since the day she'd bought them. Some people
swore by Sabatier but the best chefs chose Henckel.
The set of eight had cost more than three hundred
pounds and she had taken good care of them.

She rejected the serrated knives: they were not
right for the job. Any butcher would tell you that
selecting the right tool is crucial. The three inch knife
was too short, the eight inch too long. She picked up
the six inch and weighed it in her hand. It felt solid
and heavy.

She tested the blade with the ball of her left
thumb and watched dispassionately as beads of
scarlet bubbled up. It reminded her of something.
Ah, yes: she and Greg Summers pledging themselves to a lifelong friendship at the age of eleven

with a mingling of their blood. She placed the thumb in her mouth and sucked, finding comfort in the warm metallic taste.

Satisfied with her weapon, she went into the sitting room and switched on the spotlight above Tinker Girl. She examined it in a way she hadn't for twenty years: the dense richness of the oil paint, layered so that in places it was a quarter of an inch thick, giving the picture a third dimension. Her skin looked almost white at first glance but closer scrutiny showed a dozen — a score — of colours going to make up her complexion. Similarly her hair was not black but a porridge of browns and purples, of navy blue and aubergine.

Without allowing herself to think, she raised the knife and brought it down across the canvas in one long sweep, from top right to bottom left. Then, because she was, to a limited extent, ambidextrous, she moved the blade to her other hand and swept from top left to bottom right.

Where the gashes met in the middle the canvas began to peel back like a four-pointed star and flakes of paint dropped to the floor to lie as dazed insects on the boards, multi-coloured. She jabbed the knife repeatedly into the face of the girl, blinding her and cutting out her tongue.

When she was finished, she was panting.

'There,' she said, stepping back. 'Now it is ready for you, Antony.'

She heard a car draw up on the gravel drive and

looked at the grandfather clock in the corner. It was not yet nine o'clock. Why had he come so early? To catch her unprepared, or to be sure that she did not so catch him? She switched off the light above the picture, dropped the knife on the writing desk in the alcove to one side and went out into the hall.

She had left the front door unlocked for him.

But instead of stopping at the front, the car swung round the side of the house towards the car port. Odd, she thought: Antony never parked there. Perhaps he thought it would be easier to take the canvas out the back way. She retraced her steps and waited for him in the kitchen doorway, but when the side door opened it was Cressida who came in.

Elise had observed the changes in her daughter over the past few weeks, even before she knew the cause of them. Two months ago she might have conceded that her child was arrogant, a little conceited, but that she had a right to be. She was beautiful; she had a fine husband and two gorgeous children, a charming house, money, a talent which, if not her father's genius, enabled her to find pleasure in her art.

Now she was like a broken doll, all her confidence gone, her clear eyes dulled with suffering, her cheeks blotched with recent tears. That was what love did to you, Elise thought with a moment of clarity: not the warm blanket of marital contentment but the love that the poets wrote of so glibly — the love of Tristan and Isolde, Romeo and Juliet —

the love that destroyed everything it touched like a forest fire.

Cressida said, 'Mummy?' And her voice was breaking.

She said, 'I know, darling. I know!' and wrapped her arms round her child. She could smell whisky on her breath, too much for someone who'd been driving, but that seemed a minor matter now, not worthy of comment. Cressida was wearing a ratty old sweater of Stephen's, far too big for her, and Elise had a pang of nostalgia for the days when she would step naked out of bed and into a shirt or jersey of Joachim's.

Of such small intimacies was a true marriage made.

They stood like that, motionless, for several minutes, then Elise held her daughter away from her and looked deep into her eyes.

'Where are Stephen and the boys, Cressie?'

Her voice was steady, despite the scotch. 'Stephen's driven over to spend the evening with his mum. I was supposed to be going too but I said I had a migraine so he took the kids and left me to rest. I was alone in that house with my thoughts and I couldn't bear it. I couldn't bear it a moment longer. I had to talk to someone or I would go mad, and there was no one else I could think of.'

She had been a solitary child, not quick to make friends, and she and Joachim hadn't helped by transplanting her at the age of sixteen, just as adolescence makes a teenager awkward and self-conscious, hard to please. Since her marriage her life seemed to revolve around Stephen and the twins and there was never talk of girlfriends to giggle and be silly with.

'I thought I was going mad, Mummy.'

'Shh.' Elise made a soothing noise as if Cressida was once again two years old and had had one of the infant nightmares to which she had been prone: dragons and monsters that wanted to crunch her bones. She led her into the sitting room and made her comfortable in the armchair.

'I have something to tell you,' Cressida said. 'Something so awful I don't know where to start.'

'You've been having an affair with Antony,' Elise said evenly.

Cressida's eyes were wide in disbelief. 'How could you know! Did *he* tell you?'

Elise suddenly lost her self-control and burst out, 'How could you, Cressida? He's your *brother*. How could you be so selfish?'

'I know I've done something terribly wrong but I'm paying for it now, Mummy, believe me. He hasn't phoned me for days, for more than a week.' The words poured out of her in an unpunctuated rush. 'And I keep trying his mobile but it's dead and the receptionist at his office says he's in a meeting whenever I call and I'm sure she's laughing at me and when I ring his flat there's nothing but his answering machine.'

Which she would ring again and again to hear his voice.

She concluded, 'I can't bear it.'

'So that's why you bought a mobile of your own?' Elise said softly. 'So you could ring him in secret.'

'Yes, of course.'

'But it's over now, Cressie. You must accept that. The affair had nowhere to go and now it's ended and you've got to start rebuilding your life, if you can.'

'You don't understand.' She was the petulant teenager Elise remembered so well. 'We love each other. We've got to be together.'

'It's incestuous. It's against the law —'

'Who cares about that sort of thing nowadays? What with sperm donors and stuff like that no one even knows who's related to who half the time. We'll go away, somewhere where no one knows us —'

'And Stephen will use your blood relationship as ammunition, to get custody of the twins.'

'Then let him.'

'Cressida!'

'I can have other children, children with Antony, and they won't have two heads or anything and if they do I shan't care, I shall love them just the same.' She was growing hysterical. 'How do we know, anyway? How do we know he's who he says he is?'

'You mean he might be an imposter? A conman?'

'Or a mistake. Yes, that's it! They made a mistake. They got the birth certificates mixed up at the adoption society.'

'Now you're clutching at straws.'

'I have to!'

'Listen to me.' Elise grabbed her daughter by the neck of her sweater and pulled her round in her chair. She had always been physically the stronger of the two. 'You shall listen, Cressida.'

She spoke slowly, emphasising each word in turn, her face pushed up close to her daughter's. 'There is no mistake. They don't make mistakes like that. Antony is your half brother and you cannot be together. He does not love you, in any case. He does not want you. He has never loved you. He seduced you as part of a plan to hurt me for giving him up for adoption all those years ago.'

Cressida's lower lip trembled. 'I don't believe you! Why are you saying these awful things? You bitch!' She was sobbing now, the words wrenched out of her. She struggled helplessly in her mother's grasp. 'You spiteful bitch.'

'Then why has he broken with you now?'

'Because you warned him off!'

Elise released her abruptly. She straightened up and went to the writing desk where she took a buff folder from the top drawer. 'Then why did he show me *these*?' She flung the pictures on her daughter's lap.

Cressida gaped at them. 'No!' she said. 'No.'

If Elise had had any doubt as to the authenticity of these pictures, they were dispelled now. 'Look at yourself.' She snatched back the pile of photos and began to thrust them under Cressida's eyes, one by one. 'Look! Why do you think he took these photos?'

She closed her eyes to shut out the images and said feebly, 'To have a reminder of me when we're apart. Because he loves me.'

'Pictures of you posing like a whore? Do you think any mother should have to look at photos like that of her daughter? He's talking of posting them on the Internet, for God's sake. Why would he do that if he loves you?'

Cressida began to scream. She flung herself down on the hearthrug and beat her hands and feet on the floor as she howled piteously. It was something she had done occasionally in her childhood, usually for the most trivial of reasons, to the dismay of their neighbours in Kensington.

Who would have taken those nice Weissmans for a couple of child beaters?

Elise did what she had always done with these tantrums: let her wear herself out. Joachim had initially tried to soothe and comfort her but even he had eventually admitted that her way was best. Gradually the tempest died. Cressida lay limp on the floor, the last feeble sobs choking from her. She had never known what to do at the end of one of these scenes; simply to get up and wipe her eyes was an anti-climax.

Elise, understanding this, picked the right moment to drop to her knees by her daughter and raise her to a sitting position. She felt in the pocket of her cardigan for a handkerchief and wiped away the last of the tears. She was keeping an eye on the clock. It was twenty to ten and Antony might be here at any minute. On no account must her two children meet again but Cressida was clearly in no state to drive home.

'I think you should lie down for a while,' Elise said. 'Let's get you upstairs.'

'Stephen —'

'I'll ring Stephen later and tell him you're staying the night here. I'll say I rang and asked you to come over as I was feeling lonely, with it being the second anniversary of your father's death.'

After a pause, Cressida said, 'I had forgotten.'

'So I inferred.'

'Now I feel . . .'

'Don't worry about that. Life is for the living.'

Cressida made no further objection and stumbled to her feet. The portrait caught her eye and she stifled a scream.

'Tinker Girl!' She tore out of her mother's arms and ran across to the ruined painting, running her hands over it, sending more slivers of paint floating to the floor. 'What happened to Tinker Girl?'

' She had come to the end of her useful life.'

Cressida said dully, 'I don't understand.'

'No.'

'I thought it was your most treasured possession.'

'It was.'

'I have never really understood you.'

'No.'

Elise led her upstairs to her own bedroom. Cressida

stood like a rag doll as her mother undressed her, wrapped her in one of her own nightgowns and put her to bed.

'I'll give you something to help you sleep.'

She went to the bathroom and fetched the same medication she had given Antony the night she had tried to kill him, mixing it for Cressida in a glass, stirring it with the handle of her toothbrush. When she returned, her daughter had already fallen into an uneasy sleep, her breathing deep but ragged, curled up, her dark head sideways on the pillow. Elise placed the glass of medicine on the bedside table, stroked a hand over her child's hot brow and left her.

She closed the heavy oak door that separated the old wing from the new to deaden any noise.

Back in the sitting room, she burned the photographs in the grate.

Keeping faith

He was punctual, stopping his Golf on the drive as her clock struck ten, each tinny chime echoing for a second, merging with the next. Elise didn't move but sat in her armchair by the fire, counting his footsteps down the stone flags of the hall.

He was a quiet walker.

'I'm here,' he said awkwardly, paused in the doorway.

'So I see.'

'I'll just take the picture and get out of your —' He had seen the damage and it silenced him. Out of your what, she wondered? Hair. Way. Life. The last of these, she hoped.

He walked over to the wall like a man in a trance.

'Take it,' she said. 'It's yours.'

He stood staring at the ruined canvas for a moment then, to her surprise, he began to laugh. 'You have the power to astonish me, Elise. I don't think I've ever met anyone quite like you.'

'Joachim always said he would destroy a picture rather than let it fall into the hands of someone he despised. I have kept that faith with him.'

He looked at her with admiration. 'You know, if we had met in other circumstances, I might have liked you.'

'Then that is the difference between us. Now.' She

got to her feet. 'You promised me that if I gave you Tinker Girl you would go away and never bother me or my family again. Is there any chance that you will keep that promise?'

'I will keep my promise.' He reached up to take the painting down from its hook. 'Can you give me a hand with it?'

'You're actually taking it?'

'Sure. It will be a reminder, a memento.'

She went to help him because the canvas was a heavy one, the frame, though unobtrusive, was solid oak, painted black. 'If you have learned anything from the last few weeks, Antony, then perhaps it won't all be wasted.'

She fetched an old sheet from the linen cupboard and wrapped the canvas. Together, with a curious sense of companionship, they carried the painting out to his car. It took them some time to stow it in the Golf. He had to let down the back and move the passenger seat as far forward as it would go. Even then the tailgate wouldn't shut.

'I'll get some string,' she said.

'Some of that picture wire you keep about?'

'Actually, yes. That will do the trick.' She hesitated. 'Antony, have you thought of seeking help?'

'A psychiatrist, you mean?'

'It may not be too late. I know that you have suffered and nobody regrets that more than I, but you're still a young man and could put it all behind you and make a fresh start.'

'With my luck I'd be referred to Hannibal Lecter.'

She shrugged. No one could help him if he wouldn't help himself. She turned away and he followed her back into the house.

'How is Cressida?' he asked as they walked along the hall.

'Do you care?'

'Not much. In fact, not at all. How did an extraordinary woman like you come to produce someone so commonplace?'

'It won't bother you never to contact her again then?'

'Not in the slightest. She bores me to tears.'

Elise went into the kitchen in search of something to tie down the tailgate of the car. Antony waited in the sitting room, standing uselessly in front of the fireplace, his hands in his pockets, staring into the flames as if he might find salvation in them, a kind of *auto da fé*.

As she rummaged through drawers, trying to remember what she had done with the picture wire after the night she'd tried to throttle him, she heard a scream that almost froze her blood. It was like the battle cry of some unnatural creature, a fiend from hell.

It was over almost before it had begun. Forcing movement into her unwilling legs, she rushed back into the sitting room.

'Cressida!'

Her daughter stood by the writing desk in the alcove, clinging to it as if she would otherwise fall down. She had dressed herself again but her hair was dishevelled and flattened on one side. Her face twisted in fury, an ugly mask of hatred. Her jersey was covered in blood and she was panting as if she'd completed a marathon.

On the floor by the windows Antony lay motionless on his back with one leg contorted beneath him. The knife that Elise had used to slash the painting was protruding from the left side of his chest, the centrepiece of a red pool that was still rippling outwards, seeping its way across his shirt. His eyes were open and fixed on nothing, a bubble of bloodtinged saliva frothing on his lips.

Elise was in no doubt that her son was dead, but she knelt and placed a hand to his neck, feeling for a pulse that wasn't there.

'Commonplace, am I?' Cressida loomed over her, her eyes slightly mad as she contemplated her handiwork. 'Do I still bore you to tears, Antony?'

'What happened?' Elise felt very calm, as a person might feel at the moment of death.

Cressida was also lucid, speaking crisply. 'I woke up. I heard voices outside. I knew his at once. You were laughing together. You were bloody laughing with him.'

'I don't think I was, you know. Talking, yes.'

'I heard you! I was on the landing when you came in. I heard what he said about me and I heard you laugh at it.'

'Cressida, there was no laughter.'

'I crept down the stairs and along the hall —'

'To kill him?'

'No! To talk to him, to have it out with him. To make it up with him so that everything would be all right again.'

'Oh, Cressida!'

'He didn't hear me come in. He was staring into the fire. And then I didn't know what to say and I moved across the room behind him, trying to pluck up the courage to speak. I reached the desk and felt the knife beneath my hand so I picked it up, not knowing what it was.'

'You just picked up the knife, because it was there?'

'Yes! He must have heard something then because he turned round. When he saw me and saw the knife in my hand he was afraid — I could see it in his eyes. I liked it that he was afraid, that I was punishing him. He walked towards me with his hand held out to take the knife. I was going to give it to him, but he tripped on the edge of the hearthrug — you've always joked about how it was a death trap, that rug — and fell forward and the knife just slid into his chest. And he fell down.' She stared down at the lifeless bundle of flesh at her feet. 'Like that.'

Elise didn't believe a word of it. The hearthrug was exactly where it had been; no one had tripped on it. And surely Antony would have spoken if he had turned and seen her with the knife in her hand. He would have said, 'Give me the knife, Cressie' and she would have heard him.

No, she had taken him by stealth but there was no

point in arguing. Elise knew from experience that her daughter would stick to her story, come hell or high water. She would tell it and embellish it until she believed it herself, until it became, in her muddled head, the truth.

'And then I screamed,' Cressida said.

'Did you?'

'I must have.'

To the end of her life, Elise was never sure which of her children it was she had heard scream: the murderer or the victim.

'You must go,' Elise said. 'Do you hear me?'

Cressida, emerging from the trance-like state that had possessed her for the last few minutes, realising at last what she had done, dropped to the floor beside the body, moaning, 'Antony. No! Antony, my darling.'

Elise swung her arm back and hit her daughter very hard across the face. Stunned, the younger woman gasped as she recovered some of her senses.

'I didn't mean to kill him,' she stammered.

'Well, you made an expert job of it!'

'What am I to do? Oh, God, Mummy! Tell me what to do.'

'You're to go home at once,' Elise said sharply. 'Would Stephen lie to the police for you?'

'What? How should I know?'

Elise hauled Cressida to her feet. 'Then make sure you get back before he does. You were never here tonight. You were at home on your own all evening.

I can give you half an hour before I send for the police; after that the forensic will look too wrong.'

Still Cressida didn't move so Elise grabbed her by the arm and bundled her into the downstairs cloakroom where she made her wash the blood from her hands. She ran upstairs to the bedroom which had been Cressida's as a girl and dug some old clothes out of the wardrobe, jeans and a sweater, not dissimilar to the ones she was wearing.

Stephen would never notice the difference. When did men ever notice in detail what their wives were wearing?

Cressida was shivering as her mother helped her into the fresh clothes. She led her out of the house. She didn't know if her daughter was fit to drive but it was her best hope. At least she seemed sober now.

'Drive carefully,' she said. 'Slowly. Don't do anything to draw attention to yourself.'

Still the young woman hesitated. 'I can't let you take the blame.'

'I won't have to. We took Bellini for a short walk, Antony and I, then came home and disturbed a burglar. It's only a few weeks since I reported a prowler one night so it'll hold together. Christmas is a peak time for burglaries, anyway, what with people out at parties and lots of expensive presents lying around. Antony tried to grapple with him and was stabbed. Simple. It'll be fine.'

Cressida nodded, accepting her mother's word as law.

Elise stood watching as the engine coughed then

turned over and caught. Cressida moved off, jerkily at first, then roaring away at speed on the empty road that led west out of Alderbright.

She wrestled the portrait out of Antony's car. Without help it was a major undertaking and it suffered a lot more damage in the process, but she managed somehow. She locked the car and dragged the canvas back into the sitting room where she propped it against the wall. Above it she could clearly see the space where it had hung, an oblong lighter in hue that the surrounding paintwork.

She pulled off the sheet, stuffing it into the carved oak chest between the sofas, and eyed the painting. She wondered, just for a second, if the damage could be repaired, before she remembered that it didn't matter: Tinker Girl was dead and would never hang on this wall again.

Bellini was licking Antony's face and Elise didn't try to stop her. The little dog had always liked Antony, which proved what a lousy judge of character she was, but then he had been invariably charming, to man, woman or beast. Now the Westie was trying to wake him, or perhaps to comfort him.

She fetched a damp J cloth from the kitchen and wiped the handle of the knife clean of Cressida's fingerprints. Then she grasped the hilt herself, as she would have done had she been administering the blow, taking care not to pull the blade out or dislodge it in any way.

How perfectly Cressida had struck; no surgeon with his detailed knowledge of anatomy could have made a neater job. In her mind's eye she could see the anatomical poster that had once hung on the wall of Joachim's studio and was now his daughter's. She remembered how Cressida would stand and look at it for half an hour at a time, transfixed. She shook her head vigorously to dislodge the memory.

She knew that the story of a burglar disturbed would not hold water — she had more respect for Greg Summers than that — but that was the tale she would tell, initially. She would break down and confess when they confronted her with the evidence: her fingerprints on the handle of the knife. She would bluster that they'd got there when she had tried to pull the knife out but they wouldn't believe her.

If her confession had to be coaxed out of her then they were less likely to suspect the existence of a deeper truth, an inner doll in this succession of gaudy Russian babushkas.

She went out of the kitchen door and round to the back of the house. Picking up a fallen branch, she used it to smash a large pane of glass in the sitting room window, then reached in and unfastened it, leaving it agape.

Back inside, she removed her cardigan and pulled Cressida's blood-stained sweater on over her blouse, making a little moue of distaste at the sticky feel of it. She wiped her hands down it and let the blood dry under her nails. Her initial story would be that she had got covered with it as she cradled her dying son in her arms, a living pietà.

She knelt down by the body again and scrutinised

his face. With his eyes wide open like that, his expression was one only of surprise. 'You win, Antony,' she said, pressing his lids shut with her thumbs. 'You have destroyed my life. You have your revenge.'

'What the hell's going on?'

Her hand went to her throat, stifling a scream as she stared up at the faceless shadow in the broken window.

'My God, Jack! You scared the shit out of me.'

'I heard glass being smashed and a few minutes ago I could have sworn somebody screamed.'

'It's nothing.'

She rose to block the window but McFee thrust her roughly aside and stepped in carefully over the jagged sill, coming to an abrupt halt at the sight of the dead man.

'You call this nothing?'

He crouched down and tilted the face towards the light, nodding as he recognised the handsome features. She noticed that his voice had lost the familiar Scottish cadences she was used to. So he, too, had been playing a part all these years.

'Who did this?' he asked.

'I did.'

He scrutinised her face. 'Why would you?'

'It's too long a story.'

It flickered across her mind for a moment that she could pin this murder on McFee, the criminal, the fugitive. She and Antony had surprised him breaking into the house, stealing food from her kitchen.

He had picked up the knife and chased them into the sitting room . . .

She could knock him out, now, as he kneeled at her feet. He would never expect it of her. She glanced around for a weapon, her eyes lighting on a piece of stone sculpture that Joachim had bought on a trip to Zimbabwe fifteen years ago.

It was long and narrow and bulbous at the top, like a club.

The idea was no sooner born in her mind than it died. McFee was no angel but she had counted him a friend and you didn't frame your friends for murder.

She said, 'Jack! You have to make yourself scarce because the police will be crawling all over this house in a few minutes.'

'The police?' He scrambled to his feet. 'Have you called them?'

'Not yet.'

'Are you mad, woman? You're not just going to hold your hands up to murder. I'll help you get rid of the body. We'll dump it somewhere it won't be found in a hurry.'

Elise almost laughed: that was a true mark of friendship, if ever there was one. She shook her head. 'Jack, you're one of a kind, but it's too late for feeble attempts to cover up.'

He shrugged. 'You obviously have a story you want to tell and you're determined to tell it and I'm not going to stop you. I have problems of my own.'

'Now go, because I can't give you long.'

'I need money, a passport.'

'I haven't much in the house.'

His face hardened. 'You better hope they don't catch up with me, Elise. I had nothing much to do in that studio of yours, lying in the dark. I heard the other car that came a couple of hours ago and I heard it leave just now. I know there was someone else here tonight as well as you and the dead boy and I've got a pretty good idea who it was too.'

She looked at him for a moment, then nodded. 'Point taken. Come with me.'

McFee stepped carefully round the body and followed her into the study. She opened a safe in the wall, hidden behind the sketch of Silas Weatherby, and handed him a roll of clean bank notes which he pocketed. Then she rummaged in the desk and produced Joachim's passport, for she had thrown nothing of his away.

'There's no resemblance,' he said, examining the photograph of an old man with a shock of white hair and a thin, intelligent, ascetic face.

'When do they ever look closely?'

'They'll be watching the ports for me.'

'Catch a boat to Ireland and take a plane out of there. That's your best bet but you're on your own now.'

'Fair enough.' He turned away then hesitated. 'Why did you give me shelter, Elise?'

'I suppose because Joachim was once a refugee.'

He laughed. 'I wasn't exactly acting out of altruism, you know.'

'I know, but nor were most of the people who helped Joachim across Europe in 1938. They took everything he had of value, but they saved his life and, in the end, that was all that mattered.' She offered him her hand. 'Good luck, Jack.'

'You too.' He glanced back towards the sitting room. 'Looks like you need it more than I do.'

She gave him an old coat of her husband's. It was too big for him but it was warm and black and wouldn't show up in the dark. The pockets were capacious. She saw him off out of the front door and watched him round the corner.

He disappeared into the night, never to be heard of again.

She waited ten minutes, the longest ten minutes of her life. Then she let her breath come quick and short, injected a note of mild hysteria into her voice and dialled 999. Three quarters of an hour later Gregory Summers would interrupt his dental ablutions to answer the phone.

At Alders End, Elise sat down to wait. The best of her life was behind her and she had settled the last of her debts.

Scene of crime

'She's in here,' Barbara said, leading the way. 'She's pretty shocked.'

'I can imagine.'

The rear of the house had been sealed off as a crime scene and Elise was waiting in the dining room, amid the incongruous beauties of Christmas. He noticed that the tree had real candles on it and stifled the policeman's urge to point out the dangers thereof.

He stepped forward and took both her hands in his. She looked up and gave him a brave smile. 'Greg. Thank goodness.'

'Have you seen a doctor?' he asked.

'A doctor? I'm not injured.' She pulled out the sweater she was wearing and looked at it critically. 'This is not *my* blood.'

'I know. I meant for shock.'

'I don't think a doctor can help with that. Do you?'

'Sometimes,' but she waved the idea away with one weary hand.

'We'll need the clothes Lady Weissman is wearing,' Barbara reminded him,' for evidence.'

He frowned at her, but Elise said, 'Of course. Do you want me to come and change now, Sergeant?'

'If you will,' Barbara said. 'I'll help you.'

'Can I call anyone for you?' Greg asked. 'Your

daughter?' He searched his memory. 'Cressida, isn't it?'

Elise shook her head. 'She'll be asleep. There's no point in distressing her before morning. You'll be here for a while, will you?'

'Of course.'

'Then I could hardly be in better hands.'

She followed Barbara out of the room. Greg made his way along the hall to the sitting room where the doctor and the police photographer were already at work on the body while the SOCOs waited patiently in their white overalls to search for evidence.

'Were your son and daughter very close?' Barbara asked.

She looked with curiosity at this woman who was, apparently, such a good friend of the boss; she knew Greg Summers pretty well and had never heard him mention her name.

'Not close, no.' Elise began to rummage in her wardrobe, picking garments off the rails, then letting them drop to the floor. She made an exasperated noise. 'I can't think straight. I'm sorry.'

She was worried suddenly that there might be some evidence that her daughter had been here tonight, but what might that evidence be? There was so much to think of when you were setting up an elaborate web of lies. From the corner of her eye she saw that the bed was unmade. She should have thought of that, but she might pass as the sort of person who didn't bother to make her bed every morning.

'Something warm,' Barbara said, 'and practical.'
She took charge, selecting a pair of black woollen
trousers, a matching shirt and a pink lambswool jersey. Elise stripped off with no sign of self-conscious-
ness before the younger woman and Barbara bagged
up her soiled clothes, even down to her shoes.

'Dr Chubb,' Greg said.

'Superintendent.'

They'd worked together for five years and were
on perfectly cordial terms but had never progressed
to first names. Greg didn't even know what Dr
Chubb's first name was as he signed himself A. E.
Chubb.

Adrian: he looked like an Adrian.

'He's not been dead long,' the doctor said. 'I'd say
an hour, two at the outside.' He glanced behind him.
'Although it's cold in here with that window
smashed. I certified death at 0023 hours.'

Dr Chubb didn't suit his name since he wasn't
chubby, but tall and lean, with a handsome, rather
severe face that looked ten years younger than its
age, which was forty-two.

Greg looked down at the hollow shell of a man at
his feet. He had seen him twice while he'd been
alive and he wasn't sure that he would have recognised Antony Lucas in this pale, lifeless face, this
torso covered with congealed blood.

It *was* cold, damn cold. He rubbed his arms.

'What time did the 999 call come through?' he
asked.

Chubb shrugged. 'I was called out around midnight.'

'Me too.'

The damaged painting caught Greg's eye and he stepped over to it with a cry of dismay. 'What the hell happened here?'

Dr Chubb gave him a sardonic look. 'That's for you to find out, isn't it?'

Barbara came in at that moment and handed the bag of bloodied clothing to a SOCO.

She said 'Hello, Aidan' to Dr Chubb.

'All right, Babs?'

Aidan? Greg asked about the emergency call.

'Two minutes past eleven,' Barbara said promptly. 'Tom Reilly and Sharon Moore were here within fifteen minutes. They took one look, secured the scene and sent for CID. I was on call and was here by twenty to twelve. Since it was obviously an unlawful killing, I rang you.'

'And it was Lady Weissman who made the call?'

'Yes.'

'Where is she now?'

'Back waiting in the dining room.'

'I'll talk to her right away.'

'In what capacity?' Barbara asked.

'What?'

She said patiently, 'As a witness or a suspect?'

He was shocked. 'A witness, of course!'

Barbara nodded thoughtfully.

'Can the body be moved?' Greg asked the doctor.

'I'm done here. I'd be surprised if the cause of

death is anything other than a knife through the heart, but I'll do the post-mortem first thing tomorrow morning.' He corrected himself. '*This* morning.'

The two men shook hands and Chubb was gone. Greg checked with the photographer who also gave the all-clear to move the body and it was taken out to the waiting ambulance. He got out of the way and let the overalled men begin their meticulous search for evidence.

Elise was in the same position as before when he returned to her, sitting in the carver chair at the head of the dining table, her eyes fixed on a bowl of peach-coloured roses in the centre of the table.

He pulled a chair up next to her. He noticed that the roses gave out no smell, like most hothouse flowers. He hated flowers that had no scent. Barbara took a seat a little further down the table. She took out a notebook and pen and sat silently waiting.

Greg said, 'They've taken him out.'

'Will I get the chance to see him again?'

'We shall need a formal identification, later today, when you feel up to it.'

'But you know who he is.'

'A formality, as I say.' He hesitated. 'Is there a next of kin? I mean,' he went on awkwardly, 'legally —'

'Legally, I am not the next of kin, although I was his mother.'

'Exactly.'

'His adoptive parents are dead. I don't think there is anyone.'

'No wife, ex-wife, live-in girlfriend?'

'None of those.'

'Can I have his address?' Elise recited Antony's address in West London and Barbara wrote it down.

'Now tell me what happened tonight,' Greg said. 'Take your time but tell me all of it.'

'Antony and I had been out for a drink —'

'Where?' Barbara asked, making shorthand notations.

This lying was harder than she'd thought, but her story mustn't sound too glib. 'No, not a drink, actually. That is, we meant to go for a drink, a nightcap just before closing time, but everywhere we tried was so crowded and noisy.'

'Christmas,' Barbara said.

'Yes. Exactly. Office parties, people horribly drunk.' She began to get the hang of it. 'Can you believe, we parked at the Bell Inn at Boxford and, just as we were going in, a young man came stumbling out and vomited all over the car-park. He only just missed my shoes! Somehow the idea of a quick drink was fast losing its appeal and we came straight home.'

'So you hadn't been gone long?' Greg said. 'Anyone watching you leave wouldn't have been expecting you back so quickly.'

'I suppose not.'

'And this was what time?'

'When we returned? Five to eleven. Ten to.'

'And what happened when you got back.'

'I was dying for a pee so I veered off to the downstairs lavatory. Antony went on ahead into the sitting room.'

She paused and gulped down an obstruction in her throat. Barbara rose and examined the contents of the sideboard. She poured a glass of tonic water and handed it to Elise who nodded in gratitude. She drank down half the glass before continuing with her story.

'Then I heard a noise, a . . . a scream, only it was stifled almost at once, into a sort of horrible gurgling sound. It was terrifying. I tidied myself up as quickly as I could and ran into the sitting room. I found Antony as you saw him, lying on the floor.'

'Dead?'

'Not quite dead. Dying. I got down beside him and gathered him up in my arms. There was blood everywhere.'

Tears started in her eyes, to her own surprise. Greg passed her a clean handkerchief and she mopped them up without comment while he waited, pausing with the cotton pressed to her nose and mouth.

He said, 'You didn't phone for an ambulance right away?'

'I could see it was no use. All I could do was hold him — nurse him in my arms — while his life ebbed away. He was dead within two minutes. Nothing could have saved him.'

'And the assailant?'

'I saw no one. I suppose I was aware that the window was open, broken. He must have fled that way, horrified by what he'd done. I can't believe that he meant to kill anyone.'

'Did you look out of the window?'

'I was too busy cradling Antony.'

'What about the picture,' Greg asked. 'Tinker Girl.'

'The portrait? Yes. He must have done that too. Not so much a burglar as a vandal, come to wreak wilful destruction, lashing out when he was surprised in the act.'

With luck, Greg thought, this vandal-cum-burglar would panic and that would make him easier to find.

'I suppose it's the same man,' she ventured, 'the one you've been looking for for the local burglaries.'

He was surprised. 'We made an arrest. Haven't you heard?'

'Me? No, why?'

'It was Silas Weatherby's daughter.'

'Jennet? Are you sure. Well, of course you are. That probably explains why Silas hasn't turned up for work this last week. I wasn't bothered as there's not much to do in the garden at this time of year but I stopped at his cottage when I was driving through the village yesterday, to make sure he wasn't ill, and there was a note on the door saying he'd gone away for a few days.'

She thought for a moment, then said, 'So this is a different burglar.'

'They're like weeds: you no sooner deal with one than another springs up.'

'Yes.'

He asked, 'Did you see the knife?'

'Yes. I could see the handle.'

'Had you seen it before?'

'Oh, it's one of my kitchen knives, I'm sure of that. I've had them for years. He must have been searching the kitchen — don't people sometimes hide valuables there? — and seen the knives in their block and I suppose the picture was too much of a temptation: something beautiful and irreplaceable.'

'Did you touch the knife at all?' Greg asked. 'After the murder?'

'No,' she said fervently. 'Not at all.'

He took her fingerprints for elimination purposes. 'You'd best get some sleep,' he said gently. 'I know how difficult it is to recall details while you're in shock. In the morning you may remember more and we can talk again. Is there somewhere you can go — a friend or neighbour?'

She was startled. 'I will sleep here, in my own home.'

'But will you feel safe?'

'Of course.'

'There'll be a lot of noise,' Barbara pointed out. 'Our people will be here all night.'

'Then they will keep me safe.'

Gregory Summers sat in silence with the preliminary forensic reports in his hand. It was late afternoon on Christmas Eve and he'd snatched a few hours sleep at the police station before the belated dawn at this, the darkest time of the year.

The post-mortem had thrown up no surprises:

Antony Lucas had died from one clean blow to the heart, if clean was the right word for something so vicious. Death, said the doctor, would have been instantaneous. Otherwise he was a young man of about thirty, in the peak of health and physical condition, although some old scarring of the bronchial tubes suggested a childhood tendency to asthma.

The pathologist couldn't account for a ring of burns on the small of his back which looked to have been made by cigarettes.

Greg rang Dr Chubb. 'Are they recent, these burns?'

'God, no! At least fifteen years old.'

'They must have been deep to leave such lasting scars.'

'Believe me, they were.'

'Any theories?'

'Self harm?'

'In the small of the back? Isn't that hard to reach?' He felt round his own back. Not the obvious place to burn yourself, though it had the merit of being invisible in normal circumstances.

'So what's your theory?' the doctor was asking.

Greg shrugged them remembered that he was on the phone and Dr Chubb — *Aidan* — couldn't see him. He said a polite goodbye, exchanged wishes for a merry Christmas, and hung up.

He sat thinking for a moment. He had been lucky: in thirty years in the police force he had never had to deal with a serious case of child abuse, but he had heard the most hair-raising stories from colleagues who had. The things that people did to their own children beggared belief and he had seen the hardest of men choke back tears at the memories.

He shook his head. Whatever these old scars were they had nothing to do with Elise and, surely, had played no part in Lucas's death.

He glanced at the report again then picked up the phone and pressed the redial button.

'Chubb,' the doctor said with resignation.

'You say here he would have died instantaneously.'

'That's right.'

'His mother says she held him in her arms while he died, that it took a couple of minutes. Is that not possible?'

Chubb pondered the question. 'Let's say that I would be very surprised. She'ld have been in shock, though, so she may have convinced herself that he was still alive.'

'And the blood flow?'

'Would have stopped when the heart stopped pumping. You know that.'

'So the only person likely to be heavily spattered with blood . . .'

'Is the killer, standing right in front of him as he died.'

'Thanks.'

'I'm off home now, Summers, so if that's everything . . .'

'For the moment. Merry Christmas.'

'You too. Again.'

They hung up. Greg read on.

The pathologist had removed the dagger and passed it on for examination. Forensic had found one set of prints on the handle: those of Elise Weissman, who had sworn to him that she had not touched it.

He threw the report onto his desk and sighed. There had to be some simple explanation. He got up and went to stand by the window, looking moodily out, trying to clear his thoughts.

It was full dark in Newbury, although it was barely four o'clock, and the town was festive. Half a mile away a firework went off, scattering green and red sparks over a wide area. The police station was unusually quiet, preparing to leave a skeleton staff on duty for the next forty-eight hours.

The car-park was almost empty.

There was a knock at the closed door. Susan Habib had already gone home, clutching the bottle of perfume that Greg had given her in the ritual token exchange. A small parcel — her gift to him, technically deemed a Hanukkah present — lay unopened on his desk. It was flat and light, swathed in yellow teddy bears with red bow ties. Handkerchiefs or socks.

He yelled, 'Come in!'

It was Barbara, not looking at all as if she'd been up all night, tidy in her charcoal-grey trouser suit and pale blue blouse, although the latter had lost some of its crispness. By tacit agreement, he and Barbara did not exchange Christmas presents, which didn't mean that he felt less close to her than to Susan, rather the opposite.

He gestured her to a chair and resumed his own seat.

'The SOCO team has finished at Alders End,' she said. 'Everybody's winding down for Christmas now.'

'Do you want to get off home?' Greg asked. She shook her head. 'Then give me your opinion on these.'

He passed the forensic reports to her and she read them, her eyes moving swiftly down the sheets of printed paper, while he fiddled idly with the yellow teddy bears before stowing them safely in his pocket. As usual, she lost no time in putting her finger on the problems.

'She said he took a few minutes to die.'

'The doctor says that might have been wishful thinking.'

She read on. 'And she swore blind she didn't touch the knife.'

'She uses the knife all the time,' he said. 'It's *her* knife.' He told himself that he was merely playing devil's advocate.

'But her prints would have been blurred by those of the killer,' she pointed out, 'even if he wore gloves. The prints we took from the handle weren't even smudged, so she must have been the last person to touch it.'

'What am I to think, Barbara?'

'That we can't go on treating her as a witness, not

at the moment. There are too many inconsistencies.'

He sighed and reached for his jacket. 'Fancy a ride out to Alderbright?'

Elise made a good show of being flustered.

'Are you accusing me . . .'

'No one's accusing you of anything,' Greg butted in. 'There's just a few details I'd like to clear up. You told me categorically that you didn't touch the knife after the murder and the lab says different.'

'I remember now.' Her hand flew to her throat, in the classic gesture of the poor liar and Greg felt his heart plummet. The Elsie Riley he had known had been a good liar, the picture of injured innocence, even when caught in the act of wrong doing, but that had been half a lifetime ago.

'My first thought was to pull the knife out,' she said, 'but I realised at once that that would be a mistake, that it would increase the blood flow and make his death more sure.'

'You were already certain that he was dying,' Barbara said, referring to her notes of the previous night.

'Yes, but one really doesn't think clearly in those circumstances. I must have taken hold of the knife, then realised the futility of it and let go again.'

Greg nodded slowly. It was not impossible. He said, 'You're quite certain he didn't die instantly, that there were a couple of minutes of life left in him.'

'I . . .' Her eyes avoided his. 'That's what I thought.'

'And you hadn't seen your son from the day of his birth till he made contact with you last summer.'

'That's correct.'

'So have you any idea how he came by scars, old burn marks, on the small of his back.'

She was all puzzlement. 'I can't imagine.'

They left. Barbara said, 'Should we have arrested her, sir?' as she drove them back to Newbury.

'There's plenty of time,' he replied sadly. 'She's not going anywhere.'

'Take this.'

It wasn't the same knife, of course, but an identical one: a thin, very sharp blade some six inches in length. Greg accepted it from Deepak Gupta in the deserted forensics laboratory and looked enquiringly at it.

It was late on Christmas Eve but Deep was a Hindu and liked to pretend loftily that Christmas wasn't happening.

Gupta picked up a luridly patterned cushion from the seat of his chair and held it in front of himself at chest height. Then he lifted it a few inches, because he was a short man, barely five and a half feet tall and Antony Lucas's chest had been higher than his.

'Stab me,' he said. 'Remember the blow was struck from below, through the ribs and up into the heart.'

From below, as a woman might strike a man.

Nice way to spend Christmas Eve, Greg

thought. He bent his knees to reduce his height and brought the knife up into the cushion. He half expected a shower of feathers but the stuffing was a solid pad of kapok which accepted the blade with nothing but a faint squeak of protest. It was not, perhaps, the first abuse that this garish pillow had encountered.

'So?' he said.

'Look at how you're holding the knife.' Greg examined his fingers, clutched round the handle of the knife with the thumb pointing towards the blade. Gupta dropped to the ground and lay on his back with the cushion still doing duty as his chest. 'Come down here and cradle me in your arms,' he said. Greg obeyed, trusting that no one would walk in on them. 'Now try to pull the knife out.'

Greg did so. He instinctively grasped the handle from above, with his thumb pointing away from the blade.

'I see,' he said, releasing his colleague, who sprang nimbly to his feet.

'The fingerprints we found on the knife handle are in the first position,' the little man said.

* * *

They found her fingerprints on the branch that had been used to smash the window. The footprints on the ground outside were too muddled to be of use but there were slivers of fresh mud from that ground on the soles of the shoes she had been wearing.

Greg found that he was surprised only that she

had been so careless. Surprised and disappointed in his old friend.

He went to arrest her, taking only Barbara with him.

'She's not going to put up a fight,' he said.

Barbara was not so sure. Lady Weissman's kitchen had seemed to her to be full of knives and the blow through Antony Lucas's heart had been swift and unwavering.

They found Elise in the drive at Alders End, stowing parcels in the boot of her Lotus. She was wearing a suit of mauve silk with a black blouse, gentle mourning.

'We were all going to gather here for Christmas dinner,' she explained, 'including Antony, but in the circumstances . . .' She gestured helplessly. 'I'm driving over to Marlborough for a rather muted celebration.'

He said gently, 'I'm afraid not, Elise.'

She understood. 'May I phone, let them know I'm not coming?'

'Of course.'

He followed her into the house and she used the telephone in the study. It was Stephen who answered. She longed to ask him what sort of state Cressida was in but she didn't dare. She explained the situation. 'I am still helping the police with their enquiries.'

'On Christmas Day?'

'Justice waits for no man.'

'I don't like this, Elise. I think you should get a solicitor before you say anything more.'

She smiled at the idea of calling on her and Joachim's solicitor: he was a fastidious man, able enough at conveyancing and handling their investments; but a murder charge? She thought not.

'He'll know someone,' Stephen said, when she spoke her thoughts.

'I can't call some hot-shot criminal lawyer out, not today. Don't worry.' He continued to protest and she cut across him. 'I must go now, Stephen. Give my love to Cressida and the boys.' She hung up and turned to Greg. 'Ready when you are. Am I under arrest?'

'Not yet.' He arrested her.

So now, she thought, was the moment for the best act of her life.

Under their patient but unflinching questioning, she did not hold out long.

She might have tried harder to uphold the story of the intruder, she knew, but there was no intruder to be found and charged with the crime and, eventually, that would have become apparent. The case would have stayed open for as long as it needed to. And what would she have done if somebody — some small-time thief like Jennet Weatherby — had been arrested and charged with murder?

Better to leave the fingerprints, the footmarks, and get it over with. Close the case.

It had been she, Elise, who had brought the serpent Antony into the garden of Eden and it was she, Elise, who must pay the penalty.

For the sake of her beloved grandsons.

Unburdening

Elise spoke slowly but fluently, seemingly oblivious to the two cassette tapes turning as one, recording her words. She had refused the help of a solicitor and sat alone on her side of the interview table, facing Greg and Barbara.

'It all began over thirty years ago,' she said. 'Can I start that far back, Superintendent, because otherwise I can make no sense of it?'

'We have all the time in the world,' Greg said, which was not entirely true, since he had twenty-four hours in which to charge Elise Weissman with the murder of her son or release her. He sensed that she was not playing for time, however, and he was prepared to give her plenty of rope.

Even though it was Christmas morning, he was in no hurry to be gone. Nor, he sensed, was Barbara, who preferred a good arrest to a turkey dinner any day.

'I was eighteen,' Elise began, 'young for my age and very naive. My father worked for a Mr Brewster who had a farm near the Savernake Forest. He had a brother, Eric, who'd never fancied farming and had moved away to Portsmouth but who came to stay every so often. Eric was rather dashing, what we used to call a cad: sharp clothes, big car, breezy manner. I had a bit of a crush on him and he must have known but he never tried to take advantage of it.

'One day in September Eric told me he was going to a big party that a friend of his was throwing in Salisbury and he asked me if I fancied earning ten pounds helping out, serving drinks and so on. I jumped at the chance because ten quid was a lot of money then, or it was to me, and I suppose I thought, too, that Eric might notice for the first time that I was a proper grown-up young lady.

'It didn't take me long to realise that I'd made a mistake. It wasn't the elegant drinks party I'd envisaged. There were drugs, which weren't common in those days, and pornographic films, things that made my eyes pop. I was thoroughly embarrassed but I had no way of getting home under my own steam and no money till I'd been paid, so I decided to make the best of it and keep my head down.

'They'd put me in a maid's uniform: a black dress that barely covered my knickers and a white frilly apron and cap. That was okay: I found that quite amusing. But as the evening wore on the party got rowdier and more out of control. It was nothing short of an orgy. I was appalled, disgusted. They were behaving like animals. Men kept pestering me, trying to grab me, to get me to join in, even though Eric told them good-naturedly to leave me alone.

'Finally I took refuge in a sort of study on the ground floor. I sat down on a sofa in the bay window and began to cry because I felt so helpless.'

She paused and took a long draught of water. The two cassette tapes flowed smoothly on across the silence.

Greg said, 'In your own time, Lady Weissman.'

'A man came in, an old man. At least he seemed old to me although I suppose he was in his sixties which, somehow, now, doesn't seem so very old.' She smiled faintly. 'He was plump with fair hair and bright blue eyes. He had a benign face, or so it seemed to me, the way you imagine a bishop's face to be. I have never forgotten that face. He asked me what was wrong and sat down on the sofa next to me and put his arm round me to comfort me and I was grateful.'

She took a deep breath, then looked Greg straight in the eye.

'He raped me, there on the sofa. If I had felt helpless before ... I had no idea that a man — especially an old man — could be so strong. I struggled but that seemed to amuse him, as if it was all a game, an act I was putting on. I was a virgin. He hurt me. I was sobbing and begging him to stop but he didn't stop. He kept laughing. When he was finished he tidied himself up and walked off without a word.

'Eric came in a few minutes later. He'd found out what had happened and he looked worried. He realised that it had all gone too far and had come to carry out some kind of damage limitation. I suppose I should have been hysterical but I wasn't. I've seldom felt so calm and no doubt that reassured him.

'He decided on a carrot and stick approach, starting with the stick. I had come to the party of my own volition and no one would believe that I didn't know what I was letting myself in for. If I made a complaint against the old man it would be his word against mine. He was rich and important and I was nobody so the police would believe him. In those days they scarcely took allegations of rape seriously.'

Greg winced. He remembered those days. It had been a TV programme about his own force, the Thames Valley Police, which had provoked public outrage and a change in procedure.

'But if I was a sensible girl, as he put it, and kept my mouth shut, well, there was no real harm done and I should have five hundred pounds to compensate me.'

She looked at Barbara. 'What would you have done in my place?'

'I don't know,' Barbara said honestly.

'I was ashamed, sure that going to the police would just make things worse and five hundred pounds was a small fortune.'

'So you kept your mouth shut,' Greg said.

She nodded. 'Eric locked me in the study so that no one else could find me and at dawn he drove me home. He was cold towards me, I remember, contemptuous, and I felt soiled.

'Two months later, I realised I was pregnant. You can imagine my feelings, carrying the child of that monster. I couldn't face my parents and their questions, hurting them like that. They were such good, simple people. You remember?'

Greg nodded, recalling the honest, kindly faces of Ger and Mary Riley who had treated their only child as a precious gift, a treasure. He had always felt welcome in their humble house.

'I took my five hundred pounds and I ran away to London. I was lucky. I could have ended up on the streets but I fell in with some more good people: decent people, who went some way towards giving me back my faith in humanity.

'My baby was born at St Mary's, Paddington. I couldn't even bear to look at him and he was taken away and given up for adoption. I didn't think about him again, not in all those years. I got a job as a barmaid in a fashionable pub in Earl's Court, living in. We had lots of artists, actors and such like coming in as regulars and one of them asked me to model for him one day. He told me I was beautiful. No one had ever told me that before. It was he who rechristened me Elise and I realised I was starting a new life.'

At last Greg saw the truth. He'd been certain that Antony reminded him of someone. It had been like a fact in the back of his mind that he couldn't quite pull into conscious thought but now it was clear to him: his face was the same shape as Piers', as were his slim, elegant fingers with the middle one an inch longer than the index and third fingers. The difference in colouring had fooled him, a superficial difference, but he saw now that the two handsome young men looked like brothers.

Or cousins, at least.

There was a long pause and Greg finally prompted her. 'And thirty years later your son made contact.'

'I had no maternal feelings for him — all my mother love belonged to Cressida — but I had already rejected him once and I told myself that he wasn't responsible for what his father had done, that he was as much a victim as I was. I agreed to see him. He was handsome and intelligent, charming and personable and soon I came to like him for himself.'

Her face darkened. 'But he was his father's son, all right, blood of that blood.'

'And the night of the murder,' Greg prompted.

'Things came to a head suddenly. He'd been spending every weekend at Alders End while we got to know each other and I suggested that perhaps he might space out his visits a bit more. He lost his temper. He was shouting and I began to be afraid of him. He was blaming me for rejecting him as a baby and saying I was rejecting him all over again. He said he would make me pay for what I'd done, as he had paid.'

'What did he mean by that?' Barbara asked.

'I never found out. He called me names — vicious, hurtful names. They cut me to the core. He demanded to know who his father was and I told him my story but he called me a liar, a little whore who was inventing a story to cover up her own sins.

'I told him to get out of my house but he wouldn't go. He went into the kitchen and found one of the knives lying draining by the sink and before I knew what was happening he was slashing Tinker Girl. He knew how much that painting meant to me.

'I went berserk. I think I was literally out of my mind for a few minutes. My fury gave me strength and I ripped the knife out of his hand and threatened him with it. He laughed and it was his father's laugh. That was the final straw. He said I hadn't the guts to stick him. He was wrong. I called for help immediately but it was too late.'

'It was a "lucky" blow,' Greg said, 'up through the ribs and into the heart. Instantly fatal.'

'A lucky blow,' she echoed, and blew out a tiny laugh through her thin lips.

When the tapes were switched off, Elise leaned across the table, placing her hand over Greg's. 'Don't worry. I shall plead guilty.'

'No!' he exclaimed. Barbara stared at him in disbelief. 'There's no point in pleading guilty at a murder trial,' he went on more peaceably. 'The only sentence the judge can give you is one of life. Better take your chance in front of the jury. You never know with juries.'

He had seen some bizarre verdicts in his time, incomprehensible.

'They might accept that the balance of your mind was disturbed,' he added. 'You said so yourself, a few minutes ago: you went berserk. You could be acquitted or, at least, get off with a manslaughter verdict.'

Elise nodded at the cassette recorder. 'And let all that be played in court, for everyone to hear, about my rape? Let it be splashed all over the tabloids and let Joachim's memory be besmirched.'

'It was no shame on you,' he said.

'Wasn't it? That's not how people think, not really, and I will not play the victim.' She shook her head. 'Thank you, Greg. It's not that I don't appreciate it, but I prefer to plead guilty.'

That way the evidence need never be tested in court.

He bowed his head, accepting if not understanding. There would be time, before she had to enter a formal plea, for common sense to prevail.

She said, 'You were probably the best friend I ever had, you know, the only person who ever accepted little Elsie Riley for who she was. And now I'm going to ask one last favour of you, for the sake of those lost summers long ago. Will you take care of Bellini for me?'

He was startled. 'Me? But surely your daughter —'

'Stephen is allergic. Please. She likes you.'

'Well, I suppose I could look after her for a while, till I can find her a proper home.'

She said simply, 'Thank you,' and they took her to the charge room and charged her with murder.

A dog is not just for Christmas

Greg pulled up in his drive behind Angie's grey Renault Clio, the West Highland Terrier motionless on the passenger seat beside him with her paws stretched out in front of her, like the sphinx. She had accompanied him without demur, promiscuous in her affections.

He'd stopped at a Pakistani shop in Newbury that was open on Christmas day and bought a week's supply of dog food.

He looked at his watch as he undid his seat belt. It was a quarter to four which meant that Christmas dinner was long over and he was presumably in trouble with a capital T. It was dusk. In the front window his tinsel Christmas tree glittered with fairy lights while a rampant Santa drove his reindeer across the roof of the porch.

According to Angie, this Santa was ironic.

'Better face the music,' he told Bellini, opening his door. The dog jumped onto the driver's seat and out into the drive. Greg started to walk across the flower beds, as the quickest route to the front door, but saw that the dog had taken one look at the mud and plonked her hairy behind down on the cement, awaiting her accustomed lift. He sighed, went back and picked her up, tucking her under his arm.

'We're going to have to cure you of that,' he told her.

As he opened the front door he could hear the CD of cheesy Christmas songs that Angie had bought as a joke but had played almost incessantly since the end of term. A mid-Atlantic tenor was warbling 'Walking in a Winter Wonderland' to a syrupy rhythm beat.

When had it last snowed in the Thames Valley at Christmas? Too long ago to remember.

Angelica and her mother, Rita Lampton, were curled up on the sofa together, sated — almost sedated — with food and drink. Two pairs of identical green eyes looked at him with mild accusation as he appeared in the doorway.

He strode purposefully across the room and dropped the docile terrier into Angie's lap.

'Surprise! Merry Christmas!'

He spent Boxing Day wondering if he should call off the exhumation now that he knew that Elise, more than anyone, had the motive to kill old Mr Hamilton. But he couldn't do that, not even for his oldest friend.

Trevor Faber sat on a red padded chair with white chevrons, clutching a blue cardboard cup of coffee, and waited.

Airports, he thought. Was there a more dismal place in the world than Terminal Three at Heathrow? It was never night here: a small town perpetually glowing, with its burger bars and Tie Racks, its empty chapel and Bodyshop.

Menial workers, mostly black, mostly women, shuffled in and out of lavatories with mop and bucket.

The place was shockingly crowded. You assumed that people got off their planes and made for the exit, but no: they and their luggage queued for information, for car hire and for transfers. There was even a booth advertising passport photos. If you'd come this far without your passport then you'd surely lost the plot.

Trevor had once seen a photo booth in his local Tesco which boasted 'We take your picture until you're happy', which had struck him as an outrageously extravagant claim.

He kept one eye on the arrivals screen as he sipped the coffee, trying not to burn his mouth. It was surprisingly good actually, although he'd been under the impression that cappuccino had foam on top, not just a layer of chocolate-flavoured scum.

The United Airlines plane from Denver Colorado, via Chicago, was due to land in two minutes, on time, but he was an experienced traveller himself and knew that it would be a good half hour before Greif and his girl appeared.

That had been a good guess of Superintendent Summers, that they had gone skiing for Christmas. He liked Summers: a decent man, with the senses of humour and perspective that Krepski lacked. He had got the truth about the punch-up with Monroe out of Barbara Carey during a Boxing Day drinking session in a pub by the river and the memory of his boss's bloodied face brought a smile to his lips.

The DCI, having done such a splendid job on Operation Cuckoo, had been commended and moved to head up a new undercover drugs squad in the east end of London. Inspector Faber wouldn't miss him.

He might be found floating face down in the Thames before long.

The simplest thing had been to ask the Colorado police to keep an eye on Greif and Cole — in case McFee managed to tip them off — sit tight and wait for them to re-enter the country. He knew that they had boarded the plane in Denver twelve hours ago and they had not done a bunk at O'Hare, which meant that they were walking into his arms like long-missed siblings.

In this age of mobile phones and e-mail, it suggested that McFee wasn't bothered about anybody's fate but his own.

Not a team player, our Mr McFee.

Passengers were coming through the cavernous arrivals tunnel in bunches, pushing weary trolleys, their eyes sunken, their skin dehydrated. Sometimes the sight of a waiting loved-one would breathe new life into them but mostly they walked dazedly off, following the directions to tube, bus or taxi. Men stood patiently holding up signs, names from every language, every continent. Passengers would approach them uncertainly with a thin smile. To shake hands or not to shake?

Behind him was the Internet Exchange, where you could buy fifteen minutes surfing for a pound. Red-eyed men and women, many of them fresh off a twenty-hour flight, made eagerly for the nearest computer terminal, logging on with a sigh of relief.

He was glad he didn't have an addictive personality.

The Colorado flight had landed. Trevor crumpled his empty cup in his fist and pitched it into the nearest rubbish bin. It landed plum in the middle but bounced out again. An Asian woman with a mop and bucket gave him a sardonic look and bent to pick it up. He smiled thanks at her. She wore a full sari under her ugly nylon overall and he could see stout leather trainers poking from the hem.

He hadn't wanted the coffee but something had made him fetch it. Now he had a barely controllable urge to buy a tie with yellow elephants on it or some peppermint body lotion, maybe an airport blockbuster with silver writing on the cover. Perhaps those announcements along the lines of 'Mr Maxwell Chump, travelling on the British Airways flight from Dubai, is kindly requested to contact the airport information desk' contained subliminal advertising.

And while it might be kind of the airport authority to request Mr Chump to come for his message, was it actually their place to say so?

He mentally welded his buttocks to the chair, the better to resist temptation. On the three seats next to his an olive-skinned girl — Brazilian, to judge by the stickers on her luggage — lay stretched out fast asleep. She was snoring, a little bubble of spit forming on her dark red lips.

It reminded him of the drowned Iranians and he looked away.

He took the photograph out of the inside pocket of his jacket and studied it again. Like all policemen he was good at faces, trained to take in the details, to make no mistake. No oil painting, this Greif, but they said money was an aphrodisiac.

It was only twenty minutes, in fact, before the young haulier and his fiancée appeared, almost invisible behind their trolley which was laden with ski equipment and bags of designer shopping. They were smiling lovingly at each other despite their apparent tiredness, with no sign of the discord that had marred their engagement dinner at Boxford Hall. Trevor Faber got to his feet, as did three other men in plain clothes who had been distributed about the hall.

He let Greif get well clear of the gate before he approached him. He didn't want him darting back and losing himself in the mysterious bowels of the airport. His colleagues positioned themselves to cut off possible escape routes and he flourished his warrant card in the young man's face and spoke in an undertone.

'Mr Justin Greif? I'm a police officer. Will you come with me please.'

An elderly lady behind the couple hissed 'drug

dealers' to her companion in an ear-splitting whisper and they both stared avidly at Greif.

Greif smiled with an easy charm. 'I don't know what this is about, constable —'

'If you would just accompany me, sir, then I can explain everything.'

Faber led the way to the interview room which he had borrowed from the airport police.

'Now, what's all this about?' Greif asked, dropping his flight bag on the table. 'There must be some misunderstanding.'

'Justin Greif, I am arresting you on suspicion of involvement in the illegal trade in immigrants. You are not obliged to say anything but if you fail to mention when questioned —'

He got no further with his caution because Philippa Cole emitted a wild shriek of fury, making them all jump.

'You stupid bastard!'

Before any of the men could stop her, she grabbed a ski from the trolley and belted her beloved over the head with it, sending him crashing to the ground with blood trickling down his unconscious face.

'Only a flesh wound, apparently,' Barbara reported cheerfully. 'They brought him round and patched him up.'

'So, *now* is the wedding off?' Greg asked.

'I should think so.'

'Did Cole know what Greif was up to?'

'She's admitting nothing but she's no fool so my

guess would be yes. I think she was furious with him for getting caught, rather than for breaking the law.'

'If he's convicted, it's likely the court will order the confiscation of his assets, or a large part of them,' Greg said.

Barbara nodded. 'He's not exactly the best husband material any more.'

'Is she under arrest?'

'They had to let her go. She's not a partner in the firm and they can't prove her involvement with the trafficking. Greif wasn't about to make a complaint of assault against her either.'

'So all we're missing now is McFee,' Greg said.

* * *

A warder led Cressida into the bare room where her mother was sitting and left them without a word. The younger woman looked visibly shrunken and Elise gave her a warm smile. She was sitting on an upright chair behind a table and Cressida sank onto the one opposite, clutching her shoulder bag to her chest as she took in her surroundings.

'I thought there would be guards all around,' she said. 'I thought they would search me — you know.'

'Intimately? I hardly think so.'

'They just looked in my bag.' She stared at the black leather object in question as if it had betrayed her.

'I'm technically on remand. I have yet to be

formally convicted of a crime, so I have certain privileges denied to convicts.'

Cressida lowered her voice. 'Are there . . . is the place bugged?'

Elise laughed. 'Of course not!'

'I can't bear it, Mummy. I can't bear the thought of you in here.'

'It's not so bad.' As a murderer, she was treated with a certain respect in the remand centre. No doubt that would change when she was locked up with a lot of other murderers. 'You haven't said anything, have you?' Cressida blushed and shook her head. 'Good. Keep it that way.'

'But you said . . .' The younger woman leaned over the table and lowered her voice. 'You said it would be all right. You promised. You said they'd believe that story about a burglary gone wrong.'

'I don't think that story would ever have held water, darling. I'm sorry. I said that to get you to go, to get you safely home. You did get home before Stephen?'

'Yes, but ever since I feel like I'm playing a part. Playing it badly.'

'It's hard, I know, but things will get better.'

'But how long . . .?'

'Will I be in prison? It could be as little as seven years.'

She'd asked Greg Summers the same question and he'd answered, 'It'll be a minimum of seven years, but don't get your hopes up over that: parole boards have been getting steadily harder on lifers recently. It'll be more likely ten or twelve, probably not more than fifteen.'

He had still been trying to persuade her to plead not guilty.

'Cressie, has there been much in the newspapers?'

'No, thank God. With no papers on Christmas Day and there being such a quick arrest, it barely merited a paragraph.'

'What a relief.' The local paper might make more of it but she wasn't so worried about that.

'It was bizarre.' Cressida frowned. 'Only the papers had your name as Wiseman, so they didn't make the connection with Daddy. I can't think how that happened.'

I can, Elise thought; thank you, Greg. She changed the subject. 'How are Stephen and the children?'

'Healthy. Stephen insisted on going to the funeral. I couldn't.'

'Was there anyone else there?'

'Only a man from his office, some Welsh name. He gave a eulogy, apparently, all about what a fine young man Antony was and how he'd had all his life before him till he was so cruelly cut down.'

'That's the sort of rubbish people spout at funerals,' Elise said dismissively.

'He didn't seem to have any friends.'

Elise said, 'Poor Antony.'

'Poor us. He was cremated, in London, Mortlake. I can't bear to think of it.' She shuddered. 'The coffin, disappearing behind those curtains.'

Good, Elise thought: more evidence disposed of.

She said, 'Do you still believe you were in love with him?'

'No. Yes! If I wasn't then the terrible thing I did was so pointless.' She gulped for air. 'But, no, I didn't love him.'

'Good.' Elise took her daughter's hand. 'Darling, when all this is over and I've been sentenced I want you to start rebuilding your life. You must never tell anyone what really happened that night, for the sake of Joe and Ben. They need you.'

'There's something else I have to tell you. The Welshman, he introduced himself to Stephen at the funeral. He's Antony's executor.'

Elise understood at once. 'Oh, no!'

'He made a new will a few weeks ago, leaving everything to me.'

'I suppose he thought that if he crashed his car on the M4 then that would be the final two-finger gesture to you, to both of us. Luckily, you don't have to accept it.' The younger woman's lower lip jutted out mutinously. 'Cressida? You can't. You mustn't. It's as if he's paying you off like a whore.'

'If I refuse it then it'll go to the Crown, apparently. There is no one else.'

'Then let it go to the Crown.'

'Only we could afford a bigger house. We're a bit cramped, with the twins. It's half a million, less inheritance tax. And how would I explain to Stephen why I was refusing the money?'

Elise said desperately, 'You can move into Alders End.'

Cressida's eyes widened. 'You think I could live there! You think I could bear to see his dead body lying on the floor every time I walked into the sitting room?'

'Then it will have to be sold.'

'Then let it be sold.' She banged her fist on the table, defiant. 'He owes me, Mummy. He bloody owes me.'

'I don't know what to say, Cressida. If you can't see how destructive it would be . . .'

There was a silence while both women composed themselves, looking for a way to change the subject. Finally, Cressida said, 'I can't bear to think of you locked up in some awful place.'

'I am much stronger than you think. You've only ever known me as Lady Weissman, the society hostess, stalwart of arts and charity committees. But before that I was Elsie Riley, a little — yes! — a little *peasant* girl. My life has seen many reversals of fortune and this is only the latest. I'll probably be out by the time I'm sixty and we shall have a few last years together, if you're not too ashamed to acknowledge me.'

She took her daughter's face in her hands, scrutinising the features that had come from Joachim: the mouth with its generous lips, the snub nose, the eyes that were just a little too small for perfection. She remembered how she had once stood for hours watching this baby in its crib. She ran her fingers over her lips, as she had once run them over her husband's.

'Promise me — swear to me — that you will never reveal the truth to anyone.'

Cressida kissed her mother's fingers. 'I swear.'

Elise saw that it had not been a hard promise for Cressida to make. It was only natural to children that their parents should sacrifice their lives for them and Cressida was selfish and spoilt, because that was what she and Joachim had made her.

She said, 'Always remember that I love you.'

Cressie whispered, 'I love you too, Mummy.'

Elise sat on the narrow bed in her cell an hour later, a pad of writing paper balanced on her knee, a cheap black biro tracing a few confident lines. She was writing to the Weissman family solicitor to change her will.

She was going to leave the paintings to the nation, to Joachim's adopted homeland, to the Tate Britain. She would never cease to love Cressida but she no longer trusted her to be the custodian of her father's best-loved work. This way they would be safe forever from ownership by people Joachim would have despised.

'Hullo.'

'Piers?'

'Gregory.' Piers voice was unenthusiastic.

'I thought you'd like to know the result of the PM on Mr Hamilton.'

Piers took a deep breath. 'Fire away.'

'Nothing, not even a stake through the heart. He

had a stroke, just as the doctor diagnosed.' He heard a long sigh at the other end. It had been a relief to him too, a double relief. He said, 'I'm sorry, Piers. I know how distressing the whole exhumation business is, just after you've had the funeral and said your goodbyes.'

'It's not your fault.' Piers tone was warmer. 'You were just doing your job. Are you disappointed?'

'I wouldn't have minded pinning a murder charge on the bastard McFee.'

'You caught up with him?'

'Not yet.'

'Thanks for letting me know, anyway.'

'See you soon?'

'Sure. See you.'

Devil take you

And then there was the death of the old man, Elise thought, as she lay in her cell at the remand centre that night: could she really acquit herself of that?

Did she want to?

She thought back to the night when she'd left her son sleeping his drugged sleep and made her way on foot across the fields to Boxford Hall ...

The door of the Garden Suite opened silently and a middle-aged woman entered. She was wearing the uniform of the Boxford Hall hotel: a black knee-length skirt and white blouse, black waistcoat, sensible shoes.

And white cotton gloves.

Mr Hamilton was sitting in an armchair near the french windows that gave onto the rose garden. He wore nothing but a dressing gown, maroon silk with gold trim. He hadn't just got out of the bath as he didn't smell very clean and his bare feet were visibly grubby. On the table at his side was a half-empty bottle of brandy and he held a tumbler of the golden liquid in his withered right hand. His handsome silver-topped cane stood propped against the side of his chair.

He glanced up and said in the steady voice of the habitual drinker, 'I didn't order "room service" tonight.'

'Didn't you?'

'No.'

'Good,' Elise said, 'then we won't be disturbed.'

She shut the door behind her, turned the key in the lock and slipped it into the pocket of her waistcoat. She moved swiftly to the king-sized bed and unplugged the telephone that stood on the night table. 'Suite' was something of an overstatement implying, as it did, at least two rooms; the Garden Suite was one large room divided into sitting and sleeping areas.

Hamilton took another sip of brandy as he watched her actions without comment, although his left hand grasped his cane. Then his face broke into a leer and he said, 'You're a bit old for my taste, love, but you're wearing well. Heh?'

'I assumed you'd died a long time ago,' she said. 'You were ancient even then. I couldn't believe my eyes when I saw you in the restaurant the other evening, but I had no doubt. I knew you at once.'

He said, 'You have the advantage of me.'

'Yes,' she agreed, 'I have.'

She took a piece of picture wire from her skirt pocket and twisted it in her fingers. Hamilton watched the deft movements of her elegant hands.

'Enlighten me, my dear.'

'Salisbury,' she said. 'Thirty-odd years ago. A wild party and an innocent girl who screamed for mercy.'

His eyes were all blank indifference.

'But there were so many of us,' she said. 'I daresay.'

'And now you've come for a rematch, heh? Better late than never.'

He put down his tumbler and struggled to his feet, leaning on the cane for support. His dressing gown gaped open at the front and he made no attempt to close it. She saw to her disgust that he was semi-tumescent amid the straggle of grey pubic hair beneath the flabby paunch.

She lost her temper.

'Filthy old man!' she raged. 'Filthy, disgusting old man.'

He raised his cane as if to strike her with it but she tore it from his hand with one swift motion and hurled it away across the bed. She advanced on him, the wire stretched tight between her hands.

Hamilton laughed heartily, but the laugh turned abruptly into a choke and his hand went to the base of his throat, his eyes widening in disbelief. He fell back into his armchair. Elise stopped, staring, as he groped for his glass of brandy. His hand was shaking and he knocked it to the floor where it fell on its side and flowed out over the expensive carpet.

'Help me,' he mouthed, his voice weak, distorted.

She stood for a moment, unable to move, as he slumped in his seat and his eyes closed. His breathing was harsh and shallow.

Gathering her wits, she pocketed her wire, put the key back in the door, unbolted the french windows and darted out. She stopped outside, on a paved terrace, to catch her breath and rally her senses. It had been taken out of her hands and she was glad; for the second time that night she had been spared from committing murder.

The sounds of merrymaking in the restaurant were clearly audible to her right. She went to move, into the gardens to her left, towards the public footpath that led back to Alderbright, then checked herself, remembering.

She took a deep breath for courage and returned to the room. She crossed to the bed, avoiding the sight of the figure in the armchair, and plugged the telephone back into its socket. She picked up the cane. Then she braced herself to look at him.

His eyes were open again, pools of fear as the product of years of callousness and egoism faced the cruel reality of death. He was trying to speak but no recognisable word emerged.

There was still time to summon help, had there been anyone prepared to summon it. She propped the cane up against the chair, where it been when she arrived.

As she left the room again, she heard a little sigh from the blue lips of the old man as he breathed his final breath. He might not have sold his soul in Paris in 1947, but the devil was coming to claim it anyway.

She walked quickly away towards the lake.

Twice that night she had tried to kill a man and twice she had been thwarted, once by her own tender conscience, once pre-empted by nature. She had been lucky because she knew that she would not have hesitated the second time and she would have had that burden to carry.

So many lives ruined, she thought, by that one evil old man. It was to be hoped that Antony Lucas had been the only seed he'd sown. She could not have curtailed his life by much. He had lived, unpunished, far beyond the mortal span of man.

There was no justice in the world.

She turned over and went to sleep.

Epilogue

'Happy New Year,' Greg said, raising his glass of champagne in salute.

'And to you.' Piers clinked his flute against his friend's. 'May all your troubles be little ones and all mine hung like carthorses.'

It was lunchtime on New Year's Day and they were sharing a toast in a wine bar in Hungerford, which was deserted after the celebrations of the eve. Piers looked bright eyed, as if he'd slept at least twelve hours, while the mirror that morning had shown Greg a tired old man with grey bags under his eyes. He was also acutely aware of the tartan socks, Susan Habib's gift, that were not quite concealed under his Timberlands. No one had done any laundry lately and these were his only clean pair. He tucked his feet under his chair.

'So what's it to be?' Greg asked, when they had drained their glasses and refilled them. 'Manhattan loft conversion in Soho? A house in the marina in Brighton with a big boat?'

Piers asked slyly, 'Will you miss me, Gregory?'

'Well, you know.' He shifted uncomfortably. 'One never likes to see a friend move away.'

'Then let your beating heart be still, my darling. Great-uncle Piers left me nothing but debts.'

'What!'

'He had us all fooled. You remember how he said the lease on his mews house in Chelsea had expired? More like he got chucked out for not paying the ground rent and service charges.'

'But Boxford Hall . . . He must have run up a bill for thousands. If not tens of thousands.'

'That was the cunning of it. While he was staying there he hadn't paid a penny. They had his credit card details and so long as he kept spending lavishly he wasn't going to be presented with a bill till he left.'

'Ah!'

'So long as you act like you've got the readies, few people are going to ask you to prove it. Admittedly he didn't quite check out in the way they'd anticipated, but it seems that the cupboard is bare. According to the solicitor, even his VC will have to be sold.'

Greg was incredulous. 'He won the Victoria Cross?'

'Conspicuous valour during the evacuation from Dunkirk. Oddly, it was one of the few things he never talked about.'

'Life is full of surprises.'

'Ain't that the truth.'

'You have to admire the old bugger's cheek, in a way,' Greg said.

'Oh, he was no bugger. Always very clear on that point.'

'So was he never anything but an old con man?'

Piers shook his head. 'There was money once, no doubt about that, all those years spent racketing around South America and Africa in the 30s, 50s,

60s. His solicitor thinks he made some bad investments over the past few years, speculative to the point of recklessness, refusing all sober, solicitous advice. And there was no way he was going to cut his expenses, of course. When you're used to living like a rich man . . .'

'So you get nothing?'

'Not a penny.'

'If I'd known, I wouldn't have let you buy champagne.'

'Don't worry about that, although you can get the next bottle.' Piers drained the last of the bubbling gold into their empty glasses and glanced round impatiently. 'Why can you never get served in this place? It's not as if it's busy.'

'Chronic shortage of staff,' Greg said.

'You're not driving, are you?'

'Angie's coming to pick me up after she's dropped her mum at the station.'

'And how was Christmas with Angie's mum?' Piers asked.

'All right, actually. Better than I'd thought.'

'She knows about you and Angie now?'

'Angie told her a few weeks ago. Rita seemed . . . unsurprised.'

'Well! How's the Renault going?'

'Great.'

Piers had helped Angie pick out the second-hand hatchback that took her to college and back each day. To Greg's immense surprise he claimed to have spent half his adolescence lying under a car, covered

with oil, and had certainly proved very knowledgeable with the local used-car dealers. So much for
stereotyping, although Greg hadn't enquired as to
how the other half of Piers's adolescence had been
spent, since Piers would certainly have told him.

He went to the bar to get another bottle. On his
return he asked, 'Do you mind about the money?'

'Not really. In fact, not at all. I like Hungerford. I
like my little flat, my friends. I like my *life*. If it ain't
broke, don't fix it.'

'Can I interest you in a West Highland Terrier?'
Greg asked. 'The ideal companion for a lonely bach-
elor.'

'Thanks, but I'm allergic,' Piers said swiftly.

Greg wondered why he was the only person
who hadn't the presence of mind to claim allergy
when confronted with an unwanted bitch. Still, the
little creature was settling in well in Kintbury and
had already staked out a favourite place under the
radiator in the sitting room, although he wouldn't
let her sleep on his bed.

He realised that he would miss her if she wasn't
there.

Piers sighed. 'The old man was always full of
crap, but how I used to lap up his stories as a boy.
Him and his *orgies*! Where was it? Salisbury? All
rubbish, I suppose.'

'No,' Greg said soberly. 'I'm afraid that on that
occasion he was telling no more than the truth.'

The End